A Marriage of Convenience

Now Gareth looked across the table at Lady Althea Hawthorne. She had grown into a beauty! If she was not already betrothed, there had to be several gentlemen vying for her hand.

His keen eyes pinned her to her chair. "What I propose is this, Lady Althea. You need an escape from an intolerable position. I could do with a wife, one who could perhaps produce an heir for Chard if I do not return from the war. As I see it, we are each in the position to help the other."

Althea stared at her companion, shocked. Gareth could see from her wide-eyed expression how startling his bold proposal had been to her. But as he watched the varying emotions that began to flit over her face, he thought that he could not have hit upon a solution that would better benefit both of them.

She considered him thoughtfully with new eyes. Lord Lynley was handsome of face. The terms of the contract between them had already been established. His obligation would be to provide for and to protect her. Hers, to produce the much-needed heir for Chard. She said simply, "Yes."

D0035501

Lady Althea's Bargain

by

Gayle Buck

A SIGNET BOOK

SIGNET
Published by the Penguin Group
Penguin Books USA Inc., 375 Hudson Street,
New York, New York 10014, U.S.A.
Penguin Books Ltd, 27 Wrights Lane,
London W8 5TZ, England
Penguin Books Australia Ltd, Ringwood,
Victoria, Australia
Penguin Books Canada Ltd, 10 Alcorn Avenue,
Toronto, Ontario, Canada M4V 3B2
Penguin Books (N.Z.) Ltd, 182–190 Wairau Road,
Auckland 10, New Zealand

Penguin Books Ltd, Registered Offices:
Harmondsworth, Middlesex, England

First published by Signet, an imprint of Dutton Signet,
a division of Penguin Books USA Inc.

First Printing, September, 1995
10 9 8 7 6 5 4 3 2 1

Chapter One

"You're mad, Mama!" exclaimed Lady Althea. "Why should I ever make up such a tale? I tell you the truth. Sir Bartholomew is a cad of the rankest cut!"

Lady Bottlesby picked at the expensive fabric of her skirt. Her eyes were lowered so that she need not see her daughter's flushed, indignant face. She was not a woman of strong character and it distressed her to be at odds with anyone. "Surely you must be mistaken, Althea," she repeated.

Lady Bottlesby braved a quick upward glance at her daughter's angry expression. She added hastily, "Not that I think you have deliberately misled me, Althea, for I do not! But you are so young still, just out of seminary. You could not possibly be expected to understand gentlemen's ways. It-it is perhaps natural that you should mistake Sir Bartholomew's exquisite gallantries for-for something quite different."

"Different, indeed," said Lady Althea, very dryly.

At her mother's helpless gesture, Althea snapped, "You forget, Mama. I am not a dewy-eyed innocent of seventeen. I am nearly nineteen, and though I am not yet presented because Father's death dictated our seclusion from society, I was in a position from an early age to observe just those sorts of gallantries of which you speak!"

Lady Bottlesby's face whitened, then crumpled. She averted her head. "How could you be so cruel, Althea? When you know how-how . . . oh, my dear!" Her voice was thick with suspended tears.

Althea was at once conscience-stricken. She crossed to her mother's chair and dropped to her knees beside it. Laying her slim hand upon her mother's knee, she said contritely, "Don't, Mama. I am sorry. I should not have spoken so."

Lady Bottlesby shook her head as she hunted for, and found, a lacy scrap of handkerchief. She delicately wiped her brimming eyes and summoned up a pale, wavering smile. "So foolish of me. It should not hurt so now, I know. The earl is dead."

Lady Bottlesby raised her head so that she looked directly into her daughter's face. An intentness came into her soft blue eyes. "Althea, can you not understand? Sir Bartholomew has always had such exquisite concern for my sensibilities that I . . ."

There was a moment's silence, in which the mother's eyes pleaded for her daughter's understanding.

"Yes." Althea said it flatly. "I do know." With a quick, graceful movement and the faint rustle of skirts, Lady Althea rose to her feet. She stepped away, restlessly going to the window. She stared out at a dismal sky, though she did not really see it.

Oh yes, she knew only too well. She had seen firsthand the unhappiness of the loveless marriage that her parents had endured.

Althea had loved both of her parents, but as a child she had been helpless to make things right between them. Her mother was a fading beauty, not particularly intelligent, and needy of emotional support. The earl, ruthless and brilliant, displayed a cruel contempt for her weakness and tears.

The earl had married as society dictated, choosing for his countess a woman whose lineage and background had paralleled his own. If he had thought at all about his bride's temperament, he had counted himself fortunate that hers was a biddable character. It had not once occurred to him that his own temperament demanded one of equal strength from his mate. As a consequence, he had quickly become contemptuous of and bored with his wife. His cutting tongue had often caused her tears. Her pleading defenses had merely inflamed him further.

Even as a small child, Althea had recognized her father's hard nature. She had understood that her father detested what he perceived as weakness. Therefore, she had not patterned herself after her mother. She rarely cried. Instead, she had screamed her defiance at authority and had gone to almost any length to gain her objective.

The earl had seen something of himself in the blaze-eyed child. Though she was not the male heir he had desired, Althea came to be indulged to an amazing extent by her father. She was modeled by his careless attention and her own inclinations into a willful personality in her own right.

Through the years the earl had supported a succession of mistresses. The child Althea had seen and heard more than any young girl should have. There had been distressing scenes of anger and bitterness, accusations and cold scorn. Other scenes lodged in Althea's memory, too, scenes of subtle seduction beneath the earl's own roof.

The earl had seemed to be driven by the cruel side of his nature to inflict as much hurt as possible upon his wife, as though demanding that she respond. The countess had bitterly resented being displaced, but she had not known how to combat it.

Althea had often thought that if her mother had only stood up to the earl, even if only once, he might have relented in his barbed words and put aside his mistresses. But the countess had never tested the breach between herself and the earl, and so the years had passed in unabated misery.

It was no wonder, then, that Sir Bartholomew Bottlesby had found such rapid favor with the recently widowed countess. The baronet was unfailingly considerate and gentle of voice. He had scarcely ever been seen abroad with a frown fixed upon his florid face. On the contrary, his smiling geniality was a byword. If the gentleman was a trifle short and stout, his taste in small clothes a bit flashy, his compliments of an extravagance that bordered on the ludicrous, then that must all be excused in the face of his reputation as a dependable gallant and his obvious desire to please.

"We are caught finely, are we not, Mama?" asked Althea, without turning away from the window.

There was no answer from behind her, which did not surprise her. Althea reflected wearily that her father's dominating character had worked to put her into an untenable position from which she saw little hope of escape.

The years with the earl had served to create such a craving for tender regard in Althea's mother that the lady prized affection above all things. Lady Bottlesby had as good as declared her reluctance to disturb the utopia of her new marriage, even for the sake of her daughter.

Althea laid her forehead against the cool glass. "If only we had not been forced to leave London," she sighed.

At last Lady Bottlesby felt able to respond. "There was never any question of doing otherwise, Althea. I had hoped that you would be granted the benefit of a Season, but . . ." Lady Bottlesby's voice trailed off.

Althea turned, a faint smile touching her lips. Her green eyes were all too knowing. "But neither my cousin nor his good wife wished to be saddled with me."

Lady Bottlesby frowned. "That is not at all a well-bred expression, Althea."

Althea shrugged. "It matters not. I am not likely to grace any high-stickler's London drawing room. When Harold stepped into my father's shoes, he was quite definite in what he considered to be the limits of his duty toward us."

Lady Bottlesby sighed in agreement. "No; your cousin is not a particularly generous gentleman."

For a moment, both ladies reflected upon the fate that had carried them to Bath. The earl had never willingly associated with his cousins. Whenever he had chanced to meet them in society, he had ignored them as nearly as possible. His lady wife had once timidly questioned him why there was such distance maintained between himself and his heir presumptive. She had been answered so sharply for her pains that she had never again presumed to attempt to satisfy her natural curiosity.

Althea, however, could have enlightened her mother upon one point at least. The earl had thoroughly disliked his heir, and if he had chanced to have gotten himself a male bastard off one of his many mistresses, he would have gone to great lengths to see the boy made his legal heir.

But the earl had not fathered a son, and upon his unexpected death, his heir presumptive had naturally stepped into his lordship's shoes. Since there had never been any sort of friendly relationship fostered between the families, the new earl had not hesitated to request that Lady Hawthorne and Lady Althea remove themselves without delay from their prestigious London address so that he and his growing brood could take up residence.

Lady Hawthorne and her daughter had gone to Bath, taking a more or less permanent lease on a town house in the fashionable quarter of the town. At one sweep, they had been deprived of home and friends, and as deep mourning precluded going about establishing themselves as open to invitation, it had been a very dull six months indeed. The past few months, when they had observed half-mourning, had scarcely been less trying.

"Damn Father for dying at such a time," said Althea with suppressed violence.

"Althea!" exclaimed Lady Bottlesby, shocked. "The earl adored you."

"Did he, indeed?" An odd smile touched Althea's lips and the amused expression in her eyes made the color rise in Lady Bottlesby's face.

Lady Bottlesby took to pleating her skirt once more. "In in his own way, of course he did. At least he left you well-provided."

"There is that," agreed Althea.

The earl had been affectionate toward Althea in his cold-natured way, and he had proved it by leaving her a considerable heiress. However, Althea had never harbored illusions that she was a beloved daughter in the traditional sense. And so, within the space of a few months, she had done with her grieving and had been more than ready to go on with her life.

It was ironic that on the very eve of her long-anticipated emancipation from her father's aegis, the earl had died.

Althea had set herself to shine at the select seminary chosen by the earl for its strict curriculum and the drilling of ladylike accomplishments into young misses. She had anticipated her presentation to society because it would have granted her the opportunity to display her accomplishments and her natural attractions. Those, coupled with her substantial dowry, would have made her very eligible in the eyes of unattached gentlemen. In short, Althea had unemotionally planned a strategy that would snare a husband and so gain for herself her own establishment and with it a modicum of freedom.

Then the earl had died, and instead of a brilliant London

Season upon her emergence from the seminary, Althea had been plunged into a year's seclusion.

Lady Hawthorne had not chafed under the period of mourning as had her daughter. For her, it was a time of quiet contentment. There had been so little love lost between herself and the earl that his unexpected death came as a surprising and ultimately welcome release.

Once out of black gloves, Lady Hawthorne and Lady Althea began to emerge from total seclusion and were seen in the Pump Room or out walking sedately around the square.

Little was generally known of the Hawthorne ladies other than the fact that they had been used with regrettable brusqueness by the new earl. It was also thought that they were well-heeled. The latter was obvious from their address in Laura Place and that they were always very well attired. They also maintained a carriage, an extravagance indeed because it was impractical to use it on the steep hills of Bath proper. It was thought, too, that Lady Hawthorne possessed a more than generous widow's portion and that Lady Althea was endowed of fortune, but the specifics were unknown.

Even though Lady Hawthorne and Lady Althea were still in mourning, there were tentative invitations made to them as various personages made themselves known through the good offices of the Master of Ceremony. The initial overtures were made by ladies, but there soon came to be a few gentleman acquaintances as well.

Sir Bartholomew Bottlesby was one of the latter. He came to call upon the Hawthorne ladies more and more often. It was not long before others began to remark that the baronet seemed to have captured the ladies' favor.

Althea was not unaware that her mother particularly enjoyed Sir Bartholomew's extravagantly gallant attentions. Nor did she think it a bad thing. Her mother needed the sort of diversion and coddling that a comfortably aged admirer could bring to her.

Lady Hawthorne had blushed and blossomed under Sir Bartholomew's unceasing admiration. Althea had been astonished to realize that her mother was still a very handsome woman.

Althea had been unsurprised when her mother announced

that Sir Bartholomew had made her an offer. At Lady Hawthorne's anxious query whether she cared for the match, Althea had said in her forthright way, "The question is hardly whether *I* care for it, but rather, whether you do, dear ma'am."

"But do you like Sir Bartholomew?" Lady Hawthorne persisted.

"Come, ma'am, surely you do not mean to cry off if I do not," said Althea in a rallying tone. She saw from her mother's expression that was just exactly what Lady Hawthorne had meant, and she abandoned her levity. "Mama, I do not like nor dislike Sir Bartholomew to any strong degree. He has always been unfailingly polite toward me, so that I have nothing whatsoever to complain of in his manners."

"Yes, Sir Bartholomew treats one's sensitivities with such exquisite forbearance. Not like—" Lady Hawthorne broke off, a shadow crossing her face. She shook her head. "That tender regard is what particularly appeals to me, Althea. Sir Bartholomew is such a perfect gentleman. But I shall refuse his suit if-if it is repugnant to you, for I know that you felt the earl's passing, and it is not so very long ago, after all."

"Nonsense. Why should I object to Sir Bartholomew's suit for you?" asked Althea, setting aside an unfathomable, vague unease. "I have never seen you appear to better advantage than when you are in his company. I could not deny you that happiness out of some misplaced loyalty to my father's memory. What a ninny you must think me, Mama!"

Lady Hawthorne squeezed her daughter's hand. "Thank you, my dear. I am so glad that you do not oppose the match. I have never been happier than at this moment."

"I suspect that shopping for your bridal clothes will make you happier still," Althea had said dryly.

Chapter Two

The marriage had taken place and Sir Bartholomew had carried his new bride and stepdaughter off to his manor house in Surrey.

Althea would have preferred to have remained in Bath, having no wish to intrude on her mother's and stepfather's honeymoon. However, without the services of a respectable chaperone, there was no question that she would be able to remain in Bath. There had been a possibility of staying with the family of one of her dearest friends, but when her friend chose that inopportune time to contract a bad bout of influenza, Althea was once more cast adrift.

"You must come with us, Althea," Lady Bottlesby had said. Since both her mother and Sir Bartholomew had brushed aside Althea's observation that she would be underfoot, and really having no other choice, she had allowed herself to be persuaded to accompany them.

For three months, theirs had been an ideal household. Sir Bartholomew had proven himself as attentive a husband as he had been an admirer. He was also indulgent of Althea, calling his stepdaughter a pretty puss, and had promised to launch her to an extravagant London Season.

Then had come disillusionment. Althea was at first incredulous. But there was no question that she was mistaken. Her early childhood had made her too wise in the ways of the world. She formed quite a decided opinion about her stepfather.

Sir Bartholomew was a cad, a knave, and a lecher.

Althea had voiced her opinion on a number of occasions to the gentleman himself. Now she had broken her silence with her mother. She had not wanted to distress her mother. After all, the poor lady had endured much in her previous marriage to the earl. But Althea was not willing to immolate herself to preserve her mother's blissful ignorance. No, the time had come when she had no choice but to burst Lady Bottlesby's bubble. She had not anticipated that her mother would question the veracity of what she had to say.

Althea tried once more to convey her genuine concerns. "Mama, I am sorry that I have grieved you. But I must make you understand. I do know very well what I am saying about Sir Bartholomew. Do you recall that when I was a child I always locked my bedroom door?"

Lady Bottlesby looked unhappy.

Althea pressed her. "Do you, Mama?"

"Yes, my dear. Nurse told me," Lady Bottlesby admitted reluctantly.

"Do you know why?" Althea asked gently, but with a hint of steel in her voice.

Lady Bottlesby averted her face. Almost peevishly, she said, "Of course I do, Althea. I am not the peagoose that you obviously think me."

"I have been glad lately of that childish habit, Mama," said Althea deliberately.

Lady Bottlesby's eyes rose swift to her daughter's, consternation paling her face. Suddenly her gaze brimmed with tears. "I had thought to be done with it all," she whispered.

There had often been odd comings and goings in the earl's house and Althea had formed the habit when quite young of locking her bedroom door upon retiring for the night.

Once, a rather disheveled blonde woman had come into Althea's room after her nurse had put her to bed. Althea had sat up, regarding the intruder with sleepy, astonished eyes.

The woman had been just as surprised. "Oh! Is this your room, dearie? I must have missed my way." The woman had retreated and softly closed the door.

Althea had climbed out of bed, padded barefoot across the room, and turned the key in the lock. There had not been a night gone by since then that she had not locked her door.

Not long after Althea and her mother had settled into the house in Surrey, Althea began to be awakened at odd hours of the night by the stealthy sound of her doorknob being tried.

It did not terrify her. She had heard that sound before. Some of the riotous parties hosted by her father had resulted in the rattling of doorknobs and loud drunken complaints. On those nights, Althea's nurse had always set up a cot in the bedroom and stayed with her. It had comforted Althea's childish fears and she had always slept more soundly in the assurance that her nurse was close by.

Despite the conditioning of her childhood, however, Althea was distressed. Someone was obviously attempting to gain entrance to her bedroom. Althea was not such an innocent that she would waste a moment wondering over the purpose behind such nocturnal visits. She suspected that she knew the identity of the visitor, as well.

Some weeks before, Sir Bartholomew's attentions toward her had begun to take on a marked difference.

His paternal busses upon her cheek had begun to seek her mouth. He had made excuses to brush up against her, and his hands had surreptitiously roved where they had no business.

For Althea, the crowning incident had taken place when her stepfather had met her as she was coming back from a ride and waved away the groom, saying that he himself would help Lady Althea dismount. When her feet touched the ground, his hands had slid from her waist boldly up to her breasts. Althea had broken away from him, her cheeks aflame. "Sir! You cross the line!"

Sir Bartholomew had shrugged. "My dear Lady Althea. You are Hawthorne's daughter. There is nothing over which you should take such a pet."

Thereafter, Althea had taken to avoiding her stepfather as much as civility allowed.

Not long afterward, Althea had quietly told her dresser to move a trundle bed into the bedroom. She did not inform the maid why, nor did the woman inquire. It was simply done.

It was dark but for the embers of the dying fire. The man had snuffed the candles. Smoke was acrid in her nostrils.

The man gave a low laugh. His indistinct form swayed. "Come to me, little bird."

She shrank closer against the wall at her back. Terror swelled in her throat.

She was shaken and shaken again. "My lady! Wake up, my lady!"

Althea's eyes snapped open. Uncomprehending, still caught in the throes of the nightmare, she stared up into her anxious dresser's face. The black mists receded. "Darcy?"

"Aye, my lady. You were crying out in your sleep."

Althea passed a weary hand over her face. "It was but a dream. An old dream. Pray do not regard it, Darcy. Go back to sleep."

"Aye, my lady." The dresser slowly returned to her cot.

Two nights had passed, scored by Althea's recurring dream. The third night, there came a stealthy scratching upon Althea's door. The maid raised up on her elbow. She looked at the locked door. The scratching resumed, a little more insistently. The maid turned her head and in the firelight she met her mistress's somber gaze. In a whisper, she asked, "My lady?"

Althea nodded. Equally quiet, she said, "Let us see who it is."

The maid got out of her bed and wrapped a shawl over her shoulders. She went to the door and turned the key. Opening the door a few inches, she met the astonished face of the master of the house. Woodenly, she asked, "Was you wanting something, sir?"

Sir Bartholomew backed hurriedly from the door, shaking his head vigorously. "Er-no, no! I was only passing. I wish you good night!" He had backed completely away from the maid standing at the door. Now he turned on his heel and hurried away down the dim hallway.

The maid closed the bedroom door. She locked it. When she turned, she again met her mistress's eyes. After a long moment, she said, "We shall rest easy from now on, my lady."

Althea nodded. "Yes. So I hoped." She lay back down. Within moments, she was deeply, dreamlessly asleep.

The following day at luncheon, Sir Bartholomew had made an expansive remark. "I have noticed that you are blooming into quite a beauty, stepdaughter. We must see to it that you have the very best to set off your glowing looks. I tell you what. I shall frank you to a new wardrobe. How will that be, heh?"

Althea looked across the table at him with a hard expression in her eyes. She was at once made wary as she wondered what he was up to now.

"Oh, Sir Bartholomew! How very kind of you, and generous, too," exclaimed Lady Bottlesby. "Isn't it so, Althea?"

"Indeed, ma'am. I am quite overcome," said Althea, still on her guard. She disliked the calculating look in the gentleman's eyes. Her wariness was not misplaced.

"Then it is settled. You must pick out a few pretty notions for yourself as well, my dear wife. Nothing is too good for my two ladies. I wish only the best for you, which is why I have planned a little surprise for you, Lady Althea," said Sir Bartholomew. He turned his smile on his stepdaughter. "I am persuaded that you will thank me. I mean to engage a most superior female to have the dressing of you. When you come out next Season, there shall not be anyone to hold a candle to you, my dear." He beamed benevolence.

Althea cast a swift glance at her mother's face, which held an expression of surprise, and she knew that Sir Bartholomew had not consulted his lady. "Thank you, but it is unnecessary. I already have a dresser of superior talents," said Althea. "I need no other beside Darcy. She is head and shoulders above any others."

"Quite true, my dear. Darcy came most highly recommended by one of my dearest friends, Lady Tarper. I have never had cause to doubt the woman's abilities. Indeed, I have jealously guarded against her being stolen away from us," said Lady Bottlesby, smiling. "No doubt it would make you stare to hear how many times, and from my own friends yet, that I have turned down suggestions that Althea let Darcy go to them."

"No doubt it would, dearest lady," said Sir Bartholomew, showing his teeth with a little less than his usual amiability. "I had only thought to treat my stepdaughter to a finer dressing than she now enjoys."

"I did not realize that my appearance was wanting," said Althea with a smile.

Sir Bartholomew laughed and shook his finger at her. "It is hardly that you do not appear charming at all times, Lady Althea. Pray do not mistake my meaning. However, I had hoped to be able to spoil you a trifle. You will understand that it is my fondest wish to gratify your least whim."

Lady Bottlesby sighed. "How very affecting, to be sure."

Althea's feelings were quite different. She knew that Sir Bartholomew meant to at once put her under obligation to him and cut out the loyalty of her serving woman, who could be depended upon to protect her. Well, he would catch cold with this clumsy effort. "While I thank you for your consideration, Sir Bartholomew, I do assure you that I am completely content with my present dresser. Darcy is devoted to me. I trust her judgment and her abilities implicitly," said Althea.

"Indeed, I do not see how we could ever improve upon Darcy," said Lady Bottlesby.

"Then naturally the subject is closed," said Sir Bartholomew in almost an annoyed fashion. He turned to Lady Bottlesby. "How would you like to plan a dinner party, my dear? I should like to introduce you, and Lady Althea as well, to our neighbors."

"Oh, I should adore it! What fun it will be, will it not, Althea? Only you must tell me just how you will like it arranged, Bartholomew, for I do not wish to leave anything undone," said Lady Bottlesby.

Sir Bartholomew laughed, greatly pleased at his new wife's desire to cater to him. His good humor was completely restored. "Ah, it will be a grand affair, I promise you! And we shall invite all the young bucks of the county for my stepdaughter. She will turn all their heads. That will be something to see, will it not, my lady?"

Lady Bottlesby turned her head to smile at her daughter. She was oblivious to the barb in her husband's voice. "Indeed it will, sir."

Althea was more cognizant than her mother. She recognized the hypocrisy of Sir Bartholomew's bluff comments, but she did not challenge the baronet then. There would be time enough for that when and if the gentleman chose to skirmish with her again.

In the meantime, she needed time to think what was best done. She could not continue much longer as she was. It was very nearly impossible to avoid the gentleman when they lived under the same roof. Eventually her mother must notice the tension and explanations would have to be made. Althea had excused herself and gone upstairs to her rooms.

It had not taken a long reflection for Althea to realize that the time had come to talk to her mother. She had not relished the necessity, and it had proven every bit as bad an interview as she had anticipated.

Now Althea crossed the room to her mother. She laid a gentle hand for a brief moment upon Lady Bottlesby's shoulder. Her mother did not respond to her touch, either by word or look.

Althea sighed. "I am so very sorry, Mama." There was no more to be said.

Althea excused herself and went back to her bedroom to change into a riding habit. Riding crop in hand, she descended the stairs and went out to the stables.

Althea took a long ride. The interview with her mother had affected her. A gray depression seemed to have fallen over her spirits. But the exercise and the cool air rushing across her face blew away some of the cobwebs in her mind.

Althea returned to the manor house with much of her well-being restored. She had thought of a temporary solution to the problem that her presence posed for her mother. Surely after these months her friend Charity Comstock would have recovered sufficiently from the influenza that she would want Althea to come to stay for a time. Just the thought of returning to Bath and leaving the tension behind had raised Althea's spirits. When she entered the house, her situation seemed much less threatening than it had earlier. She intended to write to Charity at once and secure the invitation that she needed.

It was an unpleasant surprise for Althea to meet Sir Bartholomew in the hallway.

Althea greeted Sir Bartholomew civilly, but coolly, as she started for the stairs. He had obviously just descended and now he barred her way. Althea looked at the baronet, her expression inquiring. "Is there something that you wanted of me, Sir Bartholomew?"

There was a tight look about Sir Bartholomew's mouth. "Lady Althea, I would be pleased if you joined me for a moment in the sitting room," he said.

Althea raised her brows at the baronet's clipped manner, but she inclined her head in acquiescence. She preceded her step-father into the sitting room and turned to face him, wondering what he had to say to her. She had never seen him before without his full mantle of bonhomie, and the repressed air of anger about him only served to put her on her guard.

Sir Bartholomew snapped shut the door. He strode over to the mantel, taking a stance with his back to the grate and his feet spread wide. He said abruptly, "I have just come from my dear lady's rooms. Lady Bottlesby is overwrought due to a conversation that you had with her. I do not like to have my wife's peace cut up. I will have an explanation, Lady Althea."

Althea was frankly surprised that her mother had spoken to Sir Bartholomew on her behalf, but it warmed her, too. After she had comprehended just how important the success of her marriage was to her mother, Althea had scarcely hoped for even that much. Quietly, she said, "I am truly sorry that my mother is overwrought, Sir Bartholomew. However, I can readily understand it. She is my mother, after all. It cannot be a pleasant thing to learn that one's new husband is making up to one's daughter."

Sir Bartholomew smiled wide. His eyes somehow did not reflect the geniality of his expression. "Lady Althea, I am surprised at you! You have put an entirely erroneous construction upon my gestures of affection. Surely you must realize that. I am but recently wedded to your mother and I hold her in the highest esteem. If I have seemed too forward, too eager, as I have taken on my new role of father, I do assure you that nothing of ill intent was meant toward you. Of course not! It is only your imagination that has led you to think otherwise. I would not for the world distress you or place you in an awkward position. This has all been an unhappy misunderstanding."

He sighed heavily and briefly lifted his hands, palms outward, in a show of regret. "Unfortunately, it is not you or I who has suffered from it, but your dear mother. I hope that you may reassure her that there is no reason at all for her to be anxious. Lady Althea, I appeal to your good sense. Surely you will go at once to put your mother's disquiet to rest."

Althea listened to her stepfather's speech with disbelief. The baronet was actually denying to her face that there had ever been anything untoward in his actions or his words. He was actually attempting to cause her to question her own conclusions and so put the blame upon her shoulders.

Althea's cheeks flushed. She said very quietly, "Sir Bartholomew, you and I both know the truth. So does my mother, now. If you truly wish to bring peace to my mother, you will go to her and assure her that you will no longer importune me. Otherwise, I fear that she will always regard you with an uncomfortable question in her heart."

Sir Bartholomew suddenly puffed up in a rage. His normally genial face took on a ruddy hue and his small eyes flamed. "You dare to undermine my place in Lady Bottlesby's affections! I shall see you punished, so I shall!" He stepped forward, raising his wide palm to strike her.

Chapter Three

Althea's voice whipcracked. "Be very certain you know what you are about, sir!"

The baronet stopped, his hand still uplifted. Slowly, he let his hand drop, but there remained an ugly expression in his eyes. "You lack proper manners, Lady Althea. Perhaps it is time that you were taught to respect those who have been given authority over you."

Althea tightened her grip on her riding crop. Coldly, she said, "I am not a serving wench that you may abuse with impunity, Sir Bartholomew. I am my father's daughter. He would have thrashed you, and so shall I."

The baronet's hot gaze dropped to the ready whip. Sir Bartholomew took a careful step backward. Breathing heavily through his nose, he stretched his lips in the travesty of a smile. "We have misunderstood one another again, I fear. A cool head is needed in such trying circumstances. We must talk again after you have had an opportunity to reflect upon your mistaken, ill-advised representation to Lady Bottlesby. I shall naturally expect an apology from you, given to me before my dear lady."

Althea smiled. There was no fog of uncertainty in her eyes nor timorousness in her words. "You may whistle for your precious apology, Sir Bartholomew. I have made no mistake, nor have I misrepresented your behavior to my mother. I shall allow you this much, however. I shall keep my peace as long as you refrain from repeating your unwelcome attentions. Those are my terms."

Sir Bartholomew's smile had withered away. His eyes went cold. "Your terms! Do you not presume somewhat, my lady? I

am the master here. If there are to be any terms made, then
they shall be dictated by me!"

"Not in this, Sir Bartholomew. Understand me well, sir. I
am my own mistress. I shall protect myself and my honor by
any means available to me. For the sake of the peace which
you say you desire with my mother, you will abide by my
wishes in this," said Althea.

"You shall regret this day's work, miss," said Sir Bartholomew, staring at her with hatred plain in his eyes.

"I think not," said Althea. She turned on her heel and
walked quickly out of the sitting room.

Althea went upstairs to her bedroom. She shut the door and
then stood leaning against it. She was shaking. She was glad it
was over. She had not wanted a confrontation. Indeed, she saw
now that she had made a tactical error in going to her mother
before she had thought things through entirely. She should
have written to Charity and presented her mother with an unexceptional invitation that Lady Bottlesby would have been
glad to accept on her behalf. Then she could have left Sir
Bartholomew's roof quietly and without open feelings of hos-
tility.

But she had not been as wise as she had thought. She had
taken an irrevocable step and involved her mother. The
confrontation with Sir Bartholomew had come swiftly and had
been far uglier than she could ever have imagined. Sir Bartholomew's veneer of urbane geniality had been stripped off to
reveal the true nature of the man. Mean, tyrannical, self-centered, cowardly. Who would have ever have believed that all
of that had lurked beneath the skin of the ridiculous little
dandy.

Althea came away from the door and started across the
room to her wardrobe, then faltered a step at a thought. She
frowned in dawning dismay. Sir Bartholomew's strength lay in
his lavish address and easy congeniality. If it ever came to the
point, it would be his word laid against her own. It did not bear
thinking about, but she must. For Sir Bartholomew was obviously not one to accept defeat either gracefully or graciously.
As certainly as though she was again standing in the room
with him listening to his threat, Althea knew that she was not
yet done with Sir Bartholomew.

She would take what precautions she could until she had the opportunity to leave the manor house. Her faithful maid would continue to share her bedroom. In addition, Althea would take care never to be caught alone in the same room with Sir Bartholomew. If her mother retired early of an evening, so would she.

This dinner party that was being planned to honor Lady Bottlesby and herself posed a special challenge. The intent was to introduce them to the surrounding countryside and of a certainty there would be much mingling and probably dancing as well. It would tax her ingenuity, but Althea thought there was little to be gained by giving way to dismay or fear. She would mingle as assiduously as any proper daughter of the house and never allow herself to come within touching distance of Sir Bartholomew. It might prove to be a task to decline to dance with her stepfather, but Althea was determined to manage it. She would not have his hands upon her for any reason.

Althea wrote to her friend in Bath with high hopes. She was devastated when she learned by return post that Charity had been taken to the seashore for a restorative holiday. Apparently the influenza had so undermined Miss Comstock's constitution, which had never been robust, that she had not recovered as well as had been expected. Althea stared at the wall, wondering what she was going to do.

The dinner party was an overwhelming success. Lady Bottlesby was flushed with triumph. She and Althea met the neighbors and all were exceedingly gracious in welcoming the baronet's lady and her daughter to their circle. A liberal number of invitations were bestowed upon the ladies for teas and dinners and other entertainments.

Althea was also well pleased. She had always enjoyed society and she was glad to discover that she met with admiration and acceptance. The gentlemen in particular were quite taken with her. She never lacked for a dance partner or a lemonade. This circumstance was much to Althea's satisfaction because that made it impossible for her stepfather to step into the role of her rescuer. Althea enjoyed the attention and the admiration, but there was not really any single gentleman who struck her fancy.

Althea did mark one gentleman in particular, however, simply because of the oddity of his inclusion in the dinner party. She was told by one of the ladies whom she had become newly acquainted with, somewhat disparagingly, that the gentleman had recently bought a beleagered and hopelessly mortgaged estate. Mr. Craddock was attired in less than fashionable evening dress and wore a bag wig. Althea was not surprised to be told that he was a self-made gentleman with strong affiliations with trade.

What did surprise Althea was to witness the effusive welcome that Sir Bartholomew extended to the gentleman. The baronet's pride was such that Althea would not have believed that Lord Bottlesby would spend more than a moment with this particular guest, or even have bothered to invite him at all.

However, Althea did not find the odd occurrence of more than passing interest and she dismissed the strangeness of it from her mind. She enjoyed herself immensely at the dinner party even though she kept a constant eye out for Sir Bartholomew. But as the evening progressed, her stepfather did not appear inclined to seek her out and Althea was relieved. Perhaps Sir Bartholomew had taken her words to heart, after all, and she would be able to continue living under his roof with the truce that she had forced upon him.

Althea meant to hold Sir Bartholomew to his promise of a come-out. She was certain that in that at least she could count upon her mother's support.

As quickly as possible, Althea felt that she needed to snare herself a husband and establish her own household. She was uncomfortable being obligated to Sir Bartholomew for her every creature comfort with the unpleasantness that lay between them. Also, there was no guarantee how long the truce would hold up under the everyday tensions of living in the same house. Althea would rather avoid any future confrontations and spare her mother the humiliation and the upset if she could.

Surely Sir Bartholomew would have no objection to footing the bill for a Season in London, Althea thought. On the contrary, he would probably be relieved to have her gone. It could not be comfortable for the baronet to be constantly reminded by her continued presence of his foolish mistake.

It came as a shock to Althea to learn a fortnight later that Sir Bartholomew's thoughts had not only run in a similar vein to her own, but had progressed in a singularly unpleasant fashion.

Sir Bartholomew requested Althea to wait upon him in his library. The request was made in front of Lady Bottlesby so that Althea felt a measure of confidence that Sir Bartholomew would not dare to make unseeming advances to her, not when Lady Bottlesby could possibly pop into the room. In addition, her mother had nodded and smiled at her in encouragement so that Althea was able to regard the request with some measure of confidence. However, as a personal precaution Althea asked her maid to come into the room after a short length of time, using as a pretext some sort of wardrobe emergency.

When Althea entered the library, she found Sir Bartholomew seated behind his desk. He indicated a chair in front of the desk and she sat down, her face and manner composed, giving no hint of the trepidation she felt about the meeting.

"Lady Althea. I thank you for coming down so promptly," said Sir Bartholomew, smiling. "I have some important news to discuss with you."

Althea stiffened. She had learned not to trust that particular smile. She braced herself for unpleasantness. "Indeed? You will tell me, I feel certain."

Sir Bartholomew grinned wider. "Indeed I shall, and at once, if only to enjoy my little triumph. You see, stepdaughter, I have contracted your hand to a very worthy gentleman."

Althea was surprised and disturbed. Her slender brows pulled together in a faint frown as her thoughts turned quickly. "You surprise me profoundly, Sir Bartholomew. I had no notion that my interests were of such paramount importance to you."

"Oh, I assure you that I have done all in my power to stir myself upon your behalf. My efforts have met with sublime success." Sir Bartholomew smiled, his small eyes gleaming. "I have affianced you to Mr. Craddock, in fact. You are to be wed as soon as the banns are posted."

"You are mightily mistaken if you believe that I shall agree to this monstrous scheme," said Althea sharply. "I shall wed where I choose, not at your behest, Sir Bartholomew."

"Your consent has not been solicited, nor is it necessary,

Lady Althea. You are yet under age. It is your mother's right
to withhold or to give her consent upon this matter. Lady Bottlesby concurs with me that Mr. Craddock is a fine match,"
said Sir Bartholomew.

The breadth of her betrayal was shocking. Althea rocked
under it as though it was a physical blow. "I do not believe
you!" she exclaimed.

"Naturally you are free to inquire of Lady Bottlesby. You
may even attempt to persuade my lady to a change of heart."
Sir Bartholomew smiled again, this time with obvious satisfaction. "However, I think that you will find that Lady Bottlesby
cherishes the peace of her house too much—as do I!—to be
swayed by any arguments which you may muster." He paused
a moment and showed his teeth. "Lady Bottlesby *is* my lady
wife."

Althea rose from the chair. Her eyes blazed. "I am not done
yet, Sir Bartholomew." She turned and made for the door.

He called after her. "Oh, I beg to differ, my dear Lady
Althea! I told you that you would regret crossing me. I intend
to see that you regret it each and every day of your natural
life."

Althea turned to face him, her face set. "I shall not give you
that satisfaction, sir!"

Sir Bartholomew waved his hand in dismissal. "We shall
not argue the point, for it shall shortly come very clear which
of us is right. By the by, do not think of appealing to Mr. Craddock. I have naturally informed him of your regrettable insta-
bility of mind and excited imagination since the tragedy of
your father's untimely death. Mr. Craddock assures me that he
does not fear such weaknesses. On the contrary, I believe that
he quite sees it as his duty to provide firm guidance for you.
So bourgeois and yet so endearingly earnest. He assured me
that he will be a stern husband." Sir Bartholomew regarded
Lady Althea's white, expressionless face with malicious satisfaction. "You may think on this, stepdaughter. By spurning the
benevolence of which I am capable, you have acquired a mer-
ciless taskmaster."

Althea had stood immobile while the baronet flung the hate-
ful words at her. Now she inclined her head with such exag-

gerated civility that it was a studied insult. "I will not keep you, Sir Bartholomew."

As she opened the door and escaped, the baronet's last snarled curse assaulted her ears.

"I hope that he beats you, jade!"

Chapter Four

Althea's first line of action was to make some sort of appeal to her mother. She had not wanted to believe Sir Bartholomew's assertion, but deep down in her heart she had feared that it was true. Althea hoped desperately that her mother had not truly betrayed her so completely and finally. But she was disappointed.

Lady Bottlesby avoided Althea, sending messages by her expressionless maid that she was prostrated upon her couch and could see no one. After two days, Althea forced her way into her mother's rooms. The resulting interview ended with Lady Bottlesby in tears and Althea retreating in angry defeat.

Mr. Craddock came to call several times upon Sir Bartholomew in order to settle the terms of the marriage contract. Althea had the inadvertent opportunity to overhear a short exchange between the two men before they went into Sir Bartholomew's library and the door was shut. She had chanced to be descending the stairs when Sir Bartholomew had come out into the hallway to greet the arrival of Mr. Craddock with outstretched hands and a jovial word. Not wanting to draw attention to herself, Althea had paused on the landing above until they retreated into Sir Bartholomew's sanctum.

Even after Sir Bartholomew had ushered Mr. Craddock into the library and the door was safely closed, Althea stood rooted to the landing. She could scarcely believe what she had heard. A small cynical smile wavered over her face. It was no wonder that Mr. Craddock had leaped so vulgarly at the opportunity to wed her. Sir Bartholomew was selling her hand very steeply, indeed. But perhaps that enticement could be countered somewhat since she now knew how much emphasis Mr. Craddock placed upon financial opportunity.

Althea wasted little time in requesting an interview with Mr. Craddock. She had meant to meet with the gentleman in any event, but now she felt that she had a small measure of power to put behind the pleading of her case.

Althea received Mr. Craddock in the sitting room alone.

She had requested a private interview and Lady Bottlesby had agreed, though somewhat dubiously. It was not proper for a young lady to have a gentleman call upon her without being chaperoned. But Sir Bartholomew had brushed aside the convention. He seemed almost eager that Althea meet with her suitor. "My dearest lady, surely in such a case as this, we may grant Lady Althea her wish for a few minutes alone with this particular gentleman," he said.

Lady Bottlesby's eyes had widened in comprehension. "Oh, of course! What must I be thinking of? Of course you may speak privately to Mr. Craddock. But only for a quarter hour, Althea. I am persuaded that it would not be proper to allow longer, despite the circumstances."

"Thank you, Mama," said Althea ironically. She had treated Sir Bartholomew's resulting chuckle with indifference and swept off to the sitting room.

Shortly thereafter, Mr. Craddock was ushered in and the door was quietly closed. "Pray be seated, sir," said Althea. "I am glad to have this opportunity to visit with you."

"I do not see the purpose in it, but I am willing to make myself agreeable," said Mr. Craddock. He had graced Althea with a short bow and now seated himself in a wingback chair across from her.

It was not an auspicious beginning. Althea drew in her breath and mustered all of her persuasive powers to convince Mr. Craddock of the unsuitability of a match between them.

However, Sir Bartholomew had been quite correct in his assurances about her suitor. Mr. Craddock brushed aside Althea's plea to his chivalry as well as her logical reasons against the match.

"I warrant that I know better than to take you at your word, my lady. A young foolish miss such as yerself cannot decide these things for the best," he said, settling himself comfortably in the wingback chair. He crossed his heavy ankles and clasped his hands over his ample girth.

With a sharp look, he said, "Aye, ye need a firm hand, as I can well see. Sir Bartholomew explained how ye are and how ye are used to having yer own way, all due to the coddling and the spoiling. It stands to reason that yer head has been turned often with compliments and the like. Ye need an older head than yer own to guide ye and I suppose that was what unhinged ye so when yer father passed away."

"Mr. Craddock, I assure you that I am not in the least unhinged. I simply do not wish for this marriage to take place," said Althea, gritting her teeth.

Unfortunately, Mr. Craddock was willing, even eager, to take her to wed. From certain comments that Mr. Craddock then let drop, Althea gathered that the settlement that Sir Bartholomew had made over to him was even more extraordinary in terms than what she had overheard. The settlement, of course, was but the sweetener beside the consideration of her own fortune.

Mr. Craddock had wet his lips and his eyes had gleamed with a proprietory expression when he had spoken of monies. Certain of her weapon, Althea smiled at the gentleman. "My fortune is considerable, yes. However, I suspect that Sir Bartholomew is somewhat ignorant of the actual state of my affairs. Even after I wed, the major portion of my fortune remains tied up."

Mr. Craddock straightened, his complacent expression replaced with a suspicious frown. "What? What are ye saying, my lady?"

"The Earl of Hawthorne, my father, was a careful man. He did not wish me to ever be at the mercy of a wastrel husband, so he entailed the majority of my fortune to me and to my children," said Althea quietly.

Mr. Craddock levered himself out of the chair. He took a turn about the sitting room, his hands locked behind his back. A massive frown marred his face. "This is news indeed, my lady. I must speak of this to Sir Bartholomew at once. I cannot enter into a contract littered with unpleasant surprises. Yes, yes, I must speak to him at once!"

"You shall naturally do what you think best," said Althea. She rose and took leave of the gentleman. She emerged from the sitting room, her calm manner giving away nothing of the relief that she felt. Surely now she would be freed of this particular threat to her future.

She was unsurprised at Sir Bartholomew's summons later that day. Althea entered the library with a cool expression upon her face. Sir Bartholomew was standing at the window, his gaze fixed on the view. When she closed the door, he turned his head. Althea was startled by the degree of malevolence in his small eyes.

"You think yourself rather clever, do you not?" he inquired.

Althea did not pretend to misunderstand him. "I told you once that I would protect myself by any means at my disposal. I discovered Mr. Craddock's weakness and turned it to my advantage. You must forgive me if I do not commiserate with you at the overturning of your plans."

Sir Bartholomew turned to face her and laughed. The sight and sound struck ice into Althea's veins. "Overturning, my dear? Hardly that! Oh, I shall grant you that there were a few moments of distress, but it was all soon smoothed out to Mr. Craddock's and my own satisfaction. It has all turned out for the better, actually. Mr. Craddock quite saw the disadvantage of having an unstable wife and agreed that he could not be expected to provide the care that your state warrants. However, Bedlam was established for just such little problems and, of course, a Bedlamite relinquishes all rights under the law. Mr. Craddock will be a very, very wealthy man, whilst you, my dear stepdaughter, shall enjoy a vastly amusing existence!"

Althea's hand had crept up to her throat. Her eyes had gone very wide. "You are evil," she whispered. "You are truly evil."

"You have no notion how it gratifies my soul to see that look of horror," said Sir Bartholomew, very quietly. "No; I am not evil. That is merely your perception now that you have lost our little struggle of wills. Mr. Craddock will still wed you, dear Lady Althea. Whether or no he actually has you committed is entirely out of my hands. I grant you have the wit to persuade the gentleman otherwise."

Sir Bartholomew strolled over and stopped before her. He lifted a hand and ran a stroking finger along her tense jaw. Althea jerked away, her eyes flaring with hatred and fear.

He said reflectively, "Almost, I wish that you could manage

it. It will be a pity to think of such beauty wasted." Without a glance, he left the library.

Althea fled to her bedroom and locked herself inside. She paced up and down the carpet, wracking her brain for some way to escape the snare that Sir Bartholomew had set so skillfully for her.

She knew that she could not appeal to her mother. Lady Bottlesby had closed her eyes and her ears. Even if her ladyship would listen, all that Sir Bartholomew would have to do would be to deny that any such conversations had ever taken place between himself and Mr. Craddock or between himself and Althea. Lady Bottlesby was willing to seize upon any reassurance that all was well.

If by some wild chance Lady Bottlesby did get up the courage to appeal to Mr. Craddock for the truth—an unlikely scenario, indeed!—Althea knew very well that the gentleman would deny it. He would be a fool to do otherwise, for it would jeopardize everything that he had come to covet.

Recalling how Mr. Craddock had wet his lips and the avarice in his eyes when speaking about her fortune, Althea shuddered. She would not gamble the rest of her life against the gentleman's manifested spirit of greed. That was a vain hope. As certainly as she breathed, Althea knew that there would be no appeal that she could make to Mr. Craddock once she became his legal wife.

Althea saw no recourse. Cudgel her brain as much as she might, she could think of nothing better than to deny taking her vows at the altar. What with Sir Bartholomew's dastardly machinations, she thought bitterly, that would not serve in the least. He had probably already thought of that option, as it seemed to be the last one open to her, and was undoubtedly at that very moment making arrangements to close that door, as well. Althea had no clue how it could be done to have her married whether she willed it or not, but she had come to the point of believing that Sir Bartholomew was equal to nearly anything.

Althea mentally ran through every one of her acquaintances in Bath and even those whom she had known while at seminary. There was no one to whom she could appeal, really. All who were known to her or her mother would be reluctant to harbor her against her parent. She was under age and thus still legally under her mother's, and her stepfather's, protection.

She contemplated the possibility of simply disappearing. She had quite a bit of pin money left to her from previous quarters since she had done very little shopping while in mourning, with the notable exception of what her mother's wedding had required. She could take what she had and a portmanteau or two, buy a coach ticket, and drop out of sight.

Althea knew that it was mad to consider running away to London and trusting in her wits to find herself some menial post. She knew what she could face. She knew that she had her share of beauty. She could look into any mirror and see that. She knew, too, from talk she had heard among her mother's friends, or overheard from gentlemen who visited her father and who had not noticed the presence of a quiet attentive child, that comely servantwomen were held to be fair game. Her father's house had left her with few illusions about what could happen to a woman without protection.

But Althea could not think of any alternative. She could only hope that whatever faced her would be better than what she would be leaving behind.

Althea made up her mind to take her chances. She would have to take her maid into her confidence, of course. The dresser would undoubtedly object to her mistress's plans, but once she had been made to understand the alternative, Althea felt certain that the woman would wholeheartedly support her.

Althea recognized that she needed her maid's help to leave the manor house. Sir Bartholomew would not simply allow her to walk out the door with her trunks. But if the dresser carried some bandboxes and accompanied her, perhaps on the pretext of going into the village to take some gowns to a seamstress for altering, Althea thought that they might be able to leave without comment.

A worrisome thought plagued her. She did not know what Darcy would do once she was gone, for it was a foregone conclusion that the dresser would be turned out without references for playing a part in the escape. Yet Althea knew that she had no alternative but to request her maid's aid. She only hoped that the references that she would pen before her departure would be adequate enough to enable the dresser to seek another comfortable post.

Althea had actually stretched out her hand to pull the bell rope for her maid when she recalled the existence of a long forgotten great-aunt.

Althea sat down in her wingback in front of the fireplace. Her brows knitted in a frown as she thought about her great-aunt. Lady Angleton had already been approaching old age when Althea was still a child. However, she was undoubtedly still very much alive. Her ladyship was too irascible to have died in the last several months. They had last heard from Aunt Aurelia when she had sent a card of condolence upon the earl's passing. Althea thought that her mother would surely have mentioned it if Aunt Aurelia, whom she held in the greatest awe, had since died.

As she recalled, her mother was not only very much in awe of Aunt Aurelia, but perhaps even a little afraid of her ladyship. Remembering a few things from the infrequent visits that her family had made to Lady Angleton's estate during her childhood, Althea smiled faintly.

Her father had fought with Lady Angleton, often coming off the worse in the skirmishes, but he had had an affection for the old woman that had never been shaken. Her mother's feelings about Lady Angleton had been just as strong, but quite otherwise. Unlike the Earl of Hawthorne, his lady wife had always been glad to escape Lady Angleton's sphere of influence and return to London.

Althea did not think even Sir Bartholomew could override Aunt Aurelia's potent effect on Lady Bottlesby. If anyone could make Lady Bottlesby stand up to the baronet, it would be Aunt Aurelia.

Perhaps she could appeal to Aunt Aurelia. Perhaps her great-aunt could be persuaded to stand for her.

Althea closed her eyes on a fervent, winged prayer. Oh God, she hoped so. It was her best, her only, hope.

Althea rose from the chair and reached for the bell rope. It was only a moment before the dresser entered the bedroom from her own adjoining quarters. "My lady?"

"Pray sit down, Darcy. I wish to speak with you," said Althea quietly.

When Althea had put her dresser into possession of the facts of her circumstances, the woman compressed her lips and gave a sharp nod. "You'll be wanting to leave this place quick as you can, my lady."

"My thoughts precisely, Darcy," said Althea with a faint smile that did not quite eradicate the shadows in her eyes. "My reliance is upon you, for I know that I cannot simply pack my wardrobe and order out a carriage. Sir Bartholomew will not allow it. I had thought perhaps that carrying a bandbox or two, with the excuse that I needed a few things altered in the village, would do. I could drive the gig in and simply leave it at the livery stables."

"I have a better thought, my lady. I shall say that I have received a note from my sister, who is sick and needs me to nurse her. You will give me leave to be gone. Then we shall pack the portmanteaus and you will be kind enough to see me off on the coach before you go about your shopping," said the dresser.

"Yes," breathed Althea, her smile widening. "That will do very well, Darcy. I do thank you."

"I will accompany you on your journey, of course," said the dresser.

Althea looked at her tiring woman. "Will you, indeed?"

"Yes, my lady. From what you have said, it is my understanding that Lady Angleton is a high stickler. You will not want to arrive on her step without a respectable female," said the dresser primly.

"Indeed not. You are quite right, Darcy. Very well, then. You must go to Cotswold with me," said Althea. She heard the luncheon bell and turned toward the door. "I must go down and play my part of cowed stepdaughter, I suppose." Her hand upon the knob, Althea looked back at her dresser. She said softly, "I appreciate your loyalty, Darcy. Thank you."

"I should lose my position, and rightly so, if I should ever do less, my lady," said Darcy staunchly.

Althea smiled again, this time rather mistily, and exited the bedroom.

Chapter Five

After luncheon, Althea returned to her room. She found that her dresser was already sorting through the wardrobe for the scant belongings that they would be able to smuggle out of the manor. Three small, battered portmanteaus stood open at the maid's feet.

"All is in train, Darcy. I have informed Lady Bottlesby of your sister's illness and that you will be leaving on the coach on the morrow," said Althea. She smiled somewhat grimly. "Sir Bartholomew was particularly commiserative about your position. He assured me that he would see to it that I was at once supplied with a suitable lady's maid for the duration of your absence."

The dresser snorted. "That does not surprise me, my lady. That one is a snake in the grass if ever there was one!"

"Yes, indeed!" Althea went to the wardrobe and lifted out the elegant gown that she had worn for the dinner party. She took firm hold of one of the lace flounces on the skirt and very deliberately ripped it. "What a pity that you are leaving so soon, Darcy. You will not have time to repair my dress. I shall have to take it in to the village seamstress in the morning, for it is quite one of my favorites," she said.

"A pity, indeed, my lady," said Darcy woodenly, but with a twinkle in her eyes.

The remainder of the day, Althea chose to avoid Sir Bartholomew. He did not actively seek her company, which made it all the easier. Even after dinner when he had joined Lady Bottlesby and Althea in the drawing room for coffee, he was circumspect in his manner toward Althea, merely bowing to her and offering one of his genial smiles.

Lady Bottlesby anxiously watched Althea's reaction to Sir

Bartholomew. It was pitifully apparent that she hoped that there would not be any unpleasantness. Her countenance visibly relaxed when Althea turned away to sit down at the pianoforte and began quietly to play a selection.

Lady Bottlesby decided to retire early. She glanced at Sir Bartholomew when Althea said that she, too, would go upstairs, but the baronet seemed quite unaware of any possible slight.

Sir Bartholomew lifted Lady Bottlesby's hand to his lips and gallantly kissed her beringed fingers. "You are tired, my dear. I understand perfectly."

Lady Bottlesby flushed. She cast a glance at her daughter, who was waiting for her beside the door. "Yes; it has been a rather fatiguing day. I-I shall have a good night's rest, however, and be much more the thing in the morning."

Sir Bartholomew sighed and nodded. "Indeed, I believe all of us shall be the better for rest." He raised his voice slightly, adding, "Good night, Lady Althea."

Althea inclined her head, her face quite expressionless. Lady Bottlesby cast a worried glance from one to the other, then hurried over to the door. "Come, Althea. You may accompany me up the stairs."

The ladies exited the drawing room, leaving Sir Bartholomew to contemplate the fire with a thoughtful expression. After a few moments, a small, satisfied smile stretched his mouth.

As mother and daughter progressed up the stairs, Lady Bottlesby expressed once more her surprise and sadness to have learned that Althea's dresser would be leaving. "I only hope that Darcy's sister is quickly recovered so that she may soon return," said Lady Bottlesby.

"I do not expect to be without her for long, dear ma'am," said Althea with perfect truth. She parted from her mother at the head of the stairs and entered her bedroom.

Althea's dresser was waiting for her and quickly helped her to undress for bed. "Are all of your preparations made, Darcy?" Althea asked as she slipped between the sheets.

The dresser turned the key in the door. She smiled as she crossed to her own humble cot. "Yes, my lady. I shall be leaving in the morning, just as we discussed." She blew out the candle. "Sleep well, my lady."

When Sir Bartholomew and Lady Bottlesby came downstairs for breakfast, they found Althea just emerging from the breakfast room. Althea was dressed in a driving pelisse and carried whip and gloves under her arm. "Good morning," she greeted them, stopping to pull on her gloves. "Mama, I am glad to have caught you before I leave."

"Before you leave, Lady Althea?" Sir Bartholomew stared very hard at his stepdaughter.

"Yes. I am taking the gig into the village," said Althea. She was very aware of the suspicion in the baronet's gaze, but she did not glance at him as she turned toward her mother. "Mama, the most distressing thing! Darcy was going through my clothing this morning to be certain that all was left just as it should be and she found that my gown had been torn. Look, I have it here in this bandbox."

Althea lifted the lid of the bandbox that was sitting on a chair in the hallway. She displayed the torn lace flounce to her mother. Sir Bartholomew exhibited an unusual interest in the contents of the bandbox and his eyes narrowed when he saw the gown.

Lady Bottlesby uttered a sound of distress. "How annoying, to be sure! But what will you do, my dear? Darcy is leaving this very morning, and she is the only needlewoman in the house who can work lace."

"You must see my dilemma, Mama, for I should like to wear this same gown to the soiree on Friday. Darcy assured me that she has heard good things of the village seamstress's skill, so I have decided to take my gown to the woman this very morning. I can see Darcy off on the coach and run a few small errands, as well. I hope that that will give the seamstress time enough to make some progress and I shall be able to inspect the quality of her work. If it is not being done to my satisfaction, why, then there will still be time for the woman to rework it again before Friday," said Althea.

Lady Bottlesby nodded her approval. "That is a very good plan, Althea. I shall not expect you back before luncheon, of course."

"Do you think that it will take so long?" asked Althea, allowing the faintest expression of surprise to cross her face.

"Oh, most definitely it will. You must not rush the woman. That would be fatal," said Lady Bottlesby.

"Very well. I shall take tea in the village," said Althea. She smiled at her mother. "Have you any commissions for me, dear ma'am?"

Lady Bottlesby shook her head. "I do not believe so. At least, I can think of nothing at this moment. How provoking, to be sure! For undoubtedly something will leap to mind as soon as you have left!"

Althea smiled and agreed that it was always just so. She turned to Sir Bartholomew, who had been silently listening to the exchange with pursed mouth. Her voice noticeably cooler, Althea asked politely, "And you, sir? Have you any small commissions that I may discharge for you?"

Sir Bartholomew's expression cleared, as though he had come to some conclusion. "No, I think not, Lady Althea. I assume that your former dresser is already waiting patiently in the gig for you. Pray do not let us keep you standing about any longer. I should not like the woman to be late in catching the coach."

"No, indeed," agreed Althea. She picked up the bandbox and walked quickly out of the house.

A short minute later, Lady Althea, in the company of her dresser, drove away from the manor house. Neither of them looked back.

It was a short drive to the village. Althea left the gig at the livery stable and went inside the inn. When she emerged, she had in her possession two tickets for the mail coach. "Now we are set," she said with satisfaction.

The dresser shook her head dubiously. "It is not a form of travel that you are used to, my lady."

"Much I shall care for that! We shall not remain upon the coach for long, in any event," said Althea.

"What do you mean, my lady?" asked Darcy, darting a frown at her mistress.

"The coach is to be a red herring for Sir Bartholomew once he realizes that the bird has flown. He will naturally inquire for what destination our tickets were purchased. But long before that destination is reached, we shall have quietly disembarked and hired a chaise for the remainder of our journey. I imagine that shall gain us a good bit of time," said Althea cheerfully.

"Then you do expect the gentleman to give chase, my lady," said Darcy, drawing an unhappy breath.

"Oh, yes. Sir Bartholomew will give chase," said Althea quietly. "I have already learned that he does not easily accept defeat. But then, neither do I."

The mail coach arrived at the inn on time. Althea and her companion gave their baggage into the coachman's care and climbed up into the coach to take their places. The other occupants of the coach obligingly squeezed over to make room.

Althea's manner of dress was more elegant than any other individual upon the coach and gained some curious glances from two farm women. One of the women, her hand covering her mouth, leaned over toward Darcy. " 'Ere now, wot is a lady of quality doin' on the mail?"

The dresser threw a swift glance at her mistress. Althea was determinedly staring out of the window, apparently unaware that she was under discussion, but Darcy's keen eyes saw the faint tide of color in her cheeks. The dresser nodded at the farm woman and with a show of confidentiality, she leaned forward. "The poor thing has fallen upon harsh times. Her father has gone and done himself in and now she is on her way to her first post as governess."

"An evil day, I make no doubt," said the farm woman, shocked.

Thereafter the farm women whispered to one another, often glancing in Althea's direction. Althea was glad when they descended at the next stop. She turned at once to her companion. "What a positive horror story you told those poor women," she said in a low voice, mindful of the occupants who still shared the coach with them.

"Aye, but they will remember you and how you were on the mail coach," said Darcy, smiling.

Althea stared at her dresser. "How very clever of you, Darcy," she said finally.

Hours later the coach rolled into the yard of a large inn. The coachman bawled that there would be a fifteen-minute wait while the team was changed out and he recommended that his passengers go inside for a spot of tea.

Althea was one of those who alighted. The faithful Darcy was close behind her. Althea stood looking about her at the bustling inn yard. "I think—yes, I rather think that this is it, Darcy. Surely in such a crowd we shall go relatively unnoticed," she said.

"I shall manage the getting of our baggage then, my lady," said Darcy.

Althea nodded and went into the inn to arrange for the hiring of a chaise. The innkeeper was most accommodating. He did indeed have a chaise and a team for hire. If the lady would deign to wait in his own humble parlor, where she would be quite undisturbed, he would arrange the matter at once.

As Althea stood waiting for her chaise, she heard her name called. Her heart plunged into her throat. She literally froze, her mind whirling with disbelief. It was not until she was again addressed that she realized that she had not heard the voice of her stepfather, but rather that of a stranger.

"Lady Althea?"

Althea turned, and met the deep blue eyes of a gentleman dressed in military togs. His face was vaguely familiar to her. She frowned uncertainly, feeling that she must know him.

The gentleman smiled. "Surely I have not changed so very much over the years. I am Gareth Marshall."

Althea's face cleared. She at once held out her hands to him. "Of course! It was the uniform that confused me. You are still very like in face. I should have recognized you straight away."

Major Gareth Marshall released her fingers. He gestured around at the inn parlor. "I was passing the door. When I saw you, I could not imagine what Lady Althea would be doing in such a place, leagues from London. I was only assured of your identity when I addressed you."

Althea smiled, but her eyes clouded slightly. "It is a long, dull story. I will not bore you with the details. I shall not be remaining here long, in any event."

"I, too, am traveling. I have been on leave to visit my parents, but now I am returning to my duties," said Major Marshall.

"Oh, I had forgotten that the Chard country seat was in

Berkshire," said Althea. She laughed suddenly. "My word, Gareth, it does not seem possible that it has been so many years. When we last saw each other, you were on holiday from Eton!"

"And you were a skinny, shy little thing. I remember that you had found a hurt kitten and were determined to nurse it back to health," said Major Marshall.

Althea laughed again. Her eyes sparkled. "Oh, I had forgotten. That was Tommy-Cat."

"Then you did keep him?"

"Only after a long battle royal with Nurse. She detested cats. But fortunately, Tommy-Cat proved his worth by catching a mouse from under her bed. Thereafter, Nurse was his staunchest champion. Tommy-Cat lived a long, pampered life, I assure you," said Althea. "But tell me of yourself, Gareth. I have often wondered what became of you. Now, obviously, I see that you have made a place for yourself in the army. Have you been in this dreadful war from the beginning?"

"It seems so at times. But that is all coming to an end. Once Wellington meets with Bonaparte, then we shall have permanent peace," said Major Marshall. He gestured. "May I join you here in the parlor? I have ordered tea for myself and I would be honored if you would share it with me."

Althea hesitated. She glanced over at her dresser, who had come quietly into the parlor with the portmanteaus and bandbox. "That would prove unexceptional, I think." Darcy nodded understanding and moved to a discreet distance, far enough away not to overhear conversation but near enough to provide the proper chaperonage."Yes, that would be very nice. I shall ask that my chaise not be brought around immediately."

"Excellent!" Major Marshall escorted Althea to the table. They conversed well together with never an awkward pause. The tea was soon brought and Althea requested that the waiter serve her maid as well. Major Marshall was pleasantly surprised by Lady Althea's thoughtfulness. It was his experience that many social beauties spared scarcely a thought for their servants.

Althea relayed her message about her chaise through the waiter and turned back to resume her enjoyable conversation with her charming companion. She knew that she could not delay for long, but she reassured herself that a few minutes spent over tea would not matter so very much. She and Darcy had to have sustenance, after all.

Chapter Six

Althea now recalled something she had read some months previously that was rather shocking in the face of this coincidental meeting. "I was sorry to read in the lists that your brother was killed," she said.

"Yes; it was a black day for us all," said Gareth, his expression growing somber. He reflected that the tragedy was not only that he had lost a brother, but that the Earl of Chard had lost his heir.

"I must become accustomed to addressing you as Lord Lynley now. It is difficult to think of you as other than Gareth Marshall, however," said Althea with a smile.

"Yes, for me also. I never had expectations of the title. George was naturally bred to it, while I was allowed to choose my own way," said Lord Lynley, almost regretting that Lady Althea had called to mind his new persona. It was still ill-fitting to him, but he supposed that he would eventually learn to accept it.

Gareth had always been secure in the knowledge that it was his brother Lynley's responsibility to carry on the family line and shoulder the responsibilities of an earldom. He had never begrudged his brother the favored position of heir, nor bemoaned his lot as a younger son. As he perceived it, he was free to pursue whatever course in life he chose.

Now that freedom was at an end. Recalling his visit with his parents, the Earl and Countess of Chard, he sighed wearily. It had been difficult for them all.

The earl had used his considerable influence to have leave extended to his son so that the major could wait on his lordship. Major Marshall had been dismayed, though not altogether surprised, when the earl demanded that he sell out and give up his commission in the army and take up the mantle of heir apparent. The Earl of Chard had lost the hope of his house to the war; he did not wish to lose the last of his line.

There had been a terrible row. Though Gareth had fully appreciated his sire's position, he had a will and a sense of honor of his own. He meant to see the war through.

The earl had cursed him, exclaiming, "And when will that be, sirrah? Has not that Corsican escaped? All of demented Europe will flock to his banner yet again and we will see more of this same carnage!"

"I think not, sir," Gareth had said quietly. "While it is true that Bonaparte is once more at large, I do not expect his power to summon up an army to be such as it once was. The back of the French army is broken. In any event, Wellington is more than capable of settling the matter."

"The Sepoy general!" sneered the earl. "For all of his exploits, he has never faced Bonaparte himself. The duke has not a hope of defeating that brilliant madman."

"You would not speak so disparagingly of the duke, sir, if you had seen him in action on the Peninsular," said Gareth.

"Oh, I am well aware that Wellington is some sort of hero to you," said the earl, waving away his son's endorsement. "But it was while serving under his command that George was killed. You can say nothing that can defend that, sirrah!"

Gareth had known that that at least was true. Nothing would ever sway the earl from his irrational position that the Duke of Wellington was to be held personally responsible for the death of the scion of the House of Chard. Never mind that Lord Lynley had died in the company of so many others in an heroic action. The earl cared nothing about that. What mattered to him was that his heir was dead.

The only wonder of it was that the Earl of Chard had not sooner demanded that Gareth leave the army. But that had probably been due to the ceasing of the hostilities that had followed Bonaparte's surrender and the defeated emperor's subsequent exile to the island of Elba. In part, it must also have been due to the countess's influence.

On that thought, Gareth's eyes had sought and found the Countess of Chard's gaze. She had always been sympathetic to his restless desire to make his own mark upon the world, recognizing that it stood him in good stead as the younger son. She had probably counseled the earl to wait, that since the peace had come Gareth would of his own volition reach the conclusion that it was time to return home to England and take up his new responsibilities.

Then had come the shocking news of Bonaparte's escape. Shortly thereafter, Gareth had received the earl's summons and had gone home to Chard where the unfortunate confrontation had taken place.

"I am sorry, sir. I will be unable to comply with your wishes at this time. I mean to see an end put to Bonaparte," said Gareth quietly.

"You are my heir!" the earl roared, his eyes blazing. "Does that mean nothing to you?"

"It means more than I can ever express," said Gareth with perfect truth and palpable regret. The countess had winced. "However, I must finish with my sworn duty before God and king. I must see this war through to the end. Then I will sell my commission and take up my responsibilities as heir of Chard."

"Is that your final word?" snapped the earl.

"It is," said Gareth.

There was a tense silence that lengthened while the earl scowled into the fire and his hands worked on the arms of his chair. His lordship's thoughts could not be discerned from his expression. It would have astonished his son to have known that he had just earned a high measure of respect from his parent. The earl recognized the steel in his son and could not but admire its existence. His son was a man, indeed.

"Very well." The earl's tone was abrupt and dismissive. "Return to your damnable war. Now get out of my sight!"

As Gareth bowed and made his way to the door, the earl's fierce voice made him pause.

"I forbid you to be killed! I want grandsons, sirrah!"

"I shall keep it in mind, sir," Gareth had said gravely.

He had left Chard that same day, after taking tender leave of his mother. Now, as he looked across the table at Lady Althea, he was glad that he had done so. He might have missed this chance meeting otherwise. Gad, she had grown into a beauty!

If she was not already betrothed, there had to be several gentlemen vying for her hand.

On the thought, he inquired with a smile, "Have you been visiting friends? Perhaps the family of a favored gentleman?"

Althea stared at him. Startled alarm shone out of her eyes. Color suddenly flew into her cheeks and she turned her face aside.

Surprised by her reaction, Gareth began to wonder whether she was not mixed up in some sort of sordid intrigue. He had already learned that she had gone directly from the seminary into a year of mourning for her father, so she had not been given the opportunity to learn of the snares set for fashionable and wealthy young ladies. The possibility that a young innocent such as Lady Althea had been drawn into something detrimental to her immediately aroused his concern.

"Lady Althea—forgive me, but I cannot ignore your obvious discomfiture over what I intended only as an innocuous query," he said quietly. "If there is something that you would like to confide in me, or if there is some service that I might perform for you, I am willing to put myself at your disposal."

Althea did not glance at him. She knew that she had betrayed herself through her gaucherie. It was damnable not to know quite how to retrieve the situation. Embarrassment deepened her flush.

Gareth laid his fingers gently over her hand, and when it leaped like a startled deer under his, he held it firmly. "Althea, we were once friends. Can you not confide in me? I assure you of my complete discretion," he said persuasively.

There was a long moment during which he was not certain that she would respond. Then she turned fully toward him, at the same time pulling at her hand. He allowed her freedom, at least for that moment assured that she did not mean to flee.

She said abruptly, "I am on my way to join my great-aunt Lady Angleton's household in the Cotswolds. She is an invalid and lives retired from society. She likes wheezy pugs. She detests horses. She throws objects at those who displease her. She likes to play cards for hours upon hours."

Major Marshall almost laughed at this pungent description, but the complete seriousness in Althea's voice and expression stopped him. He contemplated the young woman sitting across from him. A deep frown pulled his dark brows together. "I don't understand. Is this a visit made out of duty, perhaps because you are this lady's heir?"

Althea laughed at that, but not from amusement. "No, I do not stand to inherit a penny. I would not care if I did. My great-aunt Aurelia was one of my father's few favorites, I think because she did not allow him to browbeat her. No, it is not a visit for gain and certainly not one for pleasure. I am going into self-imposed exile. I do not come into my majority until I am twenty-one, you see, and therefore I am unable to set up my own establishment until then."

Gareth asked slowly, "What has Lady Hawthorne to say to this scheme?" He was delicately feeling his way. There was such an angry and yet helpless look in her eyes that he feared she would end her confidences before he had heard the whole. And he had the gut feeling that there was a great deal more to be told.

"Several months after my father died, my mother began to enjoy the admiration of a certain gentleman. She has wed Sir Bartholomew Bottlesby." Althea hesitated, then said in a neutral voice, "I do not care for Sir Bartholomew. It will relieve my mother to have me off her hands."

There it was. The reason that Lady Althea was fleeing.

Major Marshall was hit with several impressions all at once. Lady Althea had been deprived of her rightful protector by her father's death. Her mother had remarried, with almost unseeming haste, and to a gentleman that her daughter disliked. Lady Althea disliked her stepfather with such extraordinary intensity that she was willing to bury herself alive in the household of a decrepit, demanding, crotchey old tartar who would undoubtedly make every moment of her existence a misery. If he knew anything of the ways of the world, and he did, this great-aunt would undoubtedly use Lady Althea in the manner of an unpaid drudge.

Major Marshall swore at the one, unescapable, conclusion that could be drawn. "The scoundrel! I should like to thrash him."

Althea looked at him with surprise. Real amusement leaped into her eyes. "You must not think that I was completely defenseless, Gareth."

"Then it is true. Your stepfather made unwelcome advances to you," said Gareth.

Althea nodded, then shrugged. "I am fortunate in a way, I suppose. My father's long association with a succession of mistresses left me with few illusions regarding a gentleman's wiles. I at once perceived what Sir Bartholomew was about. He naturally denied everything to my mother and she, poor thing, did not want to believe that her fairytale marriage was just that—a fairytale."

"And so you fled," said Gareth.

"Not immediately. I did not know what to do, you see. I thought perhaps that I might manage until my majority. But then Sir Bartholomew swore that he would see me wed at once to whomever he could get to come up to scratch. Before the week was out, he found a parti," said Althea. "It was then that I thought of my great-aunt."

The small hairs literally stood up on the back of Gareth's neck. Her reticence about the prospective bridegroom that Sir Bartholomew had engaged for her hand spoke volumes. Gareth's imagination raised such specters for him that the fingers of his hand, which had been lying at ease upon his thigh, clenched tightly into a fist. But he did not allow the depth of his outrage to appear in either his expression or his voice. "Your position was awkward," he said.

"Exceedingly so," agreed Althea dryly.

A half-formed thought crossed Gareth's mind. It startled him, and he brought it sharply into focus. He frowned at the young woman seated across from him. He recalled that as a girl Lady Althea had been self-possessed and all spindly limbs and long braids. She had grown into a beautiful young woman, but had retained her self-possession and reticent nature. To his sharpened gaze, her face showed signs of strain. But she met his gaze frankly, unflinchingly.

"It is an intolerable situation," he said.

"Yes, it is," she said quietly. "But I shall manage, for I must."

He could only admire her fortitude. His reflections came full-blown into existence. He said slowly, "I believe that I might be able to provide an alternative for you, Lady Althea."

Chapter Seven

Althea looked at him. There was mingled surprise and disappointment in her expression. Her voice grown noticeably cooler, she asked, "Yes?"

Gareth was startled by Lady Althea's swift change in demeanor until he suddenly recalled what she had said about being wise to the ploys of gentlemen. He realized with almost a sense of horror that she thought that he meant to offer her an indelicate proposition. Quietly, he said, "I would not insult you so, my lady."

For the second time, color flared in Althea's face. However, her eyes did not waver from his own steady gaze. Very carefully, she asked, "If it is not carte blanche that you offer, then what?"

Lady Althea had spoken with a fair amount of composure, but Gareth could see that she was holding herself very close. He had seen just such tension among his battle-scarred companions and had felt it himself many, many times. Always the feeling of being wound up tight as a screw struck just minutes before a battle was opened.

Gareth began divulging slowly what he had in mind. "As you might not know, before Lynley was killed last year he had affianced himself to an unexceptional girl. They planned to wed when he had completed his tour of duty. Lynley was killed before he was able to make the girl his wife." He stopped, frowning into the middle distance. "I am now heir to Chard and must take upon myself all the duties and obligations that have fallen upon my shoulders."

"Of course," said Althea. She fully appreciated the situation that he had explained, but what she did not understand was what any of this family history had to do with her own circumstances.

Gareth turned his dark gaze back to her. His eyes held an indefinable expression. "My father, the earl, is anxious to see the succession secured. Lynley died before he could accomplish that. My father does not wish me to return to the war, fearing that I, too, will be killed, thus erasing all chance of another generation of Marshalls to succeed him."

"But you are returning to the army," said Althea.

"Yes, I am. I swore an oath before God and for my king. I cannot in all conscience turn my back upon that. Until Bonaparte is completely defeated, I cannot take up my position here in England." Gareth smiled wryly then. "My father was not best pleased at my decision."

"Yes, I understand his lordship's concern," said Althea. She hesitated a moment. "Gareth, forgive me. But what has this to do with me?"

Gareth's expression sobered. There was a sudden intentness in his eyes that could not be ignored nor escaped. His keen gaze pinned her to her chair. "What I propose is simply this, Lady Althea. You need an escape from an intolerable position. I could do with a wife, one who could perhaps produce an heir for Chard if I do not return from the war. As I see it, we are each in the position to help the other."

He stated it baldly, without fancy dressing or false declarations. Somehow he knew that otherwise she would not even consider his outrageous suggestion.

Althea stared at her companion, shocked.

It was indeed outrageous. Gareth could see from her wide-eyed expression how startling his bold proposal had been to her. But as he watched the varying emotions that began to flit over her face, he thought that he could not have hit upon a solution that would so well benefit both of them.

Althea looked at Major Gareth Marshall, Lord Lynley, for a long, long moment. Never in her life had she expected to be offered a stark marriage of convenience.

If she had ever given a thought to accepting such an arrangement at all, she would have dismissed it out of hand. She had seen the effects of a convenient, loveless marriage that had not even had mutual respect to grace it. She did not want that for herself. She had seen the results of just such a marriage, the one that had produced herself, and the extreme disillusionment that had affected the Earl and Countess of Hawthorne.

But as Althea reflected on Lord Lynley's extraordinary proposal, she realized that the contract that he offered would not be the same as that which her parents had entered into. Her mother had told Althea more than once how fortunate she had thought herself to be chosen to become Lady Hawthorne; how excited she had been at the preparations for the social wedding; how she had enjoyed being feted as the new countess. Althea's mother had gone to the altar a dreamy-eyed romantic with scarcely a thought given to the kind of gentleman she was to wed.

Althea was not a romantic. She knew herself to be irrevocably marked by her upbringing. She was too cynical, too wise, to be caught up in the intrigues of the heart. She had meant on her come-out to identify a like-minded gentleman who shared her tastes and thus one with whom she could be comfortable. It would be a marriage of convenience, yes, but one built upon respect that would with time deepen into affection.

Love in the romantic sense was errant nonsense. How often she had observed her father's pursuits and conquests. The prize had been pleasing for a time; then his interest had inevitably waned. Love had no place in a sensible marriage; but neither did the hatred and bitterness that had plagued her parents.

Lord Lynley's direct gaze held hers while he awaited her answer. Althea liked that. He was not pressuring her or attempting to persuade her in any way. He was merely waiting.

She considered him thoughtfully with new eyes. She had known him when they had been children. Gareth Marshall had never been a cruel or a bullying boy. It was doubtful that his basic character had changed to any degree. The very fact that he was allowing her time to reflect without interruption was proof of that.

Lord Lynley was handsome of face. The hawkish set of his features was pleasing to her eyes, while his deep voice was pleasant to her ears. He was well set up. There were few gentlemen who would equal him in physical attractions, she felt.

Yet he did not appear to be puffed up in his own esteem. Not once had he glanced toward the mirror or reached up to assure himself of the set of his cravat.

She knew him to be an active man. His choice of career indicated that as much as did his lean, fit physique. That suited her very well, for she had never been a die-away miss. If she accepted him, there would be horses and holidays into the wilds of Scotland. She would be freer than she had ever been in her life.

Althea almost regretted that Lord Lynley meant to take up his obligations as heir to Chard. She rather thought that she would have enjoyed following the drum as a soldier's wife.

Lastly, she considered the fact that they were social equals. According to the world's wisdom it would not be a misalliance for either of them. If they were agreed on what the marriage was to mean to each partner, then Althea thought that they might go along very well.

The terms of the contract between them had already been established. His obligation would be to provide for and to protect her. Hers, to produce the much-needed heir for Chard.

It was a simple enough bargain, and better than she might have hoped for. She had always liked Gareth Marshall, and her former feelings had only taken firmer root upon being in his company for the hour past.

As for how he viewed her, she had already seen that he had a strong sense of chivalry. He had realized that she was in some sort of difficulty and had offered his help to her before even knowing the circumstances. A gentleman with a chivalric streak automatically offered respect to his lady.

She could not ask for more.

Done with her reflections, Althea did not hesitate. She said, simply, "Yes."

Gareth was unaware of the flow of dispassionate logic that had concluded in that one syllable. He mistakenly thought, with compassion, that Lady Althea had been engaged in a wavering conflict between fear and hope. In a gesture of reassurance, he took her hand and lifted her fingers to his lips. "You will not regret it, I promise," he said quietly.

"I know that I shall not," she said with equal quiet.

Gareth was struck once more by her calm. His admiration

for her poise under stress was strengthened. Whatever the fears she might harbor, she had placed her trust and her life in his hands and had done so in a fashion that spoke of generations of breeding. It humbled him to realize the enormity of the responsibility that he was taking on. He would not fail her.

"We must make proper arrangements. I am due back with my regiment in little more than a fortnight, so we shall have to be wed by special license," he said.

"I am under age, Gareth," said Althea softly. "And I do not know whether my mother will grant her consent."

He was surprised, not by the reminder of her age but by her uncertainty over her mother's agreement to the match. "Surely you do not believe that Lady Haw-Lady Bottlesby will object to having me for a son-in-law. Why, she has known me since I was in short coats," he said.

"Left to herself, my mother would willingly grant her blessing, I think. However, she is easily overridden. What I fear is that Sir Bartholomew will persuade her to withhold her consent," said Althea.

"Left him in a towering rage, did you?" asked Gareth, at once fully comprehending and appreciating the difficulty.

"Sir Bartholomew is known for his genial nature rather than his strength of character. He is like many such weak men. He will go to great lengths to punish those who defy him," said Althea. She smiled a little. "His choice of husband for me was to be of that nature. I was to pay for my lifetime for the sin of upsetting his applecart."

Gareth sat frowning for a moment, then asked, "Your maid has agreed to remain with you?"

"Yes. I would not otherwise have been able to travel in a respectable fashion." Althea's eyes glinted with laughter. "Though I do not care overmuch for such things, I suspected that my great-aunt would refuse to admit me if I did not present the proper appearance."

Gareth cast a keen glance at the tall, thin, lantern-jawed female in black who was sitting quietly at a discreet distance from them. "She looks the sort able and willing to throw a man into a mudpond just on the basis of a familiar glance."

"Yes, that is Darcy. She is loyal to me to a fault," said Althea.

Gareth understood what he thought was the underlying message in her words. "Then you trust her implicitly. Good; that simplifies matters, for we shall have to present a tale to the world to explain the suddenness of our marriage. The less talk there is, the better it will be."

"How do you mean?" asked Althea, her winged brows drawing together in a faint frown of puzzlement.

He smiled at her, amused that as worldly as she was in some ways she was as yet such a babe. "Any time there is a hole-in-the-wall affair, speculation runs riot. Ours will be to all intents and purposes a runaway match. I do not think that you would like it to become known that you were forced to flee from your stepfather's advances. Nor would I like it whispered that my heir must surely have been conceived before our vows were ever exchanged."

Althea flushed, feeling abruptly far less worldly than she had supposed. "No, I should not like that," she agreed. "What tale shall we put about, then?"

"That the agreement between us was of long standing and that due to the deaths in each of our families—your father and my brother—it was felt best to make the ceremony a quiet one. Thus the reason behind my leave from the army and your traveling here to Berkshire to meet me. We shall have to be wed at Gretna, but no one need know of that. My parents will endorse our tale that we were married privately at Chard. I am certain that your mother and stepfather will be anxious to avoid scandal and they will repeat the same story," said Gareth.

"I do not care for the notion of Gretna Green," said Althea, frowning a little. Though her upbringing had been unusual in one facet, she nevertheless knew what was considered to be beyond the pale. She had lived in the shadow of scandal all of her life. She did not want to be tainted by whispers for the remainder of her days, as well.

"It is reprehensible," agreed Gareth. "But I do not see what other choice we have."

"Perhaps there is a way to secure my mother's permission," said Althea thoughtfully. She looked up to meet his eyes and smiled. "My great-aunt, Lady Angleton, is a forceful character. Prodded properly, she might very well use her influence on our behalf. That is why I decided to seek out her protection in the first place. I had hoped that she would stand up for me when Mama would not."

Gareth kept an impassive expression on his face, though anger surged through him that she had had to resort to such a forlorn hope. What fear and bitterness she must have endured when she was confronted with her own mother's betrayal. "Could you persuade her to such effort? I had gathered that the lady was rather crotchety and intractable," he said.

"Oh, she is indeed all of that. However, she is also very proud. I do not think that the match proposed by Sir Bartholomew will meet with her approval, while your suit must surely prove unexceptional," said Althea.

"My thanks," said Gareth dryly. "How do you propose to enlist the lady's help?"

"I shall continue on to my great-aunt's abode. I believe that when I have put her in possession of the facts, she will at once write to my mother. My mother has always stood in great awe of my great-aunt. I am certain that under those circumstances, she will give her consent that I may be wed," said Althea. Her eyes glinted. "And I do not think that Sir Bartholomew will be able to counter Aunt Aurelia's wishes."

"It sounds a plausible enough plan." Gareth made up his mind quickly. "Very well, then; that is how we shall go about it. I shall go up to London to the Commons for the purpose of securing a special license. I shall return with it to your great-aunt's home and we shall be married from there. I take it that Lady Angleton has a chaplain or that there is a parish church?"

"Yes."

"I shall write a letter that you can carry to her, introducing myself and the reasoning behind our actions. It would be churlish to expect the lady to aid me without appealing to her good nature first," said Gareth.

He left Althea then to go out and see about her chaise.

Althea's dresser approached her mistress. Darcy's sharp eyes had missed nothing, so that even though she had not been able to hear what had been said she knew something of moment had transpired. "My lady, what are you up to now?" she asked sharply.

"I am to be married, Darcy. To Lord Lynley. He will join us at Aunt Aurelia's with a special license in hand," said Althea.

She laughed at her dresser's shocked expression. "Yes, that is precisely how I felt when his lordship first broached his offer to me. But the more I thought about it, the more strongly I felt that this is just the solution that I need."

"From the skillet into the fire," muttered Darcy, shaking her head. She said nothing more because the gentleman was returning, but her lips were pressed together in firm disapproval over the swift turn of events.

Althea and her dresser were accompanied outside to the waiting carriage. The dresser ducked into the vehicle, carrying the portmanteaus and bandbox.

When Gareth handed Althea up into the chaise, he stayed her a moment by keeping hold of her hand. Looking up at her, he asked softly, "Have you thought what should be done if we fail in this?"

"It will be Gretna," said Althea calmly.

"You do not falter at the thought?"

"My father taught me to take all my fences, but not until I was properly set," said Althea, a faint smile touching her face.

He laughed. Releasing her and closing the door, he stepped back and waved a hand as the chaise set off.

Chapter Eight

Lady Angleton was in the middle of a temper tantrum. The unexpected intelligence, conveyed by her butler, that a visitor
was awaiting her pleasure had the effect of arresting her tirade.
The object of her ladyship's fury, the denizen of the kitchens,
was dismissed, to that worthy's heartfelt relief.

"You may go. But don't think that I shall forget."

Lady Angleton's parting shot was said so fiercely that the
chef bowed himself trembling out of the room.

The chef had been guilty of chasing her ladyship's fat pugs
out of the kitchen. He was now completely convinced that
should one of her ladyship's nasty pugs again invade his
kitchen for the purpose of gobbling down the choicest meats
reserved for her ladyship's table, he would with his own hands
feed the tasty delicacies to the wheezing canines. It would be
infinitely better to so demean himself and his office rather than
endure another such dressing down. The chef thought wistfully
of packing his trunks, but such a course was not to be considered. It was truly unfortunate that the salary paid him was such
an outrageous sum.

Lady Angleton did not know of the chef's dark thoughts and
had she known she would not have cared. The purpose of servants was to faithfully serve, no more, no less.

Daughter of an earl, widow of a prominent lord, connected
through blood and marriage to a dozen or more influential
families, Lady Angleton was every inch the born aristocrat. In
her heyday, she had been much admired and courted even
though she had never been a beauty. Her ladyship's countenance was dominated by flashing black eyes and a strong
Roman nose, which some said would have done considerable
justice to a male.

However, what Lady Angleton had lacked in physical attractions she had more than made up for in force of personality. After the carriage accident that had rendered her legs useless, Lady Angleton's considerable energies had been directed from the confines of a cumbersome wheeled chair. There had not been a noticeable decline in her interests or her influence.

Althea entered the drawing room, her maid one step behind her. Althea felt herself raked by the sharpest of glances. She was not much disconcerted, for she had vivid recollections of her great-aunt. Aunt Aurelia did not appear to have changed over the intervening years; her formidable presence could literally be felt.

"Well. It is indeed Hawthorne's daughter. I would recognize those eyes and that chin however many years had passed," said Lady Angleton. "What are you doing here, gel?"

Althea was not at all dismayed by the lack of warmth in her ladyship's greeting. It was what she had expected of Lady Angleton. She advanced to bend down and kiss the elderly lady's cheek. "Aunt Aurelia, you have not changed one whit. I am glad. My father had always a grudging respect for you."

Lady Angleton pursed her mouth, unwilling to show her pleasure at the compliment. She gestured peremptorily toward a chair, ordering rather than inviting her guest to sit. "Hmph. Trying to turn me up sweet, I see. You want something, that is clear enough. Very well! Speak up, I say. What brings you to my door at this time of night?"

Althea sat down and began to remove her bonnet and gloves.

Lady Angleton watched this procedure with a jaundiced eye, but she said nothing. She was content to await events. There was very little change to disturb the flow of her days. This unexpected visit was mildly exciting.

"This is Darcy, my dresser. She has traveled up with me from Surrey," said Althea, handing the bonnet and gloves to her maid.

"Surrey?" Lady Angleton shot a sharp glance at the maid, acknowledging with a nod the tiring woman's respectful bow. "A superior female, I see. You may go tell Ferguson, my butler, that your mistress is to have the Rose Room and attend to her unpacking."

"Very good, my lady," said Darcy woodenly, taking her mistress's bonnet and gloves with her as she retreated to the door.

"And tell Ferguson that I do not wish to wait all evening for tea to be served for me and my guest!" snapped Lady Angleton.

The door closed softly.

Lady Angleton turned her attention at once to her great-niece. "I'll have the round tale now, miss. What is this about Surrey? I thought your mother to be settled in Bath."

"Mama is now become Lady Bottlesby. Sir Bartholomew's estate is in Surrey," said Althea.

"Remarried and with never the courtesy of a word to me?" Lady Angleton's bloodless lips thinned. "She was probably afraid to write me. The gel was always slack of character. She could have handled your father better if she had had an ounce of backbone." Aunt Aurelia waved her hand in dismissal. "But that is neither here nor there. Bottlesby, Bottlesby. Yes, I recall a baronet by that name. A short, somewhat stout individual with horse teeth and a braying laugh. That would be this Bottlesby's sire, no doubt. A more inane man I never encountered. If this Sir Bartholomew is anything like his father, he and your mother are well matched."

Althea was unable to restrain a laugh.

Aunt Aurelia grinned. Her eyes gleamed wickedly. "I have hit on it, have I? Well, well. So you took a disgust to the cooing and billing and shook the dust from your feet. Intelligent gel."

"Not precisely that, no. I am in need of your help, actually," said Althea. She saw instantly from the stiffening of her great-aunt's countenance that she had made an error. She tried to retrieve her mistake. "Sir Bartholomew has arranged for my marriage to a gentleman not to my taste. He is—"

"What is so heinous in that?" interrupted Aunt Aurelia. "The baronet has greater sense than I gave him credit for. It is his duty to look out for your interests, gel! If you expect me to cross your mother's and your stepfather's wishes in such a matter as this, you much mistake the matter!"

"I am not such a noddy, ma'am. However, I did feel in the need of your counsel. The gentleman in question has connections with trade," said Althea coolly.

Aunt Aurelia's expression altered with alarming effect. "With trade?"

"Yes; I believe that Mr. Craddock is in dry goods. I fear he cannot be a particularly wise businessman, for I overheard Sir Bartholomew promise a very substantial settlement to him." Althea added, reflectively, "Or perhaps such an inordinate settlement was made because Mr. Craddock is afraid that his advanced years will make him unable to enjoy all of my inheritance before he dies."

Lady Angleton's face had suffused dull red, then paled. Her black eyes glittered above her flared nostrils. Through taut lips, she declared, "I shall not allow a Hawthorne to be so demeaned. How dare Bottlesby! That imbecile, that nodcock! As for your mother—" She pinned Althea with a sharp look. "What has your mother had to say to this precious scheme?"

"Mama dislikes unpleasantness, as you must recall," said Althea.

Aunt Aurelia barked a laugh. "Aye, I warrant that is the unvarnished truth. Well, Lady Bottlesby is about to experience an exceedingly unpleasant letter. I hope it may send her into spasms! Ferguson! Ferguson, I say!"

The door was thrust open. The butler hurried in with a laden tray. "Yes, my lady! The tea is just now ready. I shall serve it at once."

"Never mind the blasted tea! Bring me my lap board and my pens and paper. Light another branch of candles. How am I to see to write? Well, man, don't just stand there like a looby!"

The butler set down the tea tray and exited on the run. In short order, several servants saw to it that Lady Angleton's requirements were met. Then the ladies were left alone again.

Aunt Aurelia trimmed her pen. "You did well to come to me, gel. I shall make very certain that this lunacy is put to a stop."

"Before you write to my mother, you might wish to read this," said Althea, withdrawing a sealed letter from her reticule. "There is information contained within it of which my mother is not yet aware."

"What are you about now?" Lady Aurelia was instantly suspicious, but nevertheless she took the letter. She glanced at the seal that marked the wax and at once recognized it. Her thin brows rose. Muttering to herself, she broke the wax and spread the sheet.

With outward calm Althea poured out tea for herself and for her great-aunt. Inwardly, she was quaking. Now would come the truly telling moment. Aunt Aurelia had been eager to dash off a blistering opinion of a bad match. It remained to be seen whether she would be willing to abet a runaway marriage.

Althea heard the crackle of folding paper. She looked up quickly, to meet Aunt Aurelia's cold gaze. Her heart beat more rapidly. Very carefully she set down her cup.

"You have played me along very skillfully, Althea. My compliments. It is not often that I am led about by the nose," said Lady Angleton with acid calm.

"As a child, I learned that one beards the dragon with boldness or not at all," said Althea.

"I am an old dragon, am I?" Aunt Aurelia clutched her chair arms. "I shall tell you, my gel!"

"I was speaking of my father. He would not have known nor cared about my existence if I had not brought myself to his attention," said Althea. "I learned also that tears do not aid one." She paused, then asked quietly, "Had I a choice, ma'am?"

There was a short silence while Althea's great-aunt stared at her with a brooding gaze. Then Lady Angleton shrugged. "You were perfectly correct. I have no patience for mealy-mouthed whining, whether from man or woman. Very well, then. Let us get down to the business at hand. You wish me to aid you to the altar with Lynley, here." Aunt Aurelia tapped the folded sheet. "It was clever of you to bring Lynley up to scratch. You have done very well for yourself, gel."

Startled, Althea realized that her ladyship was speaking of Lord Lynley, Viscount, the heir of Chard. He was not simply Major Gareth Marshall, a friend from her childhood. It had never truly penetrated until that instant that she was to eventually become a countess. Or that others would express blatant admiration for her supposedly successful ploys in landing his lordship.

Althea did not acknowledge her great-aunt's observation.

"Yes, that is it precisely. I am under age and I suspect that Sir Bartholomew will not allow Mama to grant her consent to the match."

"Why should he not? Only the greatest nodcock alive would object to it. The boy will one day be the Earl of Chard," said Aunt Aurelia.

"Sir Bartholomew holds a grudge against me. I had words with him," said Althea. She was strangely reluctant to reveal the particulars, but it proved to be unnecessary, after all.

Aunt Aurelia shot a keen glance at Althea. "Tried to give you a slip on the shoulder, did he?"

At Althea's amazed expression, Aunt Aurelia cackled. "I have lived too long not to have seen every kind of wickedness, gel. I have eyes in my head. You're a beauty. It would be wonderful indeed if Bottlesby had not also noticed. At least you had the good sense to fly to your Lord Lynley. But I am curious regarding one thing. Why did you come to me?"

Althea decided it would be a waste of time to try to explain that she had not intentionally sought out Lord Lynley's protection. The explanation could only hinder what was already in a fair way to being decided. "I disliked the notion of a Gretna Greene marriage. If at all possible I should like to procure Mama's consent to my marriage to Gareth—Lord Lynley—so that we can be wed by special license and avoid the scandal of a Gretna runaway. I thought that you would be a match for any persuasion that Sir Bartholomew might bring to bear on Mama."

Aunt Aurelia nodded. There was approval in her expression. "You have a good sense of knowing what is due your name. That is admirable. Very well; you shall have my help. I shall write to your mother and send it by private messenger. One cannot depend too much upon the mail. I shall instruct the man to wait for an answer. Be assured, Althea, Lady Bottlesby shall send back her written consent. Once we have that and your Lord Lynley has returned from London with the license, you will be wed from my own chapel."

Aunt Aurelia picked up her mended pen and dipped it into the inkwell. Her eyes glinted suddenly with wicked humor. "I shall enjoy this task. Go upstairs to bed, gel. I have already dined, but you may send down for a tray for yourself and your maid."

Thus dismissed, Althea did as she was bid. As she left the drawing room she was struck suddenly with an immense weariness. She was astounded to realize what toll the interview with her great-aunt, and indeed the past fortnight, had taken upon her. She was exceedingly glad to mount the stairs and seek out the bedroom that had been prepared for her.

Althea put herself into the competent hands of her dresser. Once she had supped, bathed, and been made ready for bed, she was grateful to slip under the coverlets. The candles were carefully extinguished and the door was softly closed. Althea's last thought before sleep claimed her was that everything was now perfectly settled.

Chapter Nine

Althea's sense of well-being lasted for a day and a half.

In that time, Lady Angleton's messenger had returned and given over into her ladyship's hand a lengthy letter from Lady Bottlesby. Aunt Aurelia snorted as she read the crossed and re-crossed sheets. She tossed the sheets over to Althea. "There it is. In the midst of protestations and declarations and tearstains, the silly woman has given her consent."

Althea swiftly perused her mother's letter. It was as Aunt Aurelia had said. Lady Bottlesby denied that she had had anything but her daughter's best interests at heart. She was shocked that Aunt Aurelia could think any differently. She was amazed that Althea had contracted such an eligible parti. Of course, she could have no objection to the connection; on the contrary, she gladly gave her consent to Althea's immediate marriage.

Althea looked up, her eyes alight with amusement. "Mama seems almost inordinately anxious that I exchange my vows."

Aunt Aurelia chuckled. "Aye, I warrant that she is. Once you are wed, the cloud hanging over her will be gone and she will settle into domestic complacency."

"I wonder whether Sir Bartholomew is aware that Mama has granted her consent," said Althea, returning the sheets.

Aunt Aurelia snorted as she tucked the letter safely away. "I would stake my pearls that he is not. Your mother is singularly poor-spirited. She will not dare to inform him."

Well into the evening of the second day, there came a pounding on the front door. Shortly thereafter, a raised voice out in the hall intruded even into the drawing room where Althea and Aunt Aurelia were playing cards.

Althea looked toward the door, then across the game table at her great-aunt. She had recognized that voice even though she had heard it raised in anger on only two previous occasions. "It is Sir Bartholomew."

"Is it, indeed. Play on, gel. Pray do not get sloppy now," said Aunt Aurelia. She kept her eyes focused on the cards that lay face up on the table, to all appearances oblivious to anything else.

The door was thrust open. Sir Bartholomew Bottlesby stood framed on the threshold. His angered gaze lighted first upon Lady Angleton, then traveled to his stepdaughter. He advanced into the drawing room toward the ladies. He showed his teeth in a broad, genial smile. "Pray forgive this unannounced intrusion, my lady. I am Sir Bartholomew Bottlesby. I am come to inquire into my stepdaughter's welfare. Lady Althea neglected to inform me of her plans to visit with you, and naturally I was made anxious upon her behalf."

Lady Angleton did not acknowledge the abrupt introduction. "Is Lady Bottlesby with you?" At her peremptory inquiry, the lady in question came shrinkingly into the drawing room. When Lady Bottlesby came level with Sir Bartholomew, she clutched his sleeve as though for support.

"You have cost me my pearls, Cecilia," said Aunt Aurelia acidly.

"I-I do not understand," said Lady Bottlesby.

Lady Angleton ignored Lady Bottlesby's bewildered expression and returned her attention to the baronet. "Sir Bartholomew. This is most unexpected. I knew your father. I must say that you favor him."

"Thank you, my lady. I am gratified, indeed," said Sir Bartholomew, puffing out his cheeks. "My dear lady wife did not tell me how gracious I would find you." He patted his wife's fluttering hand on his arm.

Althea nearly laughed, for she knew well that Aunt Aurelia had not intended a compliment. But she kept her peace, preferring to allow Aunt Aurelia to handle matters as long as her ladyship desired. Althea had little doubt of her own ability to defy Sir Bartholomew, but it was so much pleasanter when there was someone ready to do battle for her. Her thoughts went inexorably to Lord Lynley and suddenly she wished that Gareth had already returned.

"I warrant that she did not," said Lady Angleton, a smile stretching her thin lips. For a moment, her knowing gaze rested on Lady Bottlesby. When that lady flushed in discomposure, Lady Angleton cackled low in her throat. She swept her hand in a gesture of welcome. "Sir Bartholomew, pray sit down! We have a certain matter to discuss. Very well; let us get to it. I am not one to dally about, as you will soon discover."

"Of course not, my lady. I would not dream of offering such mean provocation to your good nature," said Sir Bartholomew, still smiling. He solicitously settled Lady Bottlesby on a settee and seated himself beside her.

One of the pugs trundled over to the visitors and began to sniff about the baronet's boots. A pained expression crossed Sir Bartholomew's florid face. With his foot, he surreptitiously pushed the pug away. The pug sat on its tail for a moment, mournful eyes fixed on Sir Bartholomew. It wheezed, its tongue hanging out of its mouth. Then it got up and returned to its inspection.

"Do you not like pugs, Sir Bartholomew?" inquired Lady Angleton frostily.

Sir Bartholomew smiled again. "Oh, one canine is very much like another, my lady. I prefer horses, myself. Though I must say, this is a fine specimen." He bent down to gingerly give a pat to the pug that was busily sniffing his heels.

"I am glad to hear it. What is it, Cecilia? Speak up, gel! What was that you squeaked?"

"I-I don't recall," stammered Lady Bottlesby, casting a beseeching look up at Sir Bartholomew. The baronet did not respond. Her eyes fell then to the inquisitive pug and she shuddered.

"If you cannot keep a thought in your head long enough to explain yourself, then pray do not speak. It is vastly annoying," said Lady Angleton.

Sir Bartholomew patted his wife's arm. "Never mind, my dear lady. I shall handle this matter for you, I promise you."

Lady Bottlesby cast another glance down at the busy pug. There was a look of sick apprehension in her eyes.

Althea rose, as much to swing attention from her beleaguered mother as to adhere to the civilities. "I shall ring for refreshment, my lady," she said quietly, going to the bell rope and pulling on it.

"Pray do not run away, my dear stepdaughter," said Sir Bartholomew quickly.

"I have no intention of leaving," said Althea with deliberate emphasis. She had the satisfaction of seeing by the shift in Sir Bartholomew's expression that her statement was fully comprehended.

"Aye; I should like my tea. The hour is coming late," said Aunt Aurelia.

In response to the bell, the door to the drawing room opened. The butler had anticipated the summons and he carried in a tray of small biscuits and a pot of tea. He served refreshments all around, then exited.

Lady Angleton settled her black gaze on her visitors and barked, "Well, Sir Bartholomew?"

The baronet looked momentarily disconcerted. His expression cleared. He laid down the biscuit that he had had halfway to his mouth. "Of course; I understand. You are direct, indeed, my lady! There is no roundaboutation for you. Quite the contrary!" He laughed with apparent good humor.

"I do not suffer fools gladly," said Lady Angleton.

There was an instant hardening of Sir Bartholomew's eyes. He showed his teeth, but the geniality had quite fled from his demeanor. He set down his cup with a snap. "It is as I told you, my lady. Lady Althea did not inform either her mother or me that she had planned this visit to you. We were naturally alarmed by my stepdaughter's disappearance and it was not until Lady Bottlesby received the letter from you that we knew where Lady Althea had gone."

"Did you show my letter to Sir Bartholomew, Cecilia?" asked Aunt Aurelia, swinging her gaze around upon Lady Bottlesby.

"Of course I did. The same day in which I wrote in reply to you. I knew that it would relieve Sir Bartholomew's mind to know that Althea was quite safe," said Lady Bottlesby bravely. She had been grateful for the cup of tea and took another sip, but the next words that were spoken made her strangle.

"Aye, I understand that Sir Bartholomew is . . . fond of Althea," said Aunt Aurelia with a malicious cackle.

Lady Bottlesby dropped her cup with a clatter, splashing the remainder of the tea over her skirt. Distressed, she snatched up a napkin and attempted to rub out the stains.

Sir Bartholomew flushed purple. Angrily, he snapped, "I deeply resent your inference, my lady! There has never been anything but a fatherly attachment between myself and Lady Althea. If my stepdaughter has indicated otherwise, then she is sadly at fault. Indeed, I believe her mind to be slightly disordered. She was devoted to her father. Grief has an odd effect upon some individuals, causing strange notions and imaginations."

"You interest me profoundly, Sir Bartholomew. Perhaps you would care to enlarge upon your opinion," said Lady Angleton, glancing at her great-niece's expressionless face. Althea had told her nothing. Lady Angleton herself had intuited what had taken place, and the truth of it had just been confirmed by Sir Bartholomew's hasty denials.

The baronet misinterpreted that glance. His countenance smoothed again to a confident smile. "It is enough that I have spoken so much as I have, my lady. I do not wish to cause my stepdaughter further embarrassment. No; it would be best simply to let the matter rest where it is. I am certain that you will understand now why Lady Bottlesby and I have been so anxious on Lady Althea's behalf," said Sir Bartholomew.

"So anxious that you must needs thrust her into a distasteful and unworthy marriage! Aye, Sir Bartholomew! I understand only too well," said Lady Angleton savagely.

Lady Bottlesby moaned and covered her face with her hands.

Sir Bartholomew rose to his feet, very much on his dignity. "Lady Angleton, I assure you that my intentions have been pure. Mr. Craddock is perfectly respectable. He perfectly understands my stepdaughter's circumstances and is willing to see that she is cared for in a proper manner. The banns will be read this Sunday."

The pug, having at last made up its mind, lifted its leg. A pungent stream defiled the high gloss of Sir Bartholomew's boots.

The baronet bellowed with disbelieving rage. He kicked the offending animal. The pug yelped. Aunt Aurelia screeched.

She threw her teacup with deadly aim, clipping Sir Bartholomew across the nose. Lady Bottlesby swooned and fell over onto her face on the settee. The pugs set up a stentorian barking.

Althea lay back in her chair laughing, the tears streaming down her cheeks. The release of all her pent-up tensions was exquisite.

At that moment, the door to the drawing room was thrown open. Lord Lynley strode into the room, followed by the butler and several other servants.

"What is this about?" he asked sharply.

Althea started up from her chair. "Gareth!" She held out her hands to him. "It-it is so hilarious. Oh, I am utterly undone!" She gave in to another peal of laughter.

Sir Bartholomew started toward her, his hand upraised. There was fury in his face. "This is all your doing! Laugh at *me*? By God, I shall thrash you for your temerity, so I shall!"

Gareth stepped forward, thrusting Althea behind him. "I think not, sir."

Sir Bartholomew found himself faced by a disturbingly tall and well-set-up gentleman in uniform. His rage had flamed to monumental heights and served to feed his courage. His lip curled, exposing his teeth in an unpleasant smile. "So, step-daughter! You are indeed Hawthorne's gel! You have already found yourself a protector! I wonder what Lord Lynley will say to that!"

A fist smashed his lips. Sir Bartholomew crashed to the floor.

Gareth stood over the baronet. He was white around the mouth. "I am Lynley. You are speaking of my chosen lady. If you value your life, you shall not again address her in such a fashion. Nor will you ever breathe a single malicious syllable against her name, or I shall hunt you down and kill you."

Sir Bartholomew slowly got to his feet. He felt delicately of his puffed mouth and his hand came away bloodied.

"Bartholomew!" Still dazed by her faint, Lady Bottlesby tottered to her feet. Horror was writ plain upon her face. She rushed to her spouse's side. "You are hurt!"

"It is all right, my dear. We must make allowances for these hot-tempered bloods," said Sir Bartholomew with a massive effort of will. He turned toward Lady Angleton and bowed. "My regrets, my lady, but under the circumstances I believe it best that my good lady and I take leave of your house."

"As you wish, Sir Bartholomew," said Aunt Aurelia indifferently.

Sir Bartholomew and Lady Bottlesby started for the door, arm in arm. The butler and other servants melted back from their path.

Althea put out her hand, unwilling to let her mother go without saying something to her. "Mama . . ."

Lady Bottlesby avoided Althea's anxious gaze. Without pausing, she hurried out of the door beside Sir Bartholomew.

Aunt Aurelia shot a baleful glare at her butler. "Is this a raree show, Ferguson? Should there not be someone at the door to see to my departing guests?" The butler took the hint and hurriedly swept his underlings out of the drawing room.

"Well, I never thought to be so entertained," said Aunt Aurelia with satisfaction. "By the by, your entrance was perfectly timed, Lord Lynley."

"So it would seem, my lady," said Gareth. "My only regret is that it proved necessary to resort to such means."

"That nodcock needed some sense knocked into him," said Aunt Aurelia. "Now what's amiss with you, gel? You look blue as the megrims."

"I had not wanted to lose my mother," said Althea, raising her head. "And I fear what her life with Sir Bartholomew must be now."

Aunt Aurelia snorted. "My advice to you is to put it out of your head. Your mother will do very well. She and that nodcock are two of a kind. They will choose to forget everything but the fact that you made a very advantageous marriage, and so they will crow to anyone who will listen. The Bottlesbys will beat a path to your door once you are Countess of Chard."

"You are very cynical, ma'am," said Althea with the faintest of smiles. The old lady's astringent words had soothed her spirit to a degree.

"Am I? You would not be so quick to judge if you had observed human foibles and frailties as long as I have," said Aunt Aurelia tartly. She turned her bright gaze upon the gen-

tleman. "So you are Lynley. You do not have the look about
you of your father."

"I am said to favor my mother," said Gareth. He advanced
to take the hand that her ladyship held out to him. Raising it to
his lips, he brushed a light salute across her gnarled fingers before releasing her hand. "It is my pleasure to meet you,
ma'am. I am most humbly grateful for your aiding of our
cause."

"I could not very well allow a Hawthorne to be coupled
with a dry grocer. This young woman played me like a fish,
my lord. I warn you to have a care, for she will undoubtedly
try her tricks on you," said Aunt Aurelia.

"A dry grocer?" murmured Gareth, his amused glance
touching Althea. She smiled back. "I shall certainly remember
your warning, my lady. But I believe that Althea and I know
each other too well to be surprised by anything that the other
might say. We were acquainted as children and lately have discovered that that friendship has endured."

He reached out his hand, palm upward, and Althea laid her
hand in his. His fingers closed gently around hers and they
stood thus, hands clasped. They smiled at one another.

Aunt Aurelia's thin brows rose. "Indeed! How fortunate.
Perhaps we should discuss the details of the wedding at once.
Have you the special license, Lord Lynley?"

"Here in my coat," said Gareth, laying his hand over his
heart.

At the gesture, Aunt Aurelia's lips twitched. "Good; I have
in my possession Lady Bottlesby's written consent. Very well.
We shall have my chaplain up betweentimes. You, gel, go upstairs and make yourself presentable."

"Now, my lady?" Althea was startled. She looked quickly at
Gareth and saw her own startlement reflected in his eyes.

"What better time is there?" snapped Aunt Aurelia. "Now
do as you are bid. I wish to see you wed before I am put into
bed this night. Do not keep me waiting, Althea. I am thrown
into crotchets when I tire."

Althea looked again at Gareth, this time with uncertainty.

He grinned at her. Lifting her hand to his lips, he placed a
reassuring kiss upon her fingers. Then he released her and

said, "It is her ladyship's wish, Lady Althea. I think that we must abide by it."

"Of course," said Althea, whereupon she left the drawing room.

Lord Lynley turned then to his hostess. "You are decisive, ma'am. It is a rare quality."

"I intend to see right done by my great-niece. She was clever enough to exchange a bad bargain for a superior one. I wish to make certain that it does not slip through her fingers," said Lady Angleton.

"I have already pledged my honor to Lady Althea, ma'am. You have nothing to fear," said Gareth quietly.

Aunt Aurelia cackled. "Pull the rope, my lord. We shall send a man after that fat chaplain of mine. And candles! Ferguson! Drat the man! *Ferguson!*"

Chapter Ten

When Althea told her dresser what was to take place, Darcy at once pulled on the bell rope. The housemaid who answered the summons was given a spate of instructions by the dresser. A hot bath was wanted; needlewomen were to be sent; pressing irons were to be heated; a chamomile tea was to be brewed.

"There must be no dragging of feet, girl, for Lady Althea and Lord Lynley are to be wed this very evening," said Darcy sternly.

"Aye, miss," breathed the wide-eyed housemaid. The girl scurried off, agog with the news.

The dresser threw open the doors to the massive wardrobe.

"What is all this fluster, Darcy?" asked Althea, seating herself in a wingback. She was somewhat amused at the stern-faced dresser's suppressed air of excitement.

"If you do not know what is due you, my lady, at least I do!" said Darcy. She pulled several dresses out of the wardrobe and inspected them with critical eyes. "You haven't got a proper gown, of course, but perhaps this—no! *This* one!" She held up a pale cream satin gown tied with rose-colored ribbons. The gown was deceptively simple of line but, as Darcy knew, exceptionally elegant when worn. "It is fortunate that I brought away my sewing box. There is a length of lace gauze that will do very well for an overskirt. I do hope there will be enough left for a bit of a veil. Where are those needle-women?"

In short order, the dresser's requirements were all met. Althea climbed into a warm hipbath that was set up between the cheerful fire and a screen. The dresser and two needle-women began the task of turning the satin gown into wedding attire. A pot of hot chamomile tea awaited Althea's emergence from the bath.

When Althea had questioned her maid about the tea, Darcy had stated, "It will calm your nerves, Lady Althea."

"But I am not at all nervous," said Althea.

The dresser had only smiled. "You haven't thought much about it yet, my lady."

As the minutes flew by, Althea's thoughts focused more and more on the actual exchange of vows. She finished her bath and put on her underthings. The needlewomen completed the transformation of her gown. Darcy helped Althea to dress and then turned her to the mirror.

A knock sounded on the door. When Darcy opened it, a maid delivered into the dresser's hands a small gauze-wrapped package and spoke a few short words. The dresser nodded and smiled, thanking the maid. She shut the door and returned to her mistress. "Lady Angleton's compliments, my lady. Her ladyship sends her own veil." As Darcy spoke, she had unwrapped the package and unfolded the delicate lace. The dresser placed the veil over Althea's head, letting it fall over her face.

The lingering needlewomen sighed and nodded in approval. "Ye look a proper bride, m'lady," said one.

Althea did not smile. She could only stare at herself. Her eyes had grown large with dawning comprehension that all this was really happening. She drew off the veil. "It needs a bit of pressing, Darcy."

The dresser shot a keen glance at her mistress's face. "Go on with you now," said Darcy, shooing the needlewomen out. Once she had shut the door, she returned to her mistress. "You do look a treat, my lady. I will attend to the veil in a moment. Sit down before the mirror and I shall fix your hair."

Althea did as she was bid. She seated herself in front of the mirror and watched her maid's competent fingers arrange her long hair. The true enormity of the step that she was taking felt as though it would burst through her chest. "Darcy," she whispered, "I do not believe that I can do it."

The dresser's fingers stilled for a moment as she met her mistress's wide, shadowed eyes in the mirror. "Of course you can, my lady," she said quietly. "Drink your tea, my lady."

Althea dropped her eyes. She picked up the cup and raised it to her lips. The tea had cooled and she sipped slowly at the soothing brew. The ordinary taking of tea began to unwind her tautened body. Realistic, competent Darcy. The dresser had been right, after all. Althea's nerves were strong, but fears of the unknown had threatened to overpower her.

When Althea emerged from her bedroom with Darcy in close attendance, she found that in her absence a small transformation of the house had taken place. Candles blazed and flowers had been hastily arranged in every available vase. Several servants were drawn up in the entry hall to watch the bride's descent. A collective sigh was heard at sight of the lovely veiled lady.

Althea hesitated at the bottom of the stairs. Lord Lynley awaited her, standing tall and virile in his neat red uniform. He stepped forward and offered his arm to her. It was completely untraditional, but it seemed the most natural thing in the world for the prospective groom to escort the bride through the house to the adjoining chapel. The servants came quietly behind, creating a rear guard.

Althea glanced curiously around the chapel. She had seen it last as a child and at that time it had seemed to her to be a dim and uninviting place. But here, too, a transformation had been wrought. The vaulted room was ablaze with bunches of candles. Lady Angleton had ordered a quick polishing of the chapel and the ancient wood positively glowed in the candlelight.

Althea stood before the altar beside Lord Lynley. Behind them were the witnesses: Aunt Aurelia and all of that lady's household, the reverend's wife with her numerous progeny, and the chief magistrate of the county, whom Lady Angleton had insisted must be present.

The good reverend outlined the vows that each party was to cleave to once wedded, before adding his own heartfelt explanation of the significance of their pledges to one another. He held up the set of gold rings that Gareth had had the foresight to purchase while in London. They were plain bands, not at all what one would expect of the Viscount of Chard. But they would serve as his lordship's pledge to Althea until he could obtain better.

"These rings symbolize more than the value of precious metal in the sight of Almighty God. These rings are a token of the covenant, the contract, if you will, that you forge this day between you. Just as our ancestors pledged themselves to one another till eternal rest, so do you now do the same. The rings of old were not of gold, but were cut into the flesh of the finger so that they could never be removed. Thus were fidelity and charity testified to. Though our marriage rings of today are not cut into the flesh, their significance remains the same. This covenant, once pledged between man and woman, cannot be removed. Let no man put asunder what God has joined."

Althea and Gareth exchanged the rings. The ring fitted ill on Althea's finger and its weight was foreign. Nevertheless, she knew that she had taken a step in her life that could never be revoked or reclaimed.

Through the veil she looked up into Gareth's somber, unreadable gaze. She shivered slightly, not knowing why she did so.

At the reverend's urging, Gareth folded back the veil and bent his head to claim the traditional kiss from the bride. His lips merely brushed Althea's, doing nothing to unfreeze the little core of ice that had gathered around her heart.

An audible sigh of satisfaction from the spectators went around the chapel. Lady Angleton banged her cane against the flagstones. "Enough of that, my lord! The time for that will come, when you will not have a gaggle of the curious standing about. Reverend Garnott, I wish to put down my signature as a witness. The magistrate shall be the other lawful witness. I intend to see to it that there can be no question of the legality of this marriage."

"Of course, Lady Angleton. The marriage will not be called into question in any event, since we have the clearly written consent of Lady Lynley's mother to it. I would not have performed it otherwise," said the chaplain.

"Pompous collar," muttered Aunt Aurelia. "I pay his living and this is an example of the respect with which I am treated." She raised her voice. "Very good, Reverend. I am happy to know that I am served by a man of such integrity. You and your good wife must stay for the celebration. I have arranged for a bridal dinner. It is short notice, but my chef is an excellent man. I depend upon him without reservation."

The chef would have been both startled and gratified by this accolade. Indeed, later when some of the servants who had been privileged enough to witness the ceremony told him of this praise, the emotional gentleman burst into tears and swore undying fidelity to her ladyship.

The Reverend Garnott was one who appreciated a well-set table. As the proud parent of a large family, he was aware that an invitation of this sort was not to be lightly spurned. He bowed to Lady Angleton. "We would be honored to join the wedding celebration, my lady. Indeed, I do not think that my boys would thank me if I denied them the treat."

Lady Angleton had not at all meant that the Garnott children should be present, but she could not very well deny them now without appearing mean. Instead, she nodded abruptly. "Good. We shall adjourn at once to the dining room. Ferguson, I wish to be taken back into the house."

The butler nodded to one of the footmen, a burly individual whose familiar task it was to push Lady Angleton's heavy wheeled chair. The footman took his station and turned the chair around. Lady Angleton's indomitable figure led the way out of the chapel.

Althea and Gareth had stood quietly at the altar after signing the register which Mrs. Garnott had brought over to them. As the small gathering began slowly to disperse, they hesitated, looking at one another.

Althea felt herself to be somewhat at a loss. She looked down at the ring upon her finger, turning it. It was scarcely a half hour since they had entered the chapel, but it seemed an eternity. So many conflicting emotions had rushed through her. She did not know quite what was expected of her, nor what to say. No, that was not quite true. She did know what was expected of her and it frightened her.

She felt Gareth's hand on her arm and she looked up quickly.

"It feels odd to me, also," he said quietly.

"I-I do not think that I really considered what I had agreed to," said Althea.

Quick concern flashed into his eyes. "Do you wish to reconsider?"

Althea shook her head, a small smile breaking across her face. She was hearing again the chaplain's solemn explanation of the covenanted vows between them. "It is rather late for that, do you not think?"

"There is annulment," he said slowly.

"No. I made a bargain. I shall abide by it," said Althea firmly.

He looked at her for a long moment. Then he smiled crookedly. He offered his arm to her. "We are like a pair of green subalterns, my lady. Come; let us go in to the dining room, our heads held high and high courage in our eyes, even though we are shrinking and shivering inside."

Althea cocked her head, regarding him with surprise. "You, too, Gareth?"

He grinned. "My dear lady, I am positively shaking in my boots. You have no notion!"

"Perhaps I do," said Althea. She laid her fingers upon his elbow. "But I think, with you beside me, that whatever is to come will not be so very fearsome after all."

"Good girl," he said approvingly. "All right, then. Let us be off. Lady Angleton will scold us royally if we hold up the festivities."

When Althea and Gareth entered the dining room, they were toasted by the gentry and servants alike. It was an oddly democratic gathering, especially as it took place under the roof of an absolute autocrat. But Lady Angleton smiled benignly on all. None knew that she wished for this occasion to be well-remembered. Hers was a far-reaching mind and she could foresee a time when perhaps it would be advantageous that there had been several witnesses to the joining of Viscount Lynley and Lady Althea.

When all had had their fill of costly champagne, a cold collation of meats and cheeses, and tarts, Lady Angleton announced that it was well past her bedtime.

Althea threw a quick glance around. All had apparently taken the unsubtle hint. The party had come to an end. Most of the servants faded out of the room, while some remained to clear away the evidences of the festivities.

The Reverend and Mrs. Garnott wished the newly wed couple well. Then they bid everyone good-bye and took their sleepy, well-fed sons off. The magistrate, after chuckling at something Lady Angleton said into his ear as he bent down to kiss her gnarled hand, also took a swift leave of Lord and Lady Lynley.

After the guests were gone, Aunt Aurelia said, "This day has been exciting in the extreme. I am fagged to death. I am too old for such turmoil. Althea, I am glad that you are not remaining with me, for I do not believe that I would survive long otherwise."

Althea bent down to kiss the elderly dame's withered cheek. She said quietly, "Never say so, dear ma'am. You are too fierce to give way. And I thank you for standing by me so handily."

Aunt Aurelia sniffed disparagingly, but she was pleased nonetheless. "You're a good girl, my dear. Unlike that mealy-mouthed mother of yours, you're bred true to your station." She turned her cold black gaze upon Lord Lynley. "What are your plans my lord? I do not come out of my rooms until ten of the clock. Shall I see you at luncheon?"

Gareth regretfully shook his head. "I think it will be for the best if Althea and I leave at first light, my lady. My leave from my duties is almost gone and I wish to establish her at Chard before I leave England."

"This will be good-bye, then," said Lady Angleton, giving her hand to him. His lordship bowed over her fingers and released them.

Althea had cast a swift, startled look at the viscount's face. "But I thought—Gareth, I thought that I would be accompanying you to Brussels."

"Nonsense, girl! Why should you ever think anything of the sort? Lord Lynley has more sense than to allow you to set foot on that war-torn continent," said Aunt Aurelia.

"Lady Angleton is correct, Althea," said Gareth quietly. He had been first astonished and then dismayed by her assumption that she was to accompany him overseas. "Your place is at Chard. There you will be safe. I could not balance it with my conscience if I were to expose you to the uncertainties that exist in Brussels."

"I see. I-I did not realize," said Althea, her heart sinking. It was a shattering disappointment to discover that he did not want her with him. She had simply assumed that she would go wherever he did.

"Of course you did not. When all is said and done, you are still too green to be let out on your own," said Aunt Aurelia. Her steely eyes fell on the burly footman. "You, there! Wheel me to my rooms. I want my maid and a hot toddy. I bid you good night, Althea, Lord Lynley." The footman obediently wheeled her off to her apartment, which had been relocated on the ground floor soon after the crippling accident.

Gareth bid Lady Althea a chaste good night by taking her hand and placing a correct kiss upon it. He held her fingers for a moment longer, even as he held her eyes. "I shall be up momentarily," he said.

Althea nodded, her heart suddenly pounding in her breast. At his words, all thought of the disappointment that she had just sustained flew out of her head. She turned and almost blindly made for the door. She knew that Gareth's eyes were on her and she was obscurely grateful when the door was closed, shutting her away from his thoughtful gaze.

The butler had the honor of showing Althea to the room that had been prepared for her bridal night. He bowed her inside and shut the door. Althea's dresser awaited her.

"Now, my lady, we must make you ready quick as we can," said Darcy, starting to undo the buttons on Althea's gown.

Althea wanted to say that she did not think she would ever be ready. But that was not something one confided even to the most loyal of retainers.

The gown slid down to lie in a shining circle upon the carpet. Her chemise went the same way. The dresser tossed a filmy nightgown over Althea's head and smoothed it down, tying the ribbons loosely at her mistress's breast.

Althea's hands were trembling and she clasped them in her lap when Darcy requested that she sit down before the cheval glass. She knew what to expect, and yet she did not. In a rush she wished quite passionately that she had not had the upbringing that she had. It would have been far simpler, she thought, if she had not had some idea of what went on between a man and a woman.

Darcy finished swiftly the task of brushing her mistress's hair until it shone in the firelight. Then she tucked her into the wide bed, sitting up against the pillows. The dresser said good night and quietly withdrew.

For once, Darcy had left the candle beside the bed burning and Althea stared at it. The candle flame was a symbol of her new status. She was a wife, waiting for her husband. Althea drew in her breath.

A connecting door set into the wall beside the fireplace opened. Gareth entered and paused. Althea stared across the expanse of the bedroom at him, her eyes wider and darker than usual.

Gareth closed the door softly. He smiled, saying softly, "You need not fear me, you know. I promise you that."

"No. No, I do not fear you, Gareth," said Althea with equal quiet.

He nodded. "I am glad to hear it." He approached the bed and sat down on the edge of it. He took one of her hands and gently imprisoned her fingers against his chest. The warmth of his body through the silk of the dressing gown was a shock to her. "Can you feel my heart racing, Althea? It is not every day that I take a wife. I am uncertain in this new role of mine."

"As am I," Althea admitted, her mouth lifting a little. "I am glad that you are uncertain. I do not feel so alone."

"You will never be alone again, Althea," he promised. He reached up to frame her face with both his hands. There was a tremor in his fingers. "Gad, but you are beautiful." He bent his head and tentatively, experimentally, kissed her.

Althea put up her hands around his neck and kissed him back.

He drew a long, ragged breath and pulled her to him.

Chapter Eleven

The dawn was just touching the sky with rose when a chaise left Angleton Place. The carriage was accompanied by a horseman dressed in military togs astride a magnificent bay gelding.

Seated inside the chaise, Althea watched as her husband's figure cantered past the window. At her somber thoughts, she laid her head back against the squab and sighed.

"Tired, my lady?" asked the dresser.

"Perhaps a little," Althea said. She closed her eyes to forestall any more questions or conversation. She was not actually tired, merely frustrated.

Earlier that morning, when candlelight was still throwing shadows, she had gone downstairs to find her husband. Aunt Aurelia's staff had made available a sumptuous breakfast for the travelers and she had been certain of finding his lordship already at table.

Althea had tried to talk to Gareth about his decision to take her to Chard. She had hoped that once she had explained how she felt, he would see that the best possible choice was for her to accompany him to Brussels.

But Gareth had not been moved from his stand. He shook his head gravely. "I am sorry, Althea. It is quite impossible." He reached out across the snow-white linen cloth and took hold of her hand. Very softly, he said, "If only I could have you with me. I should like that very much." His thumb caressed the inside of her wrist.

Althea blushed warmly as she recalled the night just spent. She felt suddenly incredibly shy. But she met his gaze steadily enough. "I truly do not want to be parted from you so soon."

The expression in her eyes was such that it touched a chord

of response in him. He felt himself wavering, but he could not allow himself to agree. What he wanted had to be set against the reasonable counsels of his mind.

Gareth sighed, withdrawing his hand from hers."Nor I, you. But it can be no other way. It is a very uncertain situation in Brussels at this moment and will only worsen until it is known for certain what is to be the outcome of the meeting between Wellington and Bonaparte. I would not like my wife in such a place."

"But other ladies have ventured to Brussels. Why, I have read that half the *ton* has deserted London for the Low Countries. Even the Duchess of Richmond!" said Althea, hoping to sway him.

He looked at her gravely, wondering now if this was not the key to her desire. "Is it the society that you so wish to join, my lady?"

"No, of course not! I am simply pointing out that society thinks nothing of the danger that you have foreseen," said Althea. She leaned toward him. "Gareth—"

He did not let her finish, afraid that he might yet succumb to temptation. Rioting through his mind were thoughts of what it would be like to have Althea with him each night. In pushing aside his imaginings, he spoke more abruptly than he had meant to. "Society is often made up of fools, my lady. No, Althea. The subject is closed. You must accept the fact that you are going to Chard."

Swift color rose in her cheeks at his tone. She curled her fingers. Gareth's expression eased into a teasing grin. "Come, my girl! Surely you are not jibing at the fence. My parents will not eat you, after all."

"I fear no one, sir," said Althea, raising her chin. There was the old feeling of stark aloneness welling up inside her. Once more she had to stand on her own. Already, less than a day after Gareth had promised her that she need never be alone again, she had learned that she could not trust everything that he said to her.

If he had been privy to her thoughts, he would have been appalled. But as he did not understand her, he merely felt relief that she was accepting his decision without any more resistance. "This is much better."

Gareth rose from the table. He drew her up beside him and snatched a quick kiss. She was unresponsive in his arms, but he smiled down at her anyway. "I must not shock the servants by being found making love to my wife over breakfast." When he released her, he said, "We are leaving in half an hour, Althea. Pray see that your maid has everything ready."

"As you say, my lord," said Althea, starting to sweep past him.

She was upset. He knew it. Gareth caught her wrist and stopped her. His voice was very soft. "Dear, dear Althea."

That was all he said, but it was the manner in which he said it and the look in his eyes that made Althea's breath catch. Color rising in her face, she snatched her hand away and fled from the breakfast room with the feeling that she had been scorched.

Now as she sat in the moving chaise, Althea frowned out the window. She could see how Gareth had subtly mastered her. With but a look, a touch, he had summoned up emotions that had confused her. She had been completely underminded.

She was not in love with him. *No*, Althea thought firmly, *she was not*. She was too worldy-wise, too cynical, to have committed that worst of mistakes. How then was it that he could so overset her that she completely lost sight of what she wanted?

She was going to Chard, to be deposited like some fragile package until the owner should return and lay claim to her. Althea hated it, but there was nothing she could do, short of creating a scene that would be as repugnant to her as she was certain it would be to Lord Lynley.

Althea was not at all sure that such a scene would grant her the victory, in any event. Gareth had already proven himself to be a gentleman of strong will and conviction. Since the moment that they had so providentially met, he had shown quick decision and swift action.

He was a veteran soldier, accustomed to warfare. Althea did not care to imagine what her life would be like if she should somehow turn him into an enemy. She knew that it was possible for enemy camps to exist in marriage. It had been hellish. Her mother had been a weak woman who brought the weapons of the weak to bear—tears and pleading postures that had served to escalate the mutual bitterness. There had never been a truce between her parents. She had lived through that as a child. She did not want to relive it as a wife.

Therefore, making an issue about being forced to remain in England was not the solution that Althea wanted. She did not as yet know how to approach the matter. However, she did not let go of her strong desire to be with her husband. She merely set it aside to be addressed at a more opportune time.

And so Althea traveled to Chard with all outward appearance of being submissive to her husband's wishes.

Chard was reached in early afternoon. The shadows had lengthened, casting cool pools across the graveled drive. The approach of the carriage was heard and the front door opened. A footman stepped out. He immediately recognized the scion of the house and threw a few quick words over his shoulder before he hurried down the steps.

Gareth dismounted and handed the reins of his mount to the astonished footman. He turned to open the door of the chaise and offered up a hand to help his lady to step down. When her feet touched the gravel, he looked down into her lovely face. "Do not be anxious, Althea. I shall not desert you."

Althea nodded and managed to summon up a smile. Her pride was strong. She would not let him know that his words sounded strongly of irony to her.

Lord Lynley escorted his bride into his ancestral home. He was immediately greeted by the aged butler. After responding suitably, he said, "Crockett, I present to you my wife, Lady Lynley."

"How do you do, Crockett," said Althea quietly.

The butler's smooth expression quivered, but he gave no other indication of his shock. He bowed, saying gravely, "Welcome, my lady. I shall inform the Earl and Countess of Chard of your arrival with his lordship."

"Thank you, Crockett. We shall wait in the drawing room," said Gareth.

"Very good, my lord." The butler ushered them inside the room and softly closed the door.

Althea glanced about her. The drawing room was tastefully furnished. A Persian carpet lay on the floor. Everything gleamed from polish and was well dusted. "This is a pleasant room," she said.

"Yes; Chard has always seemed most restful to my spirits. You will grow to love it as much as I," said Gareth.

There did not seem much to say between them. Both were preoccupied with their own thoughts.

It was not many minutes before the door opened and the earl, his countess on his arm, entered. The Earl of Chard nodded politely at Althea and then stared hard at his son. "This is a surprise, sir. I had thought myself well rid of you several days ago."

Lord Lynley smiled and went forward to shake his father's hand. "Indeed, sir, I thought so, too. But events transpired to bring me back." He greeted his mother.

"Yes, so we understand from Crockett," said the Countess of Chard. She transferred her smiling gaze to Althea and raised her brows. "You must think us mannerless in truth, my dear. But you must understand it is such a shock."

Lord Lynley drew his wife forward. "May I present Althea, Lady Lynley, my wife. You will recall her parents, the Earl and Countess of Hawthorne. We were married by special license day before yesterday from her great-aunt Lady Angleton's house."

After a pause, the countess went forward to kiss her daughter-in-law on the cheek. She stepped back, taking Althea's hand in hers. "Welcome, my dear. You have no notion what a flutter this news has put us in," she said.

"Thank you, my lady. I can well understand that it is a startling revelation," said Althea, smiling slightly.

"Special license, you say?" The Earl of Chard threw a narrow look at his son's composed face. "What possessed you to do such a thing? Surely you must know how this will appear. A runaway match with a libertine's daughter! I knew Hawthorne. A ramshackle man if ever there was one! I could say more, but I will not sully your mother's ears with my opinion of his lordship!"

Althea did not care for the earl's slighting of her, as though she did not exist. Her father's tainted reputation had blighted her life too long. If she did not exert herself now, she could expect to be treated with disdain for the rest of her days. That, she would not have.

"I, too, disliked my father, my lord. But he is dead and I have wed your son. Perhaps I have made the better bargain. That remains to be seen," said Althea quietly. Her eyes suddenly flashed. "Now I am Lady Lynley. It is not a name that I shall bear lightly."

"Bravo, my lady," said Gareth. He turned to his speechless parent. "Be certain that any who treat my lady with less than fairness shall answer to me."

"You are headstrong as always," complained the earl. He nodded to his daughter-in-law, his wide jaw tight. "Whilst you, my dear, have left your shy nature well behind. A fitting pair, I must say. Sit down, sit down! I cannot abide ladies standing about. My dear, send for tea. We will hear how this marriage came about."

The Countess of Chard calmly pulled the bell rope and when the butler entered, she relayed her quiet orders. The butler nodded and exited.

"Now, sirrah! I know full well that Althea is under age. I am not yet in my dotage. You will tell me now if there is anything to object to in this hasty business," said the earl.

"The knot was well and truly tied, sir. Althea's mother, Lady Bottlesby, gave her written consent. I—"

"Bottlesby? Bottlesby?" The earl looked at his countess for illumination.

"You will recall, my dear. There was a notice in the *Gazette*. Lady Hawthorne was wed to a baronet of that name less than four months ago," said the countess composedly.

"Yes, of course, I recall. Well, well, it is interesting, indeed. So you have pitchforked yourself into wedlock with my son, madam. I wonder how that came about?" said the earl, turning his hard stare upon his son. He had already accepted the fact of the marriage, but now he demanded assurance that there would be no scandal attached to it, as his heir was well aware.

"Why, it is easy enough. I took leave from the army for the express purpose of marrying Lady Althea. There has been an understanding between us of some length, of course," said Gareth.

"Oh, of course," put in the earl caustically.

Gareth ignored his father's interjection. "But the deaths in each of our respective families necessarily delayed the nuptials. Since I am still in the army and could arrange only a short leave, it was decided that a private ceremony would be best."

"A true romance, in fact," said the countess, smiling.

Gareth returned the smile. A flash of understanding passed between them. "As you say, mother."

"What have you to say to any of this, madam?" asked the earl, turning his gaze on Althea.

"I believe that Lord Lynley has told our tale well enough, my lord," said Althea quietly.

The Earl of Chard smiled, though with no particular warmth. "Indeed! There will be speculation, of course, but it will be of little account. It is a good solid tale, though I still question why the wedding was not held here at Chard. Perhaps you may shed some light upon that, my lady?"

"Other than my mother, Lady Angleton is my last living relative. She has been a cripple and a recluse for many years. It enlivened the tenor of Aunt Aurelia's days to be able to sponsor my wedding," said Althea.

Gareth laughed. His eyes were full of amusement. "That is true enough," he agreed. "Lady Angleton enjoyed the situation to the hilt, did she not?"

"I think so, indeed," said Althea, also laughing.

"Very well, the tale is spun. Now, what do you wish of me, Gareth?" asked the earl.

The viscount's expression sobered. He glanced at Althea and, taking her hand and raising her from her seat, he led her to his father. "I am placing my wife in your keeping until my return from the war."

Chapter Twelve

The Earl of Chard narrowed his eyes. He nodded abruptly. "I had not credited you with such good sense, Gareth. I accept the charge that you have laid upon me, naturally." He took Althea's hand in his and lifted her fingers to his lips. "My dear daughter, welcome. You are to feel yourself to be at home with us here at Chard."

"Thank you, my lord. I do appreciate your kindness." Althea smiled as she regained possession of her hand. "However, I must not allow you to think of me under false pretenses. I must tell you that I have most strongly disagreed with Lord Lynley's disposition of my future. I would much rather go with him to Brussels."

Lord Lynley stiffened in momentary surprise that she would raise the issue. "Althea, we have spoken of this," said Gareth with considerable constraint.

The Countess of Chard looked quickly at her son's face. She said hurriedly, "Of course you have. A lady of spirit like Althea would naturally wish to follow you, Gareth. How should it be otherwise?" The countess put her arm around her daughter-in-law's waist, smiling up at her. "My dear, I completely understand your feelings."

"Well, I do not!" said the earl, considerably affronted.

"But you are not a woman, my dear," said the countess gently. She slipped her arm from around the younger woman and turned to the earl. "Althea feels that her place is beside her husband. She has a strong sense of duty. It speaks very highly of her character."

Althea could not quite believe her good fortune to find an ally in the countess. "That is just it, my lady," she said. "I do not mind following the drum for a little while. Indeed, I should probably like it very well, for I am not a die-away miss."

"No, I do not think that you are," agreed the countess somewhat dryly. "Yet however much I sympathize with you, my dear, it cannot be." She spread her hands and, still smiling, said, "You are Viscountess Lynley, the mother of future generations of Marshalls. We cannot risk you. Gareth knows this, and though I am persuaded that he, too, would rather that you were to stay with him, he has brought you to us. So you see, my dear, you must bear your exile bravely and set your thoughts on the future."

"Precisely so!" said the Earl of Chard. "So let us have no more of this romantic nonsense. It is absurd."

Althea cast a swift glance upward at her lord's face.

Gareth met her eyes. He smiled, but his gaze remained rather somber. "I am sorry, Althea. It is part of the bargain that we made."

"Yes, I realize that now," she said, a slight edge to her voice.

The earl caught his wife's eyes and signaled her. She gave a slight understanding nod.

The countess turned to Althea. "You are undoubtedly tired from the journey, my dear. We shall not bother with tea, shall we? Let me show you to your rooms. I am persuaded that once you have had an opportunity to settle in here at Chard you will see that this has all been arranged for the best," she said.

Comprehending that it would do no good to argue, Althea made some polite rejoinder and took leave of the gentlemen. She allowed the Countess of Chard to accompany her upstairs and place her into the competent hands of her dresser.

When the countess had left the bedroom, Althea picked up an Oriental vase and quite deliberately threw it into the fireplace. It smashed into several pieces.

"My lady!" Darcy was horrified.

"It is quite all right, Darcy. None of the pieces flew out onto the carpet," Althea said, quite controlled. High color had flushed her cheekbones. "Forgive me. I am in a vile temper. Perhaps you should leave me alone for a time, Darcy."

"My lady, I do not think . . ." At the fierce look in her mistress's eyes, the dresser thought better of what she was about to say. "Very good, my lady. I shall return to waken you in an hour."

By the time that supper was announced, Althea had regained control of her emotions. She had seen nothing of Gareth in the intervening time, and perhaps it had been just as well.

Althea put on her best front to show that all was well, and she must have succeeded. The earl and countess vied to tell her about Chard and the surrounding county, their neighbors, and the social treats that could be expected. They were obviously anxious that she be put at ease.

The amiability of the occasion was spoiled when the countess inquired of her son when he had to leave. "Will it be soon?"

"Yes. I must go this very evening, in fact, if I am to make good time in crossing the channel and go on to Brussels," he said, staring down into his wine glass.

"Gareth! You cannot mean it!" exclaimed the countess.

Althea could not have expressed her own dismay any better. She tried, however. "Must you, Gareth? We have had so little time . . ."

"I am sorry, Althea, Mother. But I do not have a choice," he said, looking up. He turned toward his father. "You at least must understand, sir."

The earl reluctantly nodded. "Aye, one's duty cannot be denied. You have chosen your course and you must stick with it until it is done. I trust that you will return to us safely."

"And I, my lord," said Gareth. He was thinking of the responsibility that he now bore toward Althea. He had not forgotten the look of appeal in her eyes when she realized that she was outnumbered. He disliked leaving her. She had been such a shy, retiring young girl that he understood how much she must shrink at being left with those whom she naturally looked upon as strangers. However, the necessity could not be denied.

After supper, Gareth quietly begged pardon of his parents and bore Althea off to their private rooms. As he closed the door, he looked across the sitting room at her. He felt a stirring in his blood and a possessive feeling coursed through him. *His wife.*

She had turned to face him. Her expression was cool, faintly inquiring.

Gareth approached her and gathered her hands in his. "I wanted to have a few moments alone with you before my departure. Althea, you must believe me when I say that I wish circumstances were otherwise."

"Why can they not be, Gareth?"

"What?" He was taken aback.

Althea's fingers tightened upon his and her eyes held his gaze. She spoke urgently. "Why could we not change the circumstances, Gareth? Are things so set in stone that you cannot entertain anything else?"

"Of course not. I am not so lacking in imagination," said Gareth, but even as he spoke he felt the vague nagging conviction that he had uttered a lie. He shook his head, as much in denial of what had crossed his mind as in answer to her. "However, reason dictates our most responsible course and—"

Althea threw herself against him and on instinct his arms closed about her.

She stared up at him, crying fiercely, "I do not wish to be left alone, Gareth. Can you not understand that?"

"Althea . . ."

She wound her arms about his neck. "I want to be with you, Gareth," she whispered against his lips. Then she kissed him.

Gareth tightened his arms about her, responding swiftly to her desperate passion. His senses swam and almost he gave in to the temptation so willingly offered him.

"Oh, Gareth, do take me with you."

Gareth slid his hands up to her arms to loosen her hold about his neck. Reluctantly, he set her aside. He was breathing heavily, but he still clung to his clear vision of responsibility. With true regret, he said quietly, "I am sorry, sweetheart, but I cannot."

Althea looked at him. Her wide eyes held such an expression of vulnerability that Gareth sucked in his breath. He half raised his hand toward her.

Without a word, Althea walked away from him through the door into the bedroom. Softly, carefully, the door was shut.

Gareth stood irresolute. He wondered whether he should go to her and try to reason with her again. But there would be more pleas, perhaps even tears. He drew in a slow breath and shook his head. It would only create more unhappiness for them both, for in the end he would not have changed his mind. It was better simply to leave it as it stood.

Gareth turned and exited the sitting room.

He left within the hour.

March had given way to April and spring had come to Chard. Tender new buds covered the stately trees and the graceful gardens were coming out of their winter dreariness. The sun was shining after a fortnight of rain. There was still a chill on the air and a fire crackled quietly on the hearth in the drawing room.

Althea drew her shawl a little more securely over her shoulders as she sat back in the wingback chair. She glanced about the comfortable drawing room with an objective gaze. She still felt her position at Chard to be an awkward one. She was newly wed and had been left with her in-laws with scarcely more than an introduction. When Gareth had left, she had felt abandoned. That had been two months previous.

Althea let her thoughts reflect idly on the recent past. Gareth's reasons for leaving her at Chard had been sound, but they had never spoken true to her heart. When she tried to change his mind, he had put her off in such a way that it would have cost her a measure of pride to persist. The same thing would have been true if she had not accepted gracious defeat at the countess's hands.

Althea had never begged for anything in her life. The closest she had come was when Gareth had left. Even now she inwardly squirmed at how she had virtually offered herself in exchange for his favor. It was not in her to begin begging with virtual strangers. For that was how she had come to think even of Gareth.

Even though they had consummated their hasty marriage, Althea did not feel as though she knew much more about Gareth than she had as a child. He was not Gareth Marshall, but Viscount Lynley, heir to Chard. That was a very different thing altogether, she had discovered.

She had been lonely, but Lord Lynley was at least a faithful correspondent. She had received a letter nearly each week of their separation. Althea had read his lordship's letters and then carefully put them away. She related various tidbits of news to her in-laws as appropriate, but she never once uttered what she felt.

The Earl of Chard was agreeably surprised by his daughter-in-law's restraint. Althea was settling in nicely without the bouts of tears that he had anticipated. She was a sensible young woman, he had concluded. Though her magnificent eyes had flashed with anger at times, she had had the wisdom to keep her tongue between her teeth. When she was told that it was best if she did not ride any but the most plodding of mounts because of the possibility of being tossed, she acquiesced with scarcely a murmur. When he forbade her to take out a gun for target shooting, for fear that she would accidently wound herself, she had given way with good grace.

There was, of course, the report he had been given of the number of smashed objets d'art, but the earl brushed aside the consideration. His daughter-in-law's upbringing had undoubtedly been somewhat lacking and naturally she was high-strung, yet she was a lady to her fingertips. Measured against that, a few pieces of broken pottery were inconsequential.

All in all, he was satisfied with his heir's hasty choice. While it had been true that he had initially regarded the marriage with something less than favor, he had since come completely around. The girl's expressed desire to accompany Gareth to Brussels had been but the ill-formed romantic notion that was usual among green misses. Once she had accepted the impossibility and learned what her station as Viscountess Lynley entitled her to, she had quite sensibly forgotten all about Brussels.

Of course, the earl had thought all along that it would evolve just as it had. He had been shrewd to cut off any possibility of a scene by sending the girl away at once with his wife. It had been extremely fortunate that Gareth had wanted to leave that same evening. He had understood the advantage immediately and he had not urged his son to tarry. As a consequence of his foresight, the issue was gone the way of the wind.

The earl, complacent in his wisdom, would have been startled indeed if he had had but a hint of the tenacity that was part of his daughter-in-law's determined personality.

Althea had received another letter from Lord Lynley. She sat with his letter open in her lap, having already possessed herself of its contents. She looked out the window at the watery sunlight, wrapped in her thoughts.

Althea did not like the pattern of her life. It seemed that she did not belong anywhere. She had been *de trop* once her mother began to be courted by Sir Bartholomew, and after the wedding even more so.

Her mother had not been particularly upset to learn that she had indeed married Lord Lynley. Althea had had a letter from her mother soon after the announcement of the marriage appeared in the London *Gazette* and she had anxiously scanned Lady Bottlesby's scribbled lines for hidden meanings, but there had been nothing. Lady Bottlesby was in high spirits, for not only had her daughter succeeded in marrying well but the baronet had promised to take her to London for the Season. Incredible as it seemed, Lady Bottlesby was happy. Lady Angleton's cynical prediction had proven true.

Althea shook her head, smiling a little sadly. She could look back upon her intention to live with Aunt Aurelia as the true act of desperation that it had been. She would not have fitted in to her great-aunt's household. Sooner or later, Aunt Aurelia would have regretted her magnanimity. That formidable lady preferred to have around her those whom she could browbeat, and Althea was not cast in that mold. The two years to her majority and the gaining of her freedom would have seemed to be a purgatory. It had been fortunate indeed that she had chanced to meet Lord Lynley at that inn. At one stroke she had saved herself and Aunt Aurelia from the inevitable clashing of wills.

Althea sighed. She had assumed, so wrongly, that upon her marriage her role would be established and she would have her own responsibilities and duties. Instead, she had been left in a household that she was ill suited for. Her days were too idle. She was used to running a household. Her mother had given up the reins of that responsibility from the day that Althea had returned from the ladies' seminary. Althea was also used to managing her own stable. Most of the horses had been left in London when her cousin had stepped into the earl's shoes, but she had retained her own mount and the coach team. The horses had gone with her and her mother to Sir Bartholomew's estate. She had since sent for her horse and it was now eating its head off in the Earl of Chard's stables.

Althea was not a fool. She was on sufferance at Chard. She knew that. It was an uneasy knowledge to live under.

Not that the earl or the countess were so ill-bred that they had ever expressed anything other than polite consideration for her comfort and well-being. But Althea felt the lack of true fellowship and affection. She was an interloper. She had been thrust upon them as a duty and a responsibility.

Given time, the Earl and Countess of Chard would probably come to accept her very well. However, what with the hurried fashion of the wedding and Gareth's immediate return to duty overseas, it was inevitable that an awkward strain had been placed upon all.

Recently the earl had begun to look upon her with growing approval, but Althea knew that could be only temporary. She had tried very hard to do all that was required of her, hoping that by doing so she would win her in-laws's confidence and trust. She hoped that she could win them over enough that she could again express her continued desire to leave Chard and go to Brussels. It was not so much that she craved their approval or even their consent. She simply did not want to create unneedful strife if there could be found a better way.

However, Althea was beginning to wonder whether her efforts were worth it. The strictures and limitations of her present existence chafed her unbearably. It was but a matter of time before her temper would get the better of her and she would say something that she would later regret.

Althea felt that she had no place to call her own. The only place that she could rightfully claim was at her husband's side.

She wanted so desperately to get on with her life.

Lord Lynley had opened the door of opportunity for her by marrying her. She had thought that at last she would be able to try her wings. But he had left her to rot at Chard. Althea felt that only a saint could have been expected to accept much more.

Now she had this latest letter, which was written in a more somber vein then the others. Not that Gareth had confided his feelings to her, but even through his cheerful lines Althea could discern the truth. Events were moving swiftly. Many of the more faint-hearted had already left Brussels. Soon there would be a battle such as had never been seen. Many, many men would lose their lives.

Althea's contemplative reflections were leading her to an unmistakable conclusion. The time had come to throw over the traces. Gareth could very well be killed in this action. If she was to have any time at all with him as his wife, it had to begin now. Her decision made, Althea gave a low laugh of sheer anticipation. She was going to leave Chard.

Althea picked up Gareth's letter and folded it to be put away with his others. Thoughtfully she tapped it into one palm. In the tedious weeks spent at Chard she had learned a great deal. Lord Lynley had not exaggerated the earl's obsession to see the succession secured. Indeed, Althea had learned it was the overriding ambition for both the earl and the countess. Yet how to put her knowledge to best effect had been the main question.

Althea rather thought that she could at last answer that question.

Chapter Thirteen

The door opened and the Countess of Chard entered. Her ladyship paused, smiling, as she saw her daughter-in-law. "I was searching for my embroidery and thought I might find it in here. I hope that I do not intrude, my dear."

"Pray come in, ma'am. I am glad, for I wished to speak with you, and his lordship, too. I have had a letter from Gareth," said Althea pleasantly, at once wondering if this was opportunity opening up to her.

The countess came further into the drawing room and seated herself on the settee. "Yes, here is my basket of yarns behind this cushion. How fortunate that I thought to look in this room." She glanced at her daughter-in-law. "You wished to speak to me about something in Gareth's letter? What is it, my dear?"

"Gareth writes that all is eager expectation in Brussels. The Duke of Wellington arrived in Brussels from Vienna on the fifth of April. Everyone anticipates a swift conclusion to this business with Bonaparte," said Althea.

"That is good news, indeed. I shall be glad when this horrible war is at last done and over with and Gareth can return home," said the countess, pulling out her piecework.

"Gareth says that there is expected to be a pitched battle once Wellington and the Allied forces are squared up against the French," said Althea. "No one is quite certain what to expect, except that Bonaparte will not surrender unless he is decisively defeated."

The countess nodded, calmly embroidering. "Yes, I believe that to be so. That Corsican madman will not tamely relinquish the reins now that he is back in the saddle. It was shocking to read how readily the French flocked once more to his banner.

But I expect that the Allied forces will stand firm no matter what the French throw at them. Sadly, there will be many casualties. We can only pray that Gareth is brought home to us safely."

Althea took a deep breath. "And if he does not return, my lady?"

The countess looked up. Her eyes were very bright and hard. "We will not speak of that possibility, Lady Althea."

"I am sorry, ma'am, but I must. It is possible that Gareth might not return," said Althea. She forestalled the countess's sharp reprimand. "In view of that, ma'am, I have decided to join Gareth in Brussels."

The countess stared at Althea, quite startled. Her expression almost immediately smoothed. "I see. Perhaps you should tell me what has led you to this decision. Has Gareth hinted in his letter that he wishes you to join him after all?"

Althea hesitated, but it was not in her to lie. "No, he has not. However, that does not alter my decision. I am determined to join him in Brussels and, forgive me, for I mean no disrespect, but there is nothing that you can say that will persuade me to do otherwise."

"This is rather sudden, is it not?"

"I do not think it so sudden as all that. I wanted from the first to accompany Gareth. But I did not because Gareth cited the possible dangers and expressed his wish that I remain here at Chard until his return," said Althea.

"I believe that those considerations are still valid, Althea," said the countess gently, watching her daughter-in-law's face closely. She did not observe any wavering of the younger woman's determination.

"Yes, they are. However, circumstances must at times give way to necessity," said Althea. She smiled at the Countess of Chard. "You will agree that there is a possibility that Gareth could be killed in this last action."

The countess threw up her hand. "I have already made my sentiments clear upon this topic. Let us not speak of it, if you please, Althea. I dislike dwelling on unpleasantries, particularly those that are mere supposition."

"I am sorry, ma'am, but I feel that I must press it," said Althea. "Forgive me for indelicacy, my lady, but I am persuaded that it is your right to be made aware of this fact." She drew in her breath and said bluntly, "I am not increasing."

The Countess of Chard stared at her daughter-in-law for several moments. She was fully in her spouse's confidence and had shared in his optimism that all was well. Now she was beginning to realize just how deluded they had been, both in their perception of Althea's character and in their confidence that the future was settled.

"I see," she said at last. The countess folded away her embroidery. "As you say, Althea, at times circumstances must give way before other considerations. I shall speak to the earl upon this matter. It will not be necessary for you to broach the subject again."

"Thank you, ma'am," said Althea quietly.

The countess rose and went to pull the bell rope. She half turned toward Althea. Smiling faintly, she said, "You are a most persuasive and willful young woman, Althea. Let us hope that my son comes to appreciate those qualities."

"I trust that he will, my lady," said Althea.

The countess merely smiled again.

Althea understood, looking into the countess's eyes, that she had won her ladyship's support. Though she did not have the countess's blessing, it was enough that she had at least gained the lady's sanction. Once the earl was made aware of Althea's unanswerable argument, she knew that she would be free to leave for the Continent whenever she wished.

Althea left England three days later, taking sail from Dover. She had wasted no time in leaving Chard, preferring to be gone before either the earl or the countess thought of some delaying tactic. What that could possibly have been, under the circumstances, she was not certain. However, she did not want to allow them time to decide to write to their son. Althea thought she knew what Lord Lynley's reply would have been and it would have meant further open defiance. It was best simply to go.

On the journey from Dover to the fishing port of Ostend, from Ostend through Bruges and Ghent, Althea thrust down speculation about what her reception would be at Lord Lynley's hands. It was unprofitable to be concerned for the future.

The Countess of Chard had tried to relay a warning by her carefully chosen words, Althea knew. She only hoped that Gareth would be more amenable than his mother apparently believed he would be.

However, through force of will, Althea left that little uncertainty for the future. She refused to be anxious beforehand. She had gotten her way, and that was all that mattered at the moment. Althea settled back to enjoy her first journey on the Continent. She absorbed everything she saw eagerly and with a sense of excitement. The magnificent cities were impressive and certainly rivaled London for sweep of history. As she watched, the flats and dikes near the coast gradually gave way to sweeping fields, beech forest, and weather-worn hills. Rivers laced gracefully through the land, while canals crisscrossed in a no-nonsense style. Often in the distance she could see the roofs of tidy farmhouses or catch fleeting glimpses of grand chateaus.

Althea reached Brussels without difficulty. She and her dresser stared out of the carriage windows with wondering curiosity. The city was large and contained as many ancient edifices as London. There were striking differences from the English capital, however, in the wide boulevards and canals, in the obvious number of restaurants and shops.

The sheer magnitude of the task of finding Gareth in such a place suddenly hit Althea. A spurt of alarm went through her. However, it proved relatively simple, after all. Armed with Lord Lynley's address and through inquiry of strangers by her driver, it was easy enough for her man to find the right street.

The carriage drove past several respectable town houses and finally stopped, pulling in close to the curb. Once arrived, Althea felt an unusual trepidation take hold of her. Through the carriage window, she looked up at the front of the town house. Now was the time to begin to wonder about her reception. Certainly Gareth would be upset that she had disobeyed his express wishes. Althea did not think he would greet her with unalloyed joy. Quite the contrary, in fact.

The carriage door swung open and the driver let down the iron step.

Althea told herself that she had not come all of the way

from England to turn around now. She stiffened her flagging courage and ducked out of the carriage.

The driver had already stumped up the steps to bang the knocker on the door. The brusque summons was answered and the driver spoke in swift French to the porter. The houseservant's mouth dropped open and he sent a startled look down at the lady and her attendant standing on the walkway. He stepped back inside, disappearing from sight and leaving the door open. The driver stumped back down to the carriage and proceeded to unload Althea's baggage onto the flagged walk.

"It is a pretty street, is it not, my lady?" asked Darcy, looking approvingly up and down the length of the avenue.

"Yes, indeed," agreed Althea.

Althea paid the driver. She watched the man climb up onto his box, whip up the team, and drive away. With the going of the carriage, she felt that she had burned her last bridge behind her, and in a sense she had. She was standing in front of Gareth's town house, her baggage at her feet. Now she either gained admittance or remained marooned on the street. She almost wished that she had written to express her intention of coming to Brussels.

The porter reappeared with an expressionless individual whose exact status was not easily recognizable. This individual came down the steps and bowed to Althea. "You are Lord Lynley's wife, madam?"

"Yes, I am Lady Lynley," said Althea, drawing herself up.

The man raked her with a comprehensive glance that seemed to cut right through her to her innermost being. Althea received the distinct impression that she had failed to come up to some mark of measurement.

"Very good, my lady. I am John Applegate, his lordship's majordomo. My apologies for the delay in greeting you. We were not expecting you. Pray, will you not come in? Your baggage will naturally be taken care of."

Lifting her skirt in one gloved hand, Althea followed the man up the steps and finally set foot into her husband's home. She cast a swift glance around. The entry floor was covered with an Oriental carpet, offering a suitable relief for a few eighteenth-century Flemish chairs and a small table. The overall effect was reserved. Several doors stood off the entry hall, but she was not given an opportunity to take real stock of her surroundings.

The majordomo stood waiting at the bottom of a short flight of narrow stairs. "This way, my lady. I shall escort you up to your room. The journey was undoubtedly a long one and you will want to refresh yourself," he said.

Althea once more followed the man, this time upstairs to a small apartment. The majordomo showed Althea into a sitting room that led immediately into an adjacent bedroom. The rooms had obviously been hurriedly opened, a quick flick of a dust cloth easily observed. The windows had been pushed open to freshen the air. Here, too, the furniture was Flemish, the carpets Oriental; but an original Brussels tapestry hung on the wall of the sitting room and, in the bedroom, the warm shades of gold woven in the drapes and the bed hangings added a welcoming touch.

"Your woman's quarters are behind that door, my lady," said the majordomo, pointing at a plain door opposite Althea's own bedroom.

"Thank you. I am certain that we will be most comfortable," said Althea quietly.

The majordomo permitted himself a half-smile. "So I should hope, my lady."

Darcy had accompanied her mistress to the bedroom and at once began ordering the placement of Althea's baggage, which was being carried in by the porter. Althea had traveled lightly, preferring to have everything strapped onto the chaise that she herself was using rather than go to the expense of hiring a second chaise for luggage. As a consequence, the number of trunks and portmanteaus was small.

The fact that there was a meager amount of baggage had not escaped the majordomo's quick observation. Surely a lady of quality married to Lord Lynley would have more substance to add to her consequence. The majordomo kept his thoughts to himself, but he intended to warn his master the moment that his lordship stepped inside the front door.

This lady who had announced herself to be Lady Lynley was unmistakably of the quality. There was nothing shabby-genteel about either her manner or her dress. The porter had been correct in informing him that the lady was obviously used to patronizing the best of English shops and seamstresses. She was accompanied by an obviously superior female, as well. All of these things totally negated the possibility that Lord Lynley had been pursued by some former fancy piece.

However, it remained to be seen whether the lady's claim that she was his lordship's wife was actually true, for his lordship had said nothing about being wed while over in England. Of course, the majordomo had noticed the plain gold band on his lordship's finger and he had even entertained the boggling thought that the viscount had been caught in parson's trap at last, but he had almost as swiftly banished it. Surely if Lord Lynley had wed, he would have announced the fact to all and sundry.

Then again, Lord Lynley had been strangely reticent about his visit home. The majordomo had guessed that there had been some trouble at Chard. Now he wondered whether it was possible that this lady could be at the heart of it.

The majordomo looked with distant disfavor on the lady. His loyalties were certain and unshakable. Anything that was disturbing to the viscount was unquestionably undesirable.

"I will send up some tea and a pitcher of water, my lady. Will there be anything else?" asked the majordomo.

"Yes. Is Lord Lynley in? I should like to see him as soon as possible," said Althea, beginning to draw off her straw-colored kid gloves.

The majordomo's manner was deflating. His voice completely neutral and revealing nothing, he said, "His lordship is out, my lady. When he returns, I shall naturally inform him of your arrival."

"When do you expect Lord Lynley to return?" asked Althea.

"That I could not say, my lady," returned the majordomo. "Now if you will excuse me, my lady, I must return to my duties."

The majordomo bowed himself out of the bedroom. He retreated through the sitting room and shut the door, leaving the visitors to exchange a speaking look.

"Not a very friendly sort, is he, my lady?" observed Darcy, shaking out a dress and turning to put it away into a large wardrobe.

"No, but I suppose that it is understandable. I did not send word ahead of our arrival," said Althea, sighing. She wondered rather tiredly if she had not once more pitchforked herself into a household that would not accept her. She had finished removing her gloves. Untying the satin ribbons of her smart straw bonnet, she tossed the headgear into a nearby chair. "I have the most lowering suspicion that the worthy majordomo, John Applegate, does not approve of me or my presence here."

"Never mind. We shall do very well no matter how uppity the servants be," said Darcy stoutly.

The news that the viscount had not been apprised of their coming was unwelcome to the faithful dresser. The dresser had assumed that Lord Lynley had sent for his wife. Darcy had not seen much of his lordship, but what she had observed had given her the impression that he was a gentleman of forceful character. She glanced at her mistress's closed, brooding expression and she knew that there was trouble ahead. But what was done was done. "Why don't you let me get you unbuttoned out of that pelisse, my lady? After you have washed up and had tea, you will be able to lie down for a few minutes. Everything will appear much brighter after a short rest. Then you will be at your best when his lordship sends for you."

"My faithful, sensible Darcy," said Althea, flashing a quick, grateful smile.

"And whatever else would I be, my lady?" asked Darcy, somewhat tartly.

Chapter Fourteen

Lord Lynley was met at the front door by his majordomo. That worthy relayed in a few concise sentences what had happened earlier that afternoon. He finished by saying, "The lady is presently in the drawing room, my lord. She wished to wait for you downstairs and so I showed her in there. Do you wish me to inform her of your arrival?"

"No; no, I shall do so myself," said the viscount, frowning darkly.

The majordomo nodded and withdrew, understanding that further words were unnecessary. He had already had some of his own suspicions put to rest. The viscount had not been surprised to hear that the lady claimed to be his lawful wife, but only that she had arrived. Therefore, the lady was in actuality his lordship's wife. It was all very interesting, indeed.

For a moment Lord Lynley stood immobile, irresolute. He glanced toward the closed drawing room door. In truth, Gareth was appalled.

He had done what was honorable by Althea. He had done his clear duty by Chard, as well. He had assumed that chapter of his life to be well in hand. The earl was appeased for the time being, which meant that Lynley had a reprieve from the condemnation and guilt that had plagued him when he had withstood his sire's wishes. Though Althea had not wanted to stay at Chard and had childishly and naively insisted that she would like to be a soldier's wife, his had been the wiser head. He had successfully resisted the reckless temptation to bring her back to Brussels with him, where she could possibly be exposed to all manner of horror before the war was done. No, he had done what was best for her by placing her under the earl's protection.

Gareth had therefore returned to his military duties satisfied that he could place all his concentration on those things most pressing and immediate.

His wife's unanticipated appearance threatened to disrupt not only his peace of mind, but also his well-ordered existence. He had come back to his quarters expecting to put off his uniform and go out again to join friends for dinner. Now not only did his plans for the evening have to be rearranged, but everything else that he had assumed to have well in train up to this point was thrown into immediate jeopardy.

Shortly after Lord Lynley's return to Brussels, those who were acquainted with him discovered the notice that appeared in the London *Gazette*. The astonishing news that Viscount Lynley was wed had created a pelter of curiosity. Gareth had disclosed the simple tale that had been concocted. When asked if Lady Lynley would be joining him in Brussels, he had laughed and shaken his head. "It is too anxious a time to bring a new bride to Brussels," he had said. Many had agreed and applauded his lordship's wisdom.

Gareth's jaw tightened. He could not allow distractions to close in around him, not now when every day there was the chance that the call to arms would sound. The city had been thrown into one panic already. It was but a hair's breadth from it again.

Many of those English who had fled Brussels on the 24th of March at the false report of Bonaparte's imminent invasion of the city had since returned. However, a disquieting effect had lingered on in the minds of the resident British and the holidaymakers.

The Duke of Wellington's arrival just three weeks previously had resulted in a tremendous boost of morale. There had not been a great deal of public confidence felt in the young and excitable Prince of Orange, who was commander-in-chief of the Allied forces until his superior arrived. The Duke of Wellington's hearty and confident manner had subsequently succeeded in soothing much of the apprehension that permeated the atmosphere wherever people congregated.

The duke had entertained every week at his town house overlooking the Park. He appeared often enough at the balls and soirees held by others to assure all who observed him so closely that he had not a care in the world. His reply to every anxious query about Bonaparte was a braying laugh and the same reassuring words. Indeed, his manner was so careless as to have given a small number of individuals the impression that he must be somewhat lacking in intelligence.

Nevertheless, most in Brussels held the opinion—and stated it with fervent conviction—that the Duke of Wellington, once he came to grips with the enemy, would put Bonaparte to rout.

There were naturally factions that disagreed, but for the most part these parties kept silent. They quietly went about the business of appearing as neutral as possible, and in secret made blue and white cockades that they could wear on their hats when the French entered Brussels, symbolizing their support of the victor, Napoleon Bonaparte.

What everyone could agree on was that there would be a battle and that it would be one of titan proportions.

Attached in his duties to the Duke of Brunswick, Gareth knew perhaps better than many others that the face that Wellington presented to the world covered most successfully his grace's own grave concerns over the coming conflict. The Allied forces were not a unified whole and had not all come up yet. In addition, the rumors were that Bonaparte's forces outnumbered the Allies by two to one. Brussels was an unfortified city and therefore lay open before the gathering French forces as virtually indefensible.

Most of the royalty of Europe had gathered in Brussels and the blue bloods represented the cosmopolitan mix of the Allied forces. British, Belgian, German, Flemish, and Spanish soldiers were quartered all over the city. The congregation of royalty had its inevitable effect. Civilians from nearly every country on the map had flocked to Brussels to disport themselves in this most fashionable of European capitals. Gaiety and laughter, the flash of jewels and the strains of music in crowded ballrooms were the order of each and every day. Nowhere else could be found such sumptuous and riotous living, and it was made all the more titillating because it existed under the great grim shadow of war.

If the tide of the battle should turn against the Allies, it was extremely unlikely that everything that had been brought into Brussels would be safely spirited away again. Many men thought of their wives and daughters and wondered whether they were wise to remain. If the Allies lost, there would indeed be plunder enough for all the enemy.

But more than that, if the battle were lost, the European powers that opposed Bonaparte and were centered in Brussels would be shattered and exposed as weak and ineffectual. The star of French ascendency would once more rise over the Continent.

Brussels would be a prize, indeed, for Napoleon Bonaparte.

There was no question about it. Brussels was not the place for Lord Lynley's wife.

Gareth strode quickly to the door of the drawing room and thrust it open. He paused on the threshold, taken aback by the sight of the lovely woman who looked up quickly upon his entrance. His wife calmly regarded him with her beautiful eyes. His physical reaction was swift and immediate. His blood began to pound heavily in his veins.

"What are you doing here?" he asked, more harshly than he had intended. He stepped inside and shut the door with a sharp click.

Althea had risen at his entrance. She had already felt some trepidation at how he would receive her. Now she reacted to his tone and hard expression. She lifted her chin. "I did not wish to stay at Chard."

It was not an auspicious beginning. Her statement struck him as being childishly selfish and willful. "Well, you cannot remain here," snapped Gareth, his irritation mounting. "You will have to go back to Chard as soon as I can arrange it. Brussels is not the place for you. The situation here is altogether too uncertain."

"Gareth." Althea approached him, but she did not quite dare to touch his sleeve. Given the grim expression on his face, he looked magnificent and altogether unapproachable in his well-fitted uniform. He was angry, and rightly so, but she had to make him see. "I wasn't comfortable at Chard. And though the earl and your mother did everything to make me welcome, they were not made comfortable by my presence. I am a stranger to them. There was not time for any of us to adjust before you had left. It was all very awkward."

"Of course it was awkward. All of the circumstances of our

wedding were awkward," said Gareth shortly. He could smell her perfume and instantly memories of the sweet night they had spent together invaded his thoughts. The impulse to sweep her up into his arms and express his passion was overwhelming.

He took a turn about the room, as much to put distance between them as to clear his head and order his thoughts. He raked his fingers through his hair before he swung around to face her. His mouth was held in an exceedingly grim line. "Althea, you must see that this is impossible. You cannot remain here. Do you not understand? The city could be placed under siege at any moment. No one knows when Bonaparte will move or what he will do. The call to arms is expected any day. I cannot have you here where you could be placed in danger of your life."

"Surely there are other officer's wives here," said Althea.

"Yes, of course! But—"

"Then I do not see why I should not also take my place at my husband's side," said Althea. She lifted her hands, palm upward, in an uncharacteristic pleading gesture. "Gareth, I am not afraid. I assure you that I shall not be a burden to you. Indeed, I suspect that I might rather enjoy following the drum."

"You have not the least notion of what you are talking about. In any event, that is all quite beside the point, Althea. If you remained, I would be made anxious on your account. I would be forced to consider your safety and well-being first above my duty," said Gareth, trying very hard to explain things in a reasonable way.

"That I would not permit. Your duty must always come first. I shall do very well on my own, and so I assure you," said Althea firmly.

She saw that her declaration had not served to reassure him. She smiled and tried to lighten his frowning expression. "I have always been disgustingly self-sufficient, you know." Her attempt at humor fell sadly flat.

There was a bleak look in his eyes. Gareth shook his head, realizing that she could not, or would not, understand. He said quietly, "Althea, I do not like to order you, but in this instance I must. You are to return to Chard and remain there until I come for you."

Althea turned and walked to the window. She lifted the drape so that she could see the street below. The cobbles were cut by the long late-afternoon shadows. Several pedestrians were strolling leisurely about. Nearly all of the men were attired in some uniform or other. When she had arrived in Brussels, it had struck her forcibly that she had never seen so many uniforms, or so many that she did not recognize. It was the outward evidence of a city that had been cast as the stage for war.

"Althea, you cannot hope to ignore my wishes," said Gareth, wondering at what he perceived to be her stubborn childishness.

Without looking around, Althea said over her shoulder, "Everywhere one looks there are soldiers. There will be a great horrible battle, will there not?"

Gareth gestured impatiently. "Yes, of course. That is what I have been trying to convey to you. It will in all likelihood be the bloodiest action that anyone has ever seen. Althea, I cannot be responsible for you when the call to arms is sounded. I cannot have my thoughts divided between my concern for you and my duty. Despite your desire to the contrary, Althea, my thoughts would naturally and inevitably turn to you and your safety."

Gareth stepped closer until there was but an arm's length between them. He did not dare to touch her, however, fearing that the control he exercised over himself would dissolve. He said softly, "Althea, surely you must realize how much I want you here, with me. But if I were to be so selfish, and you were hurt through my disregard of wisdom, I would never be able to forgive myself."

The sincerity and force of his concern carried clearly to her. Althea breathed deeply, closing her eyes a moment. She could scarcely withstand his plea. But she must if she was to achieve her goal. She could not endure being alone again.

Althea abruptly dropped the drape and turned away from the window, facing him directly. Her gaze was steady when meeting his. "You might be killed," she stated quietly.

Gareth's brows snapped together. He did not understand what she was getting at by taking this tack, but he disliked it.

He had not suspected that Althea had a morbid streak. It was an unpleasant revelation.

"That is a possibility for any one of us," he said slowly. "All the more reason for you to have remained at Chard. In the event of my untimely death, you would not know where to turn. And if Brussels was overrun, you would be absolutely swallowed up in the resulting confusion. There would be no one to help you or even willing to do so."

"Gareth, I am willing to take that chance. Pray allow me the wit to understand and accept the risk," said Althea.

He sighed and shook his head. "Althea, you have no notion what it is like to be in a city that has suffered through battle. I do. I have seen pitiful, horrible sights. The most heartrending are those of women, with their young children gathered around them, who have lost their men. They are anchorless and left prey to others. I cannot entertain the thought that that same fate may be yours. No! It is far better that you return to Chard, where I know that you will be safe and will be with those who will support you were I to die."

Althea studied his face. The expression in his eyes, in the firmness of his jaw, was implacable. There would be no appeal that she could make that would move him, she realized. It was distasteful in the extreme, but she felt she had now no other option except to fall back upon the same argument that had enabled her to leave Chard in the first place.

"I shall not return to Chard. Indeed, I cannot. The earl and countess would be most displeased if I should do so," said Althea quietly.

Gareth narrowed his eyes. He suspected that she had quarreled royally with his parents, but that still did not adequately explain her presence here in Brussels. Surely his father would have had the good sense to override any breach of feelings, however strong.

His growing frustration got the better of him. He smashed his fist down on the occasional table. "God, I do not understand why my father ever allowed you to leave England at all!"

Althea had jumped at his fierce gesture. It astonished and dismayed her, for she had never thought that Gareth was capable of such a display of overt violence. It reminded her unpleasantly of her father's too-frequent tempers. She shook off the feeling and concentrated instead on what he had said. Very deliberately she played her last hand.

"It is perfectly understandable. His lordship felt that he had little choice, for I am not increasing," said Althea.

At his expression, a faint flush rose in her face. She discovered that it had been easier to inform the Countess of Chard of her lack than it was to admit it to her own husband.

Gareth continued to stare at her, stunned. Suddenly Lady Angleton's words about Althea's playing off her tricks against him came back to haunt him. At the time he had brushed aside her ladyship's statement as mere rhetoric that was voiced by an elderly and perhaps somewhat malicious tongue. Now he was not so certain.

Doubt rushed in on him even faster when he recalled how she had thrown herself at him in an effort to seduce him into changing his mind. In every detail he remembered how she had felt in his arms, the passion of her kiss. She had turned away from him when he had denied her wishes. Gareth pushed away the memory of the look in her eyes as his anger gathered. She had not even had the courtesy to say good-bye.

Gareth saw quite clearly how Lady Althea had attempted to manipulate him, how she was still attempting to do so. The devil of it was that she had struck unerringly on the one chink in his defense that he could not refute.

His expression abruptly altered. There was anger and something else in his hard blue eyes. "I see. As you say, it all becomes perfectly understandable." His lips tightened as his thoughts carried him forward. "You are clever, my lady. I somehow did not expect that in you. No doubt you found Chard dull and you anticipate that the society here will be more to your liking. Perhaps you are right. There is a mad whirl of amusements that must appeal to one who has never enjoyed a London Season."

Althea flushed even more hotly at his scathing words. "I do not deserve your condemnation, my lord."

"No, I suppose that I must not condemn you. You are, after all a product of your upbringing. Nevertheless, you are my wife." He stepped forward suddenly and grasped her wrist. His fingers were bruising. "You say you are here for a specific reason, Althea. Very well! I allow you to remain only for that. Otherwise I would insist upon your conceding to my wishes."

"I understand perfectly, Gareth," said Althea. She had grown somewhat pale with his harsh treatment, but she spoke with unbroken composure.

Gareth released her wrist and turned away. His voice was cold. "I shall get out of my dirt so that I may join you for dinner. We will discuss this matter further then."

He yanked open the door and strode out of the drawing room. As the door crashed shut behind him, Althea grasped a chair back for support. Her legs weakened and she sat down abruptly.

The interview had gone much worse than she had ever anticipated. She had expected annoyance, perhaps even anger. She had never thought that she would come up against fury and contempt. How could Gareth, who had been so sensitive to her plight with Sir Bartholomew, now turn about and so blindly spurn her? It was utterly incomprehensible.

But nothing had been right from the moment that Gareth had informed her that he was taking her to Chard. He had seemed to change before her very eyes, moment by moment, to become someone who was nothing like the boy that she had once known.

Chapter Fifteen

The door opened and the majordomo entered. Wooden-faced, he inquired, "Will his lordship be staying in for dinner, my lady?"

Althea pulled herself together. Somewhat pale, but perfectly composed, she said, "Yes. Yes, he will." She stood up. "I shall go upstairs to rest before the hour. Pray send my maid to me."

John Applegate bowed. "Very well, my lady."

Althea brushed past the man, knowing full well that he disapproved of her presence and was perhaps even suspicious of her. The thought crossed her mind yet again that she did not fit into the frame in which she found herself. It was a very old and lonely feeling.

But she would make herself fit. She was Lady Lynley, Gareth's wife. Her place was at his side, whether he wanted her there or not.

Althea lifted her skirt and went swiftly up the stairs. Her heart cried forlornly, but she would not heed it. At least, not yet. Perhaps she could cause Gareth to change his mind about her. How very much she wanted a home, a place of her own, to be loved for herself, to be cherished for herself.

Acceptance was something that she had never really had. Her father had taken notice of her only because she had forced him to through her tantrums and her willful behavior. Her mother had disassociated herself with much that should have been her concern, and Althea had left girlhood emotionally closer to her nanny than to her own mother. She had certainly made friends, but none to whom she could ever confide her deepest distresses. As a consequence, there had always been a part of her that stood back from true commitment. It had given her early an air of dignity. The very coolness of her manners had offered her a certain measure of protection from becoming too vulnerable.

Althea had hoped that with Gareth, she might have a chance of attaining the elusive quality of acceptance in her life. It was her only chance, actually.

She was looked upon simply as breeding stock by the Earl and Countess of Chard. That she had known—and used, to have her way in coming to Brussels. At the moment, Gareth suffered her presence only because he had accepted that same excuse. He could not see that she wanted to be with him for other reasons, as well. Nor would he have allowed her to remain under any other argument that she could have put forward. Althea knew that well enough. He had not been swayed by her earlier pleas. Emotional needs did not tip the balance, in his estimation. No, it was better for the moment to let Gareth think what he pleased. Yet his blatant insinuation that she had arranged her presence in Brussels solely for frivolous pursuits particularly stung.

On the surface of it, the situation appeared bleak. However, Althea was not one to give up a fight before it was well and truly lost. She would prove to Gareth that she was more than the woman that he had taken pity on and wed, more than a female who would bear him children, more than an inconvenient wife who flouted his wishes for selfish motives.

Althea had not the foggiest notion how she was to accomplish any of these things. However, she was here in Brussels, with Gareth, and opportunities must show themselves.

Althea and her husband dined *en famille*. It was at first a somewhat stilted atmosphere, but slowly as the dinner progressed both Althea and Gareth began to relax. Despite the disagreement between them, they discovered with mutual surprise that their original ease in conversing with one another had not been impaired.

Althea was impressed by the quality of the dishes that were brought to the table. She had assumed that bachelor fare would be simple and inelegant. But the roasted chicken, tomatoes stuffed with shrimp, and several side dishes gave testimony of a talented overseer of the kitchen. Althea filed away the fact and wondered what the rest of the household was like. The majordomo was certainly capable, but surely the man did not oversee the housekeeping.

"You must relay my compliments to your cook, my lord. This is superlative, indeed," said Althea, buttering a light roll.

"John Applegate, my majordomo, will attend to it," said Gareth.

The majordomo, who was presiding over serving of the table, bowed acknowledgment.

"Have you a large staff?" asked Althea.

"No, I have not needed one since it is a small establishment. There is my majordomo, a footman, the porter, a couple of housemaids, and the kitchen staff. With the exception of John, all the staff came with the town house when I rented it," said Gareth.

As he answered, it suddenly occurred to him that there would need to be an upgrading of the staff since his wife was remaining in Brussels. His was no longer a bachelor establishment where he had often welcomed his cronies. Now there was a lady in the house and those easy days were over. With dawning resignation, Gareth accepted the fact. It would be thought odd, indeed, if Lord and Lady Lynley did not formally entertain. Before they did so, however, he was obligated to introduce his wife into Brussels society.

There was seemingly no end to the complications that Althea would pose in his life. This one, at least, could be handled with relative ease. He caught the majordomo's eyes. "Wait upon me in the morning, John," he said quietly.

"Very good, my lord."

Over dinner, the conversation was by mutual consent kept on an impersonal level while they were served by the majordomo and the footman. Gareth spoke of the political and military situation, no doubt in order to show Althea just how foolish she had been to come. Nevertheless, Althea found what he had to say to be fascinating. Of particular interest to her was his opinion of how the society in Brussels was reacting to what was in essence a powder-keg situation. In return, Althea told him about his parents and the sentiments about the war that had appeared in the English newspapers. She also told him about her impressions of the Low Countries and what she had seen.

Dessert was a rich cake laden with nuts. Once it had been consumed and his lordship's wine poured, the servants left them.

Gareth's smiling expression faded. He was reluctant to fracture what had proven to be a surprisingly companionable hour. Althea had a keen mind that he had taken delight in. However, what he had to say could not be put off. He steeled himself and said, "I should like to return to our discussion of this afternoon, my lady."

"Of course, Gareth," said Althea calmly, though her heart constricted. There was a hard look now about his eyes and in the set of his jaw that warned her that it would not be a pleasant conversation. For an instant, he had almost the same look as her father. How very odd it was, she thought.

Gareth smiled, but even that did not serve to lighten the sudden severity of his countenance. "I am glad that you are of a mind to be sensible, Althea. For what I have to say will seem very harsh to you."

Her heart sank, yet she managed to smile. "I am unused to soft gloves in any event. Pray speak your mind, my lord. I am willing to listen."

He nodded. He fingered his wine glass. It was more difficult than he had imagined to lay down his ultimatum. But looking up, he said, "Good. This is it, then. You have come to Brussels with the express intent to be got with child. Is that correct?"

Althea flushed, but if he took note of her embarrassment he ignored it. She sidestepped, answering the question obliquely. "I suppose that one could say that was the impression that I left with the Earl and Countess of Chard."

"Very well. On that one condition, I will suffer you to stay. But my stipulation is this." His eyes were as hard as agate and as unyielding. "Once you are with child, you will return to England—to Chard—immediately. Have I made myself perfectly clear?"

"Perfectly," said Althea through stiff lips. Her pulse beat heavily in her veins. She felt ready to sink into the floor. But she was made of stern stuff and her pride upheld her. "I agree to your stipulation, my lord."

"What, is there to be no questioning of my wishes?" he

asked, his mouth curling in a sardonic smile at the too-easily-won victory.

He had been right. She had manipulated him finely, by God, and now that she had her way she could afford to be magnanimous, even gracious.

His lady wife was a very capable, deceiving female who acted with cold premeditation. Gareth recalled that it had been he who had first voiced anything about her stepfather's advances. Perhaps there had actually been no such advances. Perhaps she had simply seized upon his assumption and built on it because she saw in him an opportunity to spectacularly advance herself.

Gareth recalled, too, the distasteful expression on the Earl of Chard's face when he had heard Althea's name. Althea's background was against her in every way.

Althea shook her head. Almost bitterly, she said, "There is no reason that I should. I have gained my objective, have I not?" She did not know how her words served to inflame him. She rose from the table. "I shall leave you to your wine, my lord."

He inclined his head, giving her permission for her to leave him, his thoughts still racing. Gareth regarded his wife with cynicism, hurt, and a strong sense of outrage and betrayal. She had virtually tricked him into marrying her.

As Althea started to walk past her husband, he shot out his hand to grasp her above the elbow. With a quick pull, he tumbled her into his lap.

Gareth caught her chin in one strong hand while his arm tightened about her. He lowered his head and took her lips, already half-parted on a gasp of astonishment. It was a deliberately branding kiss. Althea's fingers tightened into a fist around the fabric of his coat. His hand dropped from her jaw to her throat, then traced her breast.

When at last he raised his head, she knew what it was to have been thoroughly kissed. Her cheeks were crimson. Althea stared up into his face, breathing quickly, but he was not looking into her eyes. The front of her gown lay open to his lingering gaze. Althea put up her hand to shield herself, but he caught her wrist and would not let her.

Gareth's eyes were half hooded, but their depths still revealed a smoldering passion. "I am committed this evening to friends or otherwise I would finish what I have started. You see, dear Althea, I wish to send you back to Chard as soon as possible." The cruel words said, without further ado he released her and set her onto her feet.

Althea turned her back to him. Tears stung her eyes as she pulled her gown back up onto her shoulder and straightened the laces at her bodice. If he had set out to humiliate her, he had succeeded. Moreover, there was not a thing that she could do about it. As long as he believed that the only two reasons she had come to Brussels were to be able to later present an heir for Chard and to dissipate herself in silly amusements, she could not complain of his manner toward her.

The humiliation he had dealt her, however, was not all that had transpired. She was stunned and frightened by the taste of latent power that he had revealed. It was something to remember and to be on guard against.

Without a word or backward glance, Althea left the dining room. She did not go to the drawing room, where evening coffee was traditionally served. Instead, she went directly upstairs to her private sitting room.

Althea heard when Gareth left his rooms, which she knew to be situated adjacent to her own bedroom. She went to her window and lifted the drapery. After a few moments, the viscount emerged from the house. She watched his tall upright figure stride away. Althea dropped the drape and turned away. Almost indifferently she replied to her dresser's inquiry about whether she wished to be made ready for sleep.

For the first time in many years Althea made the conscious choice not to lock her bedroom door. Though habit was strong, especially in light of what she had discovered about Gareth in the dining room, she forced herself to leave the key undisturbed. Her honor was involved. In England she had made a bargain. This evening she had accepted the stipulation that would enable her to remain in Brussels.

Hours later the door to Althea's bedroom opened. She had not been asleep. She sat up; the covers fell to her waist and she retrieved them hastily. The fire was dying, but there was enough of a red glow for her to make out details.

Gareth stood on the threshold, attired in his dressing gown.

He closed the door and advanced on the bed. His eyes had caught hers and his gaze never left her face.

Althea's heart started racing. There was something in his eyes, in his face, that raised again the specter of fear that she had felt in the dining room. She thrust it down with difficulty, but it would not be stilled. *The dying embers of the fire . . . The man in her bedroom, coming closer and closer . . . The old terror rising like bile in her throat . . .*

Althea's heart pounded. Her private nightmare was merging with reality. In her head, she heard the man's drunken voice. "*Come to me, little bird.*"

When Gareth reached for her, Althea's iron control snapped and she tried to evade him. But he caught her close. His breath was hot on her cheek and smelled of brandy.

"My wife, so eager to do her duty and present me with an heir."

Althea tried again to escape, but his arms tightened unmercifully. He carried her down onto the mattress, his lips fastening upon hers and smothering her inarticulate cry.

He was not gentle, or forbearing.

Afterward, Althea drew as far away from the stranger in her bed as she could. She was in a state of shock.

The first time Gareth had possessed her there had been a passing pain, but he had treated her with a tender consideration that had succeeded in wiping it away. What had been done this night had unlocked old fears, old memories of things she had heard and seen. It was alien to any of the finer emotions. She had been used just like the parade of mistresses kept by her father and his like-minded friends. It was exactly how Sir Bartholomew had intended to use her.

She squeezed shut her eyes, but two slow tears coursed down from under her hot lids.

"Althea . . ."

She recoiled from his touch.

Gareth had raised himself upon his elbow and reached out to touch her hair. Now he dropped his hand and regarded her unsmilingly. His expression was unreadable in the shadows.

Althea forced herself to return his gaze. He was not to know, now or ever, how deeply he had wounded her.

"You will want to sleep." Gareth reached across her and snuffed the candle flame with his fingertips.

In the dark she felt his weight shift and rise from the tumbled bed. A short moment later and his silhouette crossed between her and the dying fire. She could see that he had replaced his dressing gown. The boards creaked under his steps. Then the connecting door opened and shut. She was alone again.

Althea slid out of bed. Her nightgown was torn. She removed it and let it drop to the floor. Her eyes had adjusted to the firelight and by that dim illumination she bathed herself from the water basin.

Donning a fresh gown, Althea climbed into bed. The sheets smelled of him. She pressed her face into her pillow until she could scarcely breathe. Finally, she slept.

Chapter Sixteen

Althea slept late the following morning. Upon rising, she avoided her dresser's sympathetic and curious eyes. Unwilling to enter into conversation, she merely commanded that she be readied for the day.

Attired in an attractive day dress, Althea ventured downstairs. She had steeled herself to meet Gareth in the breakfast room. It was with mingled relief and dismay that she learned from the majordomo that Lord Lynley had already gone out.

Althea stood irresolute. "I see. Thank you, John."

The majordomo shot her ladyship a comprehensive glance. He read only dissatisfaction in her expression. He wondered whether she had any notion what impact her sudden appearance was having on the house.

John Applegate had met with Lord Lynley early that morning as requested and had been astonished to be given orders to expand the household staff. He was to hire another footman, two more housemaids, and a scullery maid.

John Applegate oversaw the functioning of the house, while also serving as his lordship's valet; but this too, was to change shortly. Lord Lynley had informed him that her ladyship would naturally wish to entertain and thus a housekeeper had become necessary. It was not his lordship's wish that John Applegate's duel duties become too onerous with the changes in the house.

The majordomo was always swift to implement his lordship's orders. Already he had found a new footman, a likely lad who happened to be related to the chef, and had begun on the task of training him when her ladyship came into the breakfast room.

At Lady Althea's entrance, John Applegate waved the new

footman away, indicating that he would wait on the mistress of the house himself if she so desired.

Althea seated herself at the table. "I require only tea and toast."

The majordomo bowed and went to the sideboard to attend to her request. Upon serving her, he said, "I trust that my lady slept well?"

Althea's startled eyes flew to the majordomo's face.

She flushed suddenly. How stupid of her. Of course the man could not have known. It was but an ordinary question. She felt like all sorts of fool for betraying herself. She tried to cover her mistake. "No, not well. I am unused to the house and its noises."

John Applegate had been surprised by Lady Althea's reaction. His countenance smoothed as his training reasserted itself. Tactfully, he accepted the explanation even as his sharp mind speculated. "I believe it is often the way upon coming into a different household. It will soon become familiar, however, my lady."

Althea stared down at her toast. She was not at all hungry. "Yes," she said slowly, "I suppose that it will."

The majordomo suspected that her ladyship was not referring to house noises at all.

Althea looked up. "I wish to go out this morning. Is there a carriage available?"

"Yes, my lady. I shall send word for it to be brought around. Perhaps in an hour?"

"Yes, thank you." Althea dismissed the servant. When he retired from the breakfast room, she forced herself to finish her meager breakfast. Then she returned upstairs to change for her drive.

In the company with her dresser, Althea rode in the carriage through the wide boulevards of Brussels. The women exclaimed together over the beauty of many of the buildings and other sights. The city was full of restaurants and shops.

Brussels did not look like a city preparing for siege. Business was going on as usual at the shops. Respectably dressed tradespeople and housewives haggled over the price of the goods and when each was satisfied with the transaction the participants shook hands. Along the Rue de Namur were the cafés. At the outside tables were several groups of people enjoying refreshments. Many were obviously families, while other tables were occupied by uniformed officers lifting tankards of the Belgian brew.

It did not take long before Althea realized that Brussels was truly a cosmopolitan city. Everywhere she looked there were uniforms and she heard a dozen different languages spoken.

The place that truly awed Althea was the great square, known as the Place Royale. Facing the square were the magnificent edifices of state, including the ornate Maison du Roi. Hundreds of windows and elaborate gilded carvings looked down on the paving stones. Birdsellers sat beside tiers of cages containing pigeons and canaries, and the square was awash with color as flower vendors offered roses, carnations, and other blooms to the promenading gentlemen and their ladies.

"Isn't it beautiful, my lady!" exclaimed Darcy. "I have never seen so many flowers in one place."

"Darcy, do let us get out," said Althea, banging on the carriage wall to get the driver to stop. "I should like to purchase some to take home with us."

"Very well, my lady," said Darcy.

The carriage stopped and the driver got down to open the door. Althea lifted her skirt and stepped down to the paving stones. She waited while Darcy joined her. Then, accompanied by her maid, Althea approached the vendors. In a very short while both women had their arms full and were up to their chins in riotous blooms. They looked at one another and burst out laughing.

"What do we do now, my lady?" asked Darcy, looking helplessly at her fragrant armful.

"Why, I mean to take them all back to the town house and fill every available vase and bowl," said Althea, her eyes sparkling. The pall that had hung over her spirits lifted. "It is spring, Darcy! Isn't it glorious?"

" 'Tis wonderful indeed, my lady," said Darcy, smiling.

They turned to retrace their steps to the carriage.

A gentleman in a Belgian cavalry uniform suddenly stepped in front of them. He bowed, and held out a bouquet of red roses. Addressing Althea, he said, "Forgive me, ma'am. I could not but notice that you had dropped these magnificent roses."

Althea graciously inclined her head, but she was wary. This could possibly be but a ploy on the gentleman's part to make her acquaintance. She had, after all, several dozens of roses and it was impossible to know whether those held by the cavalry officer were in fact hers. "Thank you, sir. You are indeed kind. If you will give them to my maid I would be most grateful."

The gentleman placed the bouquet on the top of the dresser's burden and then, before they could walk away, he said swiftly, "I am a mannerless dog, indeed! I am Baron Gaston dePlier, at your service. This lady . . ." He turned and smiled, holding out his hand to a young woman who had just then come up to join them. "May I present my sister, Mademoiselle Fleurette dePlier."

Mademoiselle dePlier flashed a shy smile. She was a tiny young woman attired in a fashionable corded walking dress. "Gaston, you have shocked the English ladies. They are not used to being accosted by strange gentlemen, *non?*" She threw a laughing glance up at her brother.

"No, indeed," said Althea, instantly thawing. She liked the friendly light in the girl's deep brown eyes. She decided that they really must be brother and sister, for there was a strong resemblance between the two. Both were black-haired and possessed strongly crafted noses. But in contrast to his sister's dark gaze, Gaston dePlier's eyes were an icy blue.

"I must reassure you, ma'am, the roses did indeed drop from your arms. Gaston would not otherwise have put himself forward so boldly," said Mademoiselle dePlier.

Althea smiled. "Once more, I thank you. My maid and I never noticed, and I would not want to lose even one of the beautiful blooms."

"They are lovely, are they not? It is always so here in Brussels. We Bruxellois appreciate beauty," said Mademoiselle dePlier. Her brother murmured agreement as his gaze rested on the lovely English face.

"I am Althea, Lady Lynley and this is Darcy. We have recently arrived from England and are admiring your city," said Althea.

"There is much to admire," said Baron dePlier. "Perhaps when our acquaintance becomes such, my lady, you will allow my sister and me to act as your guides. We will be able to show you some things of interest that possibly many of your countrymen have not yet discovered."

"Oh, yes! That would be so very amusing," said Mademoiselle dePlier in her prettily accented English. "Gaston is a very good companion, I assure you. He will take very good care of us."

"Perhaps one day, then," said Althea, glancing up at the tall Belgian cavalry officer. She turned to her silent maid. "Darcy, if we do not put these lovely flowers in water soon, we will lose them all. Mademoiselle, monsieur, it has been a pleasure. I apologize for not having a hand free to offer to you!"

Mademoiselle dePlier and her brother laughed appreciatively. "It is of no matter, my lady," said Mademoiselle, shaking her head. "I shall perhaps call upon you one day, *non?*"

The dePliers immediately took gracious leave and walked on. Althea and her maid walked back to their carriage and stepped up into it, being careful not to drop any of the flowers. The driver shut the door. He climbed up on the box and turned the horses for the town house.

Inside, Althea remarked, "That was an interesting encounter. The dePliers were remarkably friendly, I thought."

"Have you noticed how these Belgians are always shaking hands, my lady? I have seen it over and over this morning. They are a polite folk," said Darcy.

Althea nodded. "Yes." She looked around at the flowers piled on the seats and suddenly smiled. "I think that I shall like it here, Darcy."

When they returned to the town house, Althea and Darcy left most of the flowers in the carriage, carrying only as many as they could comfortably handle in one arm. Althea requested the footman and the porter to bring in the rest.

The majordomo came into the entry hall. His grizzled brows shot up at the sight of the flowers overflowing the women's arms. "May I be of assistance, my lady?"

"Indeed you may, John. Darcy and I have bought out the flower vendors and now we require every vase and bowl in the house," said Althea, smiling at him. Not even John Applegate's disapproval could have deflated her at that moment, though the majordomo looked too surprised to register anything else.

"I shall see to it immediately, my lady," said the majordomo. His gaze went to the door, where the footman and the porter were entering. His eyes widened at their armfuls. "I believe that we shall all be rather busy for a time," he observed somewhat dryly.

Althea spent the rest of the day clipping stems and arranging flowers in a multitude of vases and bowls. Arrangements and sprays of riotous blooms appeared in every room and in the entry hall. The delicate perfume of a profuse flower garden filled the air and bright splashes of color transformed the rather dour inside of the town house.

Althea sat down to a late tea feeling a sense of immense satisfaction. Cutting and arranging the flowers had been utterly enjoyable. There had been so many that every room had been filled to overflowing, even those rooms abovestairs. Wondering at her own temerity, she had sent a housemaid into Lord Lynley's rooms with bowls of carnations and chrysanthemums. The servant had seemed to think nothing of it, thereby affording Althea an instructive experience.

Althea lifted the teacup to her lips and sipped, her eyes above it thoughtful in expression. For the first time she felt that she was mistress of her own household. In the course of the day, she had learned that the servants thought of her as such, even John Applegate, who had regarded her so suspiciously and still retained much reserve in his manner toward her. But what did the majordomo's private opinion matter as long as he showed her the respect to which she was entitled as the viscountess? She was Althea, Viscountess Lynley, the future Countess of Chard.

Several small changes that could be done to the interior of the town house began to occur to her and she decided to implement them at once. Of course, there would have to be some money spent here and there, but it was of little consequence. She had seen enough regarding the shops that day to know that practically anything that she could possibly want was available to her.

She realized that she had never been happier in her life.

*   *   *

When Lord Lynley made his way home that evening, he wore a deep frown. A heavy weight was laid against his conscience. Fury had exploded in him upon discovering, as he thought, the duplicity of his wife's nature and his own stupidity in being used as a convenient dupe. The fury had been all-consuming.

Last night he had deliberately set out to drink himself senseless in an effort to forget, at least for a time. But instead of obtaining oblivion, he had merely destroyed his self-control and finer instincts. Knowing only that he desired the woman that bore his name, and hating himself and her for the weakness, he had sought her out.

No matter what connivings Althea had resorted to, she was now his lady wife and entitled to his honor and protection. There was nothing which could excuse his brutish behavior. Lord Lynley hoped only that he could somehow convey the depth of his regret.

When Lord Lynley stepped inside the front door, he abruptly stopped and stared. The entry hall looked entirely different and a thousand times more welcoming. A mirror had appeared from somewhere and the candles were already lit in the wall sconces. On the front table, a tall crystal vase was almost hidden under a cascade of roses of every hue. Beside the stairs stood another huge arrangement.

The majordomo had anticipated Lord Lynley's arrival and now came to meet his lordship. There was a twinkle in his rather hard eyes.

"John, what has happened here?" asked Gareth, giving over his hat. "I almost thought that I had entered the wrong house."

"Her ladyship discovered the flower vendors in the Place Royale, my lord," said the majordomo with a slight grin.

"She must have bought out the lot of them," said Gareth, with a slight lifting of his spirits. Perhaps he was already in a fair way to being forgiven. Surely the myriad of flowers was a good sign.

The majordomo coughed. "I believe that is precisely what her ladyship said she had done, my lord."

Lord Lynley shot a startled glance at his manservant's expressionless face. "You don't mean to say that there are more!"

The majordomo's face quivered. "Yes, my lord, as you will undoubtedly notice when you enter the drawing room or the dining room or the—"

Gareth threw up his hand, laughing. "Very well, enough! I have grasped the picture, John. It is fortunate that I have a partiality for flowers."

"As you say, my lord."

"Pray inform her ladyship that I shall be joining her for dinner this evening," said Gareth, and went on up the stairs.

When he returned downstairs again, he passed down the entry hall opening doors and silently regarding each room. When he had closed the last door again, he found the majordomo standing at his elbow. Almost in awe, he said, "I would not have believed it if I had not seen it with my own eyes."

"Her ladyship requested every vase and bowl in the house. When that proved somewhat inadequate, I sent the footman out to purchase others," said the majordomo.

Gareth shook his head and said thoughtfully, "I believe the old days are really gone, John. One cannot repine overmuch, however."

"I hope not, indeed, my lord."

"I will await Lady Lynley in the drawing room, John," said Gareth. When he walked into the drawing room and shut the door, he looked around slowly. Then he laughed out loud. He liked the flowers. He liked having a beautiful, forbearing wife. In that moment, at least, he was glad that she had flouted his wishes and followed him to Brussels.

Chapter Seventeen

Gareth was reading a newspaper when Althea came into the room. He immediately rose to his feet, tossing aside the newspaper. She was gowned in a flattering pale peach muslin that was tied under the breast with satin ribbons. Over her shoulders lay a cashmere shawl. She looked breathtakingly lovely. He went to meet her, holding out his hands to her.

"Althea. I have been waiting for you."

"My lord." The acknowledgment was perfectly civil, but it lacked warmth in either her eyes or her expression.

Gareth took a deep breath. "Althea, I behaved badly. I can only ask that you forgive me."

"Of course, my lord."

Althea's response was less than what Gareth had looked for, but at the same time he was relieved. She had spoken with complete calm. He was glad that he was not to be treated to tearful reproaches or cold condemnation. Once again, he was struck by her self-possession in difficult circumstances. If it was indeed true that he had been duped into marriage, at least he need not be ashamed of his wife's breeding.

Althea had laid her fingers in his, looking up at him with something of a questioning look. Her manner was hesitant, as though she was uncertain what he might say next.

Gareth thought that she was probably wondering what his reaction had been to finding his home transformed into a bower, and he was swift to reassure her. "The flowers are beautiful, Althea. I had no notion how spartan my existence had become before coming home this evening. You have done wonders."

A faint flush rose in her face. She inclined her head. "Thank you, my lord. I am glad that you are pleased."

Gareth smiled on her warmly. Her reticence was just what he might have expected of the shy girl that he had once known. He glanced down at her fingers, which he still held. "I must take you to a jeweler's as soon as possible. The ring is too plain, as is my own. We will commission something better."

"Oh, I do not mind this one, my lord," said Althea.

"It will please me to give you another," said Gareth. "As Viscountess Lynley you should have something more befitting your station."

She dropped her eyes, then raised them again to his face. There was a peculiarly unreadable expression in her eyes. "Of course, my lord. Let it be just as you wish."

He gestured toward the door and at the same time offered his arm. She laid her fingers lightly on his elbow. He led her out of the drawing room into dinner, all the while speaking. "You must feel free to do whatever you wish with the house, Althea. I shall leave it in your obviously capable hands. I have asked John Applegate to engage a housekeeper and hire a few more servants, so that you will be able to make plans to entertain. We shall have to introduce you into society first, of course, so that you can form acquaintances. But you will soon find your feet, I daresay."

He seated her at his right hand and then took his own place. She was regarding him with a sort of fascinated gaze, as she had done ever since he had started telling her about the arrangements he had already started to make for her accommodation. A slight frown formed between his brows. "Is there anything wrong, Althea?"

She shook her head. "No, of course not. I was just listening. I hadn't given a thought to entertaining."

Gareth laughed. "Well, you must do so now. Once it is known what a lovely wife I possess, we shall have hundreds clamoring for an invitation to our table."

A smile quivered on her lips. "Hundreds, Gareth?"

"I shall not spare your blushes, my lady. Thousands!" he teased.

She laughed then, her eyes beginning to sparkle. "I suspect that you are overly optimistic now, my lord. I shall settle for hundreds."

"Good enough," said Gareth. He tasted the mussels redolent of garlic and instantly hailed the chef's genius.

Althea, too, voiced her compliments to be carried by the footman to the denizen of the kitchen. Thereafter the couple applied themselves to silken slices of Ardennes ham, tiny boiled shrimp, and roast *poulet de Bruxelles,* removed by several vegetables. For dessert there was a wonderful honey cake.

Althea told Gareth of her meeting with the dePliers and her impressions of the city. "I thought the dePliers rather nice. Do you know them?"

"I have met Baron Gaston dePlier, but not his sister. The dePliers are one of the older families. He is a good man, well liked by the other Walloons and our own English officers," said Gareth.

"Walloons? What are they, pray?" asked Althea.

"The Belgians are composed of two groups. The Walloons are of Celtic stock and are the French-speaking inhabitants of the south and east of the country. The Flemings are found along the coast and north. They were originally a Germanic people, but their language is nearly incomprehensible to outsiders. Even their countrymen, the Walloons, claim that Flemish is impossible to learn," said Gareth.

"It is a fascinating country. And Brussels is a beautiful city. Gareth, in your letters you said that there is much anxiety over what Napoleon Bonaparte will do. But today while I was out I saw no signs of distress. There were soldiers everywhere, of course, but no one seemed to give their significance much thought. I saw that the shops were busy and at the outdoor cafés there were several laughing parties, of both soldiery and Belgian families," said Althea.

Gareth had listened gravely and now he nodded. "The gaiety is unbounded on all sides. Everywhere you go, you will hear people discussing Napoleon Bonaparte and the extraordinary response of the French as troops continue to flock to his banner. It is very much the *on-dit* and is treated just that lightly in society. But there is a tangible suppressed tension, an almost feverish look to people's faces, and a brittleness in their bright laughter. You will observe it for yourself once you have come out into society. The specter of war is in actuality never really far from anyone's mind."

Althea shivered. "It frightens me a little. The contrast that you speak of, I mean. How can one laugh and make merry while believing that at any moment death will come riding through the streets? It is macabre."

Gareth smiled, fleetingly. "And yet the dance goes on. With the Duke of Wellington's arrival in Brussels to take over command of the Allied armies there was a genuine boost of morale, in both the military and the populace. He has only to stand among us and all is said to be well."

"What of the other Allied leaders? Surely there are some jealousies?" asked Althea.

Gareth laughed, shaking his head. "It is uniformly realized what a mess we could have been in if his grace had not arrived to take over the reins from Long Billy."

"Long Billy? Gareth, really, these nicknames are disreputable. Surely you cannot possibly be referring to the Prince of Orange."

Lord Lynley's grin was swift. "Wellington is called Old Hooky for his great beak of a nose," he offered.

Althea shook her head, a smile lurking in her eyes. "What of the prince?"

"His highness was commander-in-chief of the armed forces in Brussels when news of Bonaparte's escape from Elba became known. William, the Prince of Orange, is liked well enough, but he is young, inexperienced, and excitable. I understand that only with difficulty was he dissuaded from charging after Bonaparte on his own," said Gareth.

"Did not his highness resent having to relinquish the command to the Duke of Wellington?" asked Althea curiously.

"Of course not. The prince is an intelligent fellow. He stands in awe of the duke, as do we all," said Gareth. "There is no one better suited to challenge Napoleon Bonaparte at his own game and win."

"Gareth, just how do we stand?" asked Althea quietly.

He looked at her for a long, thoughtful moment. "I can tell you this much, Althea. When Wellington took command, he was given authority over a combined Allied force of 700,000 troops. None of the promised Russian or Austrian troops have yet arrived. We are said to be outnumbered by the French two to one."

"It could turn out very badly, then," said Althea.

Gareth reached for the wine bottle and refilled his glass.

Althea's eyes followed his movements, and then her gaze lifted swiftly to search his face for signs of inebriation. Gareth had already drunk freely of the wine over the course of dinner. Althea feared to discover the telltale mask that had inevitably slipped over her father's face and that of his cronies when they had been indulging. It was that same mask that Gareth had worn when he had come to her bedroom the night before. But she saw only a meditative expression on Gareth's face as he responded to her observation.

"Wellington has been outnumbered before. His grace appears to thrive on long odds. I am convinced that the Allies will carry the day. And when we do, I shall be among the first to shout huzzah!"

"I should like to meet the Duke of Wellington," said Althea. "He sounds to be a great man."

"You shall undoubtedly have an opportunity to do so. The duke continually gives balls at his house and he is seen at nearly every function besides. You will meet various other illustrious personages, as well, such as Sir Charles Stuart, our British ambassador, and the Duke and Duchess of Richmond," said Gareth. "I must introduce you to some ladies of my acquaintance who may be trusted to take you under their wings. You will no doubt enjoy quite a social success, Althea."

Althea thoughtfully regarded him. She did not quite believe what he had said, but even so it was nice to have heard it. "Thank you, Gareth. You are kind to say so."

He looked at her, surprised. "I am not being kind, Althea; rather, I am being quite fair and honest. You are a lovely woman of birth and position, possessing both wit and a gracious manner. You will have little difficulty in establishing a place for yourself in society. It would be strange indeed if it were to be found otherwise."

Althea did not know what to say. So few sincere compliments had ever chanced her way that she scarcely knew how to react. "Th-thank you, my lord. I hope I shall be a credit to you."

"I have no doubts at all on that head, Althea," said Gareth gently.

For a moment their gazes held. Almost, Althea felt herself to be back in the inn in Gloucester. He had been Gareth Marshall to her then. He had been understanding and patient and sensitive. There was that same tender, understanding light in his eyes now. Althea tore her eyes away, confused.

The footman began clearing away the remains of dinner.

"I did not realize that it had grown so late. You will want to enjoy your wine," Althea said, rising.

"I have bespoken coffee in half an hour in the drawing room," said Gareth. "I hope that I may join you then."

"Of course," she said.

Althea excused herself and repaired to the drawing room. She occupied herself with some embroidery while waiting for her lord. She was less tense than she might have been. She had been astonished that she could sit down at the table and converse so companionably with a man that had used her so basely. But so it had happened.

It was Gareth's doing, of course. He had treated her with perfect courtesy and respect. Althea sighed. She did not understand how a man could display such utter differences in character.

Lord Lynley joined his wife for coffee. They sat together, talking quietly. He became more and more astonished at the ease with which they conversed and at how comfortable he felt with her. He had dreaded the loss of his privacy and of his freedom, particularly the evening gatherings of his fellow bachelor officers for games of chance. No doubt he would miss those times, but he suspected that these new times might prove more satisfying to his memory in later years.

When the clock struck eleven, Althea folded her work and put it away. "I shall bid you good night, Gareth. It has been a rather exciting day and a very pleasant evening. Indeed, I cannot recall when I have enjoyed myself more. However, I find that I am astonishingly weary."

Gareth nodded his understanding. "I shall be up directly, Althea."

He toed a log further into the fire and so he did not see how she paused, staring at him with widening eyes, before she hurried to the door.

As she went swiftly upstairs, Althea's thoughts turned first one way, then the other. She knew that Gareth meant to visit her. What she did not know was which Gareth to expect—the kind, considerate lover or the other. The possibility of reliving her nightmare set a frisson of panic crawling up her spine.

Darcy readied her mistress for bed and left the bedroom. Even as she lay in bed, Althea's thoughts remained disordered. Reason told her to accept Gareth's apology at face value. He had already proven himself to be both honorable and chivalrous in the past, so now, surely, she must grant him the benefit of the doubt.

As the minutes passed away, however, so did her resolution. Perhaps Gareth was even then consuming a bottle of brandy. Her knowledge of his habits was so limited.

Althea left her bed to lock her bedroom door, excusing her cowardice to herself. Gareth would be disappointed, but it was of no great moment, after all. She was tired. She had told him so. She would apologize to her husband in the morning and plead the headache as her excuse.

When Gareth went upstairs, he was smiling to himself. His wife was waiting for him. He anticipated the coming hour. He took care with his toilette and dismissed John Applegate to bed. The servant bowed and quietly left the bedroom, closing the door.

Gareth sounded a tuneless whistle as he went to the connecting door between his own bedroom and that of his wife. But when he tried the knob at her door, it would not turn. He tried it again, stupidly. Then it burst upon him that the door was locked against him. Fury such as he had never known came upon him.

Gareth turned on his heel and swiftly strode across his bedroom. He wrenched open the door. Striding down the hallway, he entered what he knew to be Althea's dresser's room.

The dresser sat up in her bed with a startled cry, clutching the blankets to her chin. Gareth ignored the servant and yanked open the door opposite the one he had just entered.

With the dresser following him, Gareth burst into his wife's bedroom.

Althea sat up in the wide bed, her hair tumbling about her face. Her eyes glimmered fearfully in the firelight.

Gareth crossed the bedroom to the locked door, twisted the

key, then wrenched it out of the lock. He turned, the key in his hand. His narrowed eyes glittered beneath their lids. He jerked his head at the dresser, who stood just inside the bedroom. "Go! Get out now!"

The dresser hesitated. Then, with obvious reluctance, she stepped back out of the bedroom and closed the door.

Althea had put out her hand as though she would stop the woman, then pulled it back. She turned her head, her face a pale oval in the firelight.

Gareth advanced upon the bed, but stopped before he reached it. He held up the key between his fingers so that she could see it. "There will never be a locked door between us, Althea! Never! Do you understand?"

Her voice was a bare thread of sound. "Yes."

Gareth dropped the key into the pocket of his dressing gown. For a long moment he stared down at his wife. She was visibly trembling, but her face was set as though in stone. Her fathomless eyes never wavered from his face.

Gareth turned away, an expression of disgust crossing his features. Without a word, he reentered his own bedroom and sharply closed the door.

For several days after, Gareth did not visit his wife's bedroom. But eventually there did come a time. He was unfailingly considerate; but he came away from her bed filled with a disquieting discontent.

Chapter Eighteen

Lord Lynley requested a few days' leave from his duties so that he could see that his wife was properly settled in.

"What? Have you sent for the viscountess to join you, after all?" asked one of his fellow officers.

"No, I did not send for her. She brought herself," said Gareth with a good-natured laugh. "I wrote too many letters detailing our pleasant pursuits and the unending amusements that occupy us. Of course, I mentioned the possibility of war as well, but that seemed not to make as strong an impression."

Amid hoots of laughter, another officer said loudly, "A tactical error, my boy. Never tell a female what she is missing. She'll be on your doorstep next morning. And a wife is worse than any other, for you cannot bid her Godspeed that same evening!"

Society was mildly amused by the story that Lady Lynley had defied her lord's sanction and had followed him to Brussels in expectation of entertainment.

Gareth was attached as an aide-de-camp to the Duke of Brunswick. He was a general favorite with his fellow staff officers as well as with the most influential hostesses in Brussels. He was told to be certain to bring his wife to all the functions. It had been Gareth's intention to amuse and to create friendly curiosity in the breasts of those who would be best suited to oversee Althea's entrance into society and he succeeded admirably.

It was noted that Lord Lynley took time from his staff duties to escort his wife into society. Lady Greville, one of the best-known hostesses, remarked, "Obviously Lynley takes a serious view of his responsibilities toward his lady. It is to his credit."

The new viscountess was soon made to feel welcome by her ladyship and others.

Althea made friends readily with several ladies, among both the Belgians and the British. Mademoiselle dePlier had kept her promise to call on Althea and the two quickly became fast friends. They shopped together and one day when Gaston dePlier was free, he escorted both ladies about Brussels and the surrounding countryside. Lord Lynley had been invited to make one of the party, but at the last minute he was called back to his duties. He assured them that to put off the outing on his account was nonsense, and so it was a very merry trio that set off to explore the beauties of Belgium.

However, Lord Lynley made arrangements to be free a few days later. After an early breakfast he requested that Althea come outside on the front step with him. Althea complied, wondering what possible reason there could be for his grave insistence.

When she stepped out, she saw instantly an elegant mare held at curbside by a groom. The trim mare was built for speed and on its back was a sidesaddle. "Oh," Althea breathed, at once envying the fortunate female to whom the horse belonged. It had been too many weeks since she had last been up on a fast mount, she thought with regret.

"She's yours, Althea," said Gareth, watching his wife's face closely.

Althea turned swiftly, a startled and amazed look on her face. "Mine?"

He smiled and nodded.

"Oh, Gareth!" Althea caught up his hand and pressed it between her own. Her green eyes were suddenly bright with unshed tears. Only a moment did she stand thus expressing her gratitude. Then she winged down the steps to make friends with the mare.

Gareth followed more sedately, enjoying her obvious happiness. He had at last done something right. He stood beside the groom, continuing to smile as Althea exclaimed and crooned over the mare.

After a few moments, he said, "I am free until luncheon. Would you like to try her paces?"

Althea turned a glowing face to him. "Of course I would! Only give me a moment to climb into my habit."

Gareth laughed at her enthusiasm. "Very well. I shall meet you downstairs in the entry hall in a quarter hour."

"It shan't take me even half as long," retorted Althea, picking up her skirt. Flashing a bit of trim ankle, she dashed back up the steps and nipped inside the front door.

" 'er ladyship seems pleased, m'lord," said the groom with a grin.

"Yes, she does," said Gareth with deep satisfaction. "My own mount is being brought around shortly. See to it that he behaves himself. He'll be restive." The groom nodded understanding and Gareth went back into the house.

Althea was true to her word. She returned down the stairs fully habited, carrying her whip under her arm as she drew on her gloves. A jaunty hat was set over her dancing eyes. "I am ready, as you can see!" she called out when she saw Lord Lynley waiting for her below.

Gareth was appreciative of the pretty picture she made. As she left the last step, he stepped forward and took her hand to bow over it with an elaborate gallantry. "You are lovely, my lady."

Althea cast a fleeting look up into his face. Then she nodded a smiling acknowledgment. "I thank you, my lord."

Gareth offered his arm and escorted his wife outside to the waiting mounts. He did not wait for the groom to offer a helping hand, but himself tossed her up into the saddle.

Althea could scarcely contain her eagerness to be off while Lord Lynley mounted his own horse. Her impatience communicated itself to her mount and the mare danced a little. Althea laughed and bent to pat the mare's arching neck. "She is ready to run."

"I suspect that her mistress is just as keen," said Gareth dryly, drawing up the reins on his mount. The stallion jibed a little, but it knew its master and settled down easily enough.

Althea laughed again and started the mare down the street. She glanced over at her companion as he drew abreast of her. "Where shall we go?"

"I thought the Allée Verte, beyond the walls of the town. It is still early enough that it should be fairly well deserted. The Allée will afford us a good gallop," said Gareth.

"Capital!" exclaimed Althea, her eyes shining.

Together they cantered toward their destination. Few others were in the streets at that outlandish hour and Lord and Lady Lynley were virtually alone in a pristine sunlit world of their own.

Upon reaching the Allée Verte, Gareth and Althea gave the horses their heads. The horses raced down the Allée past the still shining waters of the canal.

Althea laughed aloud for the sheer joy of feeling the rush of the wind and the powerful bunching movement of the horse beneath her. It was good to be alive, to be free.

They raced to the bridge that led over the canal to the Laekon road. Gareth drew up just short of the bridge, turning his stallion to meet her.

Althea pulled up before him, her face alight and laughing. The wind had whipped color into her cheeks and snatched golden tendrils of hair from confinement. She looked beautiful and Gareth caught his breath.

"She is a sweet little goer. But she cannot hold a candle to that brute of yours!"

Gareth reached down to pat his stallion's neck. "Indeed, Wild Nick is the very devil for speed. I would back him against any comers." He nudged his mount forward as he pointed. "There is a bench further on under that set of lime trees. Would you like to get down for a few moments while these two crop a few blades?"

"Very well," said Althea, smiling.

They rode companionably together, talking of nothing of importance but nevertheless enjoying their conversation. For both, there was the feeling that a better understanding was being forged between them.

When the bench was reached, Gareth dismounted and saw to his horse. Then he reached up to help Althea dismount. His strong hands nearly spanned her slender waist. She laid her hands on his shoulders and looked down into his eyes as he lifted her out of the saddle. For an instant Gareth held her thus, then he slowly lowered her until her feet touched the ground.

He did not remove his hands at once. Their eyes had never wavered from one another's face.

Suddenly Althea's lashes swept down, hiding the unfathomable expression in her eyes. "Pray do not look at me like that," she whispered.

"Should I not?" he asked quietly.

"No, you should not. It-it unmans me," she said.

Gareth gave a shout of laughter. Althea cocked her head, a flush coming into her face. "What is so amusing, pray?" she asked, though not at all angrily. She could see that he was not laughing in a malicious way at her expense.

"You are hardly a man to be unmanned, Althea!" said Gareth, still grinning.

Her lips quivered. "True," she acknowledged. "My choice of expression was scarcely appropriate. My preceptress at seminary would have scolded me most heartily for such unladylike usage."

Gareth stepped away from her and swept the bench dry with his handkerchief. Offering the seat to her, he asked, "Were you a difficult pupil, then?"

"Oh no," said Althea, smiling up at him as she sat down. "I was the model of propriety, I assure you. I had to be, you see. My father's reputation followed me. I was regarded with constant suspicion and garnered the strictest attention from the instructresses. It was thought that if any of the girls was bent to do the outrageous, it would be me. However, I proved to be a disappointment. I set myself to excel in all my studies and lessons, so that I was in actuality a very boring pupil."

Gareth smiled at her easy disparagement of herself, but he was troubled nevertheless by the picture that she drew. He felt sympathy for the young girl who had tried so hard to distance herself from an unwelcome cloud of scandal, but he would not embarrass her by making comment on it. "You put me to shame, I fear. Unlike you, I did not attend to my studies as I should. I was always mad for the army and I could not see any point to Latin verbs and the like. My father was a harsh taskmaster, however, and he had his own methods of ingraining learning into a wayward son."

"You did not have a tutor, then?" Althea asked, surprised.

"None ever lasted for more than a year or two," said Gareth

cheerfully. "I was always up to some lark or other, bringing the earl's wrath down on all our heads; on me for ignoring my lessons and leading George astray, and on the poor tutors for not controlling me better. I believe that my parents were very glad when they could finally send me up to Eton."

Althea laughed and shook her head. "I wish I had known you then, but I was still such a babe it would have been marvelous indeed if you had paid the least heed to me. In any event, it is difficult to believe that you were such an incorrigible, Gareth."

"I have shaped up considerably," he agreed, a smile in his eyes. The easy amusement faded a little. "Althea, have you ever regretted your decision to marry me?"

She looked at him in astonishment. "Why, of course I have not. You have done more for me than any other person in my life, I think. It would be strange, indeed, if I had."

"I see." He was silent a moment. He was unsure what he had hoped to gain by the question. He knew, however, that her answer had left him dissatisfied in some way. He rose and held down his hand. "It is time that we give the horses some exercise. Are you game for a long ride?"

"There is nothing that I would like better," said Althea, allowing him to draw her up from the bench.

Gareth helped her to mount and then leapt astride the stallion. "I shall show you some of the countryside this morning. The dePliers have naturally treated you to a good tour, but I think that you will find the sights different from horseback than they were from a carriage."

Althea agreed to it and they set out. They did not return home for hours and when they did, Althea said, "I have never enjoyed anything so much, Gareth. Thank you for taking me about, and thank you especially for my girl here." She gave a last pat to the mare as it was led away to the stables.

"It was my pleasure. Perhaps we should ride out together often," said Gareth.

Althea looked up at him, a smile in her eyes. "Yes, let's." Thus it became a formed habit for them to ride out every morning, except when inclement weather or Gareth's duties interfered.

Althea settled readily into her new life, happy that she had gained a riding companion in Gareth and enjoying also the social obligations that they were both sought out for. She was becoming almost blasé about the constant round of amusements and greeting the same set of people at nearly every entertainment, but occasionally she did come across someone that she had not previously met.

One afternoon at a formal tea, Althea was astonished and glad to discover that her dear friend Miss Charity Comstock was also in Brussels.

"Charity! I had no notion that you were here!" exclaimed Althea, catching hold of her friend's hands. "How long since you left England?"

The Comstocks had taken up residence in Brussels in March.

"It was so dreary in Bath after I was ill that there was simply no bearing it. I was moped to death. Dear Papa wanted to present me with a London Season so that my thoughts were given a new turn, but Mama convinced him to bring us to Brussels instead because, she said, there was no one of consequence left in London! How was I to make a proper match under those circumstances?" explained Miss Comstock with a prim look, belied by the twinkle in her deep green eyes.

Althea laughed and gently squeezed her friend's hands once more before letting go. "I *am* glad to see you, Charity! You can have no notion. I wanted to stay with you so badly rather than to go with Mama after she married Sir Bartholomew, but you were too ill to allow for it. I missed you dreadfully."

"But just see how well things have turned out! We are both here in the most exciting capital in the world. And you are a viscountess, no less!" Miss Comstock shook a reproachful finger at her taller friend. "You sly boots, Althea! Whyever did you not tell me that you were betrothed to Lynley? I nearly swooned from surprise when Mama read me the notice of your marriage. It quite set up my competitive spirit, I can tell you! And now I am betrothed."

"Oh, not really! Charity, how wonderful for you. Do I know the fortunate gentleman?" asked Althea.

"If you do not, you soon will for I mean to introduce him to you. Fancy!" she said proudly with a toss of her head. "George is an officer in the Guards."

"That is impressive, indeed. Lynley is only one of the Duke of Brunswick's staff," said Althea, tongue in cheek.

Miss Comstock shook her head. "Such paltry fortune." Her smile was wide and teasing, for she knew well enough that Lord Lynley was an aide-de-camp. She confided, "It is the Guards that will do the job, says George. And he should know. He knows everything there is to know about the army. I shall be following the drum for a good many years, I suppose. But George says that he is sure to be promoted after this action."

"Of course he will," agreed Althea, amused by her friend's partisanship.

Miss Comstock leaned closer. There was now a rather more serious cast to her pretty features. "Althea, did you know that the Earl of Hawthorne is in Brussels?"

Althea's face registered her shock. "No, I did not. Are you certain, Charity?"

"Oh, yes. I have seen his lordship myself, as well as his wife. I must say, you and your cousin favor one another somewhat, Althea. He is tall and blond just as you are, but he holds himself apart in a way that you never did. I suppose it is excess pride," said Miss Comstock. She grimaced. "Lady Hawthorne is definitely high in the instep. She gives one the impression that she is constantly looking down her long nose."

Althea smiled, nodding. "Yes, that sounds just like Minerva. I met her but once, at the reading of my father's will. We took an instant dislike to one another, possibly because I did not behave with what she considered to be the proper humility toward her."

"Pooh!" Miss Comstock tossed her head. "She is but married to an earl. You are the daughter of an earl, and one day you will be the Countess of Chard, which is an even older line than the Hawthornes. If anyone is to look down her nose, it should be you, dear Althea."

Althea laughed, shaking her head. "Oh, you *are* good for me, Charity!"

"Come, you must come greet Mama. She will be very glad to see you, I promise you," said Miss Comstock, taking Althea's hand and drawing her over a few feet to where her mother had made herself cozy with an old acquaintance. "Mama, only see whom I have found."

"Why, Althea! What a pleasant surprise. We had read of your marriage, of course, but we had no notion that you would be coming to Brussels," said Mrs. Comstock, putting up her cheek to be kissed.

"I did not know it myself until a short time ago," said Althea, straightening from making the affectionate salute.

"Have you met up with your cousin, the Earl of Hawthorne? I believe that your arrival in Brussels must almost have coincided with that of his lordship and Lady Hawthorne," said Mrs. Comstock.

"No, ma'am, I have not. In fact, I did not know that they were in the city until Charity told me just now," said Althea.

"I see. I met Lady Hawthorne in Bath once years ago. Of course, that was before the succession. We must trust that her ladyship is more content with her lot than previously," said Mrs. Comstock.

"I have met the lady but once, on the occasion of the reading of my father's will. It was not a particularly enjoyable hour for any one of us, I fear," said Althea, restraining her opinion of her cousin-in-law through the polite words.

Mrs. Comstock looked thoughtfully at Althea, her eyes wise and understanding. "Althea, pray let me present you to one of my dearest and oldest friends, Lady Greville," said Mrs. Comstock.

Lady Greville laughed. "My dear Margaret, Lady Lynley and I have already met. She has graced my parties any time these weeks past."

"Oh, I make no doubt of that! However, there is a perfectly good reason why I have brought Lady Lynley to your particular notice, Charlotte, and that is this. Althea is very much like my own daughter to me. She and Charity attended a ladies' seminary together and have been the closest of friends ever since. I have never had cause to be less than proud of either of these misses," said Mrs. Comstock.

Lady Greville cast a quick glance at Mrs. Comstock. Then she smiled again and held out her hand to the young viscountess. "I am glad to learn something about you, my dear Lady Lynley. You will find in me a good friend, I promise you."

The younger women were dismissed and walked a little

ways off. Miss Comstock's brows were creased. "What an odd thing for my mother to do!"

"Was it not?" agreed Althea. However, she was far less puzzled than her friend. She was sensitive to undercurrents and she had understood that Mrs. Comstock had been conveying an endorsement to Lady Greville upon her behalf. What Althea did not understand was why.

The prospect of war seemed to have been all but forgotten in a whirl of social activity. Napoleon Bonaparte's extraordinary welcome by the French was still alluded to, but everyone apparently preferred not to think of him. Althea at first regarded this phenomenon with wonder, for how could one forget what was happening when all around one was the sight of military uniforms. However, as she was drawn more and more into the social waters, she, too, stopped thinking about the threat that loomed just over the frontier in France. One day, without realizing that she had done so, she stopped seeing anything out of the ordinary in the astonishing number of uniforms that paraded the streets of Brussels.

The society that enlivened Brussels was glittering. It was cosmopolitan. It was made up of the privileged and titled, the influential and the favored, from perhaps a dozen or more countries. The same personages attended one another's entertainments day after day, night after night. It was therefore inevitable that Althea should come face to face with her cousin, the Earl of Hawthorne.

The earl greeted her, if not effusively, at least with courtesy. "Cousin, well met. It is a happier occasion than when we last saw one another."

"Quite true. Brussels is nothing like that grim time," said Althea, giving her hand to him. "I hope that I find you well, my lord?"

"Quite well, thank you. You are quite in looks, Althea." The earl smiled slightly. There was a glint of respect and speculation in his eyes. "I must say that you have done very well for yourself in marrying Lynley."

"Thank you, cousin," said Althea quietly.

He retained her hand, now frowning a little. "I hope that you and your mother do not hold any animosity toward me, Althea.

I realized later that I was rather unfeeling in thrusting you so soon out of your home. It would perhaps have been better if I had allowed you to remain there through your period of mourning."

Althea guessed shrewdly that her cousin had been criticized for his arbitrary action and that his pride had smarted under the sting. "It is in the past, my lord. I do not believe that it would have made any difference, in any event. I would not have wanted to stay. And once my mother removed to Bath, her spirits improved considerably," she said.

The earl nodded, satisfied. Apparently he had acted more wisely than even he had known, and so he could mention whenever it proved necessary. He squeezed her hand with a show of sympathy before releasing her fingers. "I quite understand. Unhappy memories and all that."

"Just as you say," said Althea, her thoughts covered by a gracious smile. How little her cousin understood! She hoped for his sake that there were no ghosts roaming her childhood home.

His lady joined the earl and slipped her hand inside his elbow. She had obviously been quite beautiful once, but dissatisfied lines had pulled down the corners of her mouth to give her a permanent appearance of sourness. The earl glanced down, his expression unchanging. "Ah, here is my lady wife. Minerva, you will naturally recall my cousin Althea, Lady Lynley," he said.

"Indeed, I do." Lady Hawthorne showed her small pointed teeth in a thin smile. She did not offer her hand, a deliberate insult. "Lady Lynley and I were introduced on the occasion of your succession, my dear. How odd that we should now meet again in Brussels. It quite makes one ponder the fates, does it not?"

"Indeed it does, my dear. I was just complimenting my cousin upon her marriage. It was an extraordinary coup," said the earl.

"I was fortunate, indeed," said Althea, lifting her fan and slowly moving it, wondering when she could best make her escape. Her cousin was one thing, but his wife was intolerable.

The flash of diamonds on Althea's hand caught Lady

Hawthorne's sharp eyes. "Is that your wedding band, Lady Lynley? Pray do let me see it! I adore fine jewels."

Althea transferred her fan to her other hand and reluctantly extended her left.

Lady Hawthorne gazed upon Althea's marriage ring only a moment before she lost interest. "How disappointing, to be sure! It is not near as large nor as ornate as I would have expected of Viscount Lynley."

Althea was suddenly, fiercely, glad that she had allowed Gareth to procure new rings for her and for himself. She said quietly, "I do not care for a gaudy show, Minerva." She gazed for a pointed instant at her cousin-in-law's ostentatious display of necklaces. Bright spots of dull color surged into the countess's face. Althea turned a smile upon her cousin. "These diamonds were cut in Antwerp. They suit me very well."

Though the information had meant nothing to Lady Hawthorne, the earl was better informed. He glanced down at Lady Althea's hand quickly. "Exceptional indeed, cousin. Lynley does well by you. You must be grateful to him."

Althea retained her smile with difficulty. Her cousin had spoken in a congratulatory tone that told Althea which of them, herself or Lynley, her cousin considered to have made the better bargain. She fanned herself again. "You must meet Lynley. I am quite proud of him. He is attached to the Duke of Brunswick as aide-de-camp."

The earl was suitably impressed. He had always set great store by those with high social standing and, by extension, those associated with them. "Indeed! That is quite a responsible position for a younger man. I trust that Lynley is aware of his good fortune."

Before Althea could make a suitable reply, Lady Hawthorne broke in. "I am actually much astonished to see you here in Brussels, Lady Lynley. I had thought that you and your mother were suitably retired in Bath, but you have surprised us very much. Your mother's remarriage took place before the period of mourning was done, but one must not criticize too much."

"I do not believe that there was any criticism," said Althea gently. "My mother was already out of black gloves."

"Quite so," nodded the earl, beginning to feel uncomfortable. There was an expression in Althea's eyes that was quite at variance with her quiet rejoinder.

Lady Hawthorne gave a trill of laughter and shrugged dismissively. "Why, as to that, I suppose one must bow to the shocking changes in convention. Lady Lynley, your own marriage was equally . . . precipitous, shall we say?" Her swift glance over Althea's person was speculative, probing, and left one in little doubt as to the direction of her thoughts. She might as well have openly asked whether Althea had gotten Lynley to the altar by getting herself with his child.

"Have you brought the children with you to Brussels, Minerva?" asked Althea sweetly, closing her fan with a quiet snap. "I understood that you were so devoted to your brood that you could not bear the crowding that they endured any longer, so that you had to have the house in London without delay. But perhaps you are enjoying a convenient holiday from matronly concerns."

Lady Hawthorne's eyes sparked.

"The children remain in London with our retainers," said the Earl of Hawthorne repressively.

"Oh, I see! I perfectly understand. Brussels is certainly not the place for children," said Althea with a brilliant smile. She inclined her head and passed on. Inwardly she was seething. Her cousin was as pompous and self-serving as ever, while his wife was a veritable slandermonger. Lady Hawthorne could probably scrape dirt from the inside of a white kid glove, she thought distastefully.

The earl did not know what it was that Lady Lynley had understood, but it had greatly annoyed his countess. Lady Hawthorne was fairly quivering with anger. "That baggage! She is no better than she should be! There are tales to be told in her train, I'll warrant!"

"Possibly; but we know of none of them," said the earl judiciously. "I would just as soon not know, actually. I have the Hawthorne name to think of. It will take a lifetime to rid the title of the libertine stink that still clings to it. Whatever she is or may have done, my cousin at least had sense enough to toss over the Hawthorne name. Would that I could do the same. The mantle of a black-hearted libertine! It is a bitter legacy that was left me."

As Lady Hawthorne stared after her cousin-in-law, Lady Lynley, her lips thinned in an unpleasant smile. "The libertine's daughter," she murmured. "How utterly delicious!"

Before the evening was done, Lady Hawthorne had told a dozen individuals, in the strictest confidence, of her husband's fears that the former earl's wicked reputation would overshadow his own good consequence.

"It is ridiculous, of course. But one must naturally be sensitive to these things, especially when one's own cousin was that same libertine's daughter," said Lady Hawthorne solemnly.

"Do you mean that Lady Lynley . . .?" Lady Hawthorne's confidante looked in the viscountess's direction and noted with disapprobation that Lady Lynley was laughing in quite a free way at a gentleman's sally.

Lady Hawthorne followed her companion's gaze. She smiled slightly, but hastily she made her disclaimer. "Oh, I have nothing to say against Lady Lynley. I believe she must be quite the favorite, for she is rather beautiful in a flashy sort of way. Her manner is charming, too. I am told that her father was just so charming, but of course one must not judge the viscountess according to her sire's attributes."

"Of course not, indeed," said the lady slowly.

Lady Hawthorne passed on, well pleased, and went in search of another attentive ear.

Chapter Nineteen

As Althea had forged friendships with several ladies, she had also swiftly acquired a court of admiring gentlemen. For the first time in her life, Althea was accepted by a large circle of acquaintances. She blossomed and gained confidence as she moved through Brussels society. She enjoyed particularly being able herself to entertain. Her parties came to be known for a certain cachet of graciousness, lavish displays of flowers, and superlative culinary achievements.

On many occasions, and at times with even a note of envy, Lord Lynley was told that he was fortunate in his wife. He agreed, not once by the flicker of an eye or the intonation of his voice hinting that his was less than a perfect marriage. He had his pride and it would remain intact.

It was an unfortunate time for Lord Lynley to be ordered to Ghent with military dispatches. He was gone for two days. When he returned he discovered with consternation and slow-gathering anger that his viscountess no longer enjoyed the social success she had attained. Her popularity was dangerously eroded by rumor and counter-rumor.

Whispers had begun slowly at first, and then with gathering effect. Lady Lynley came under a great deal of renewed scrutiny, this time of a kind that was hardly disposed toward friendly curiosity.

Althea felt the undercurrents first. All of her life she had been sensitive to slight and when it began in Brussels, her heart plummeted to her feet. Then she chanced to hear the whispers, too, and knew that what she feared most—what she thought she would always fear—had happened: Her father's reputation had once more risen up to haunt her.

Some of the gentlemen who had previously spoken of their

admiration for Viscountess Lynley simply faded away. A small number of others began to couch their compliments in terms that bordered on the offensive. Those, Althea cut directly from her acquaintance. Her defensive action engendered anger in certain quarters and her name was bandied about with even greater vigor by the gentlemen who had been so slighted.

Ladies who had previously thought nothing ill of Lady Lynley suddenly recalled how relaxed was her particular style. It was only with her husband, Lord Lynley, that a certain reserve of manner had at times become apparent.

None had previously thought this to be unusual. On the contrary, it was not considered at all fashionable to sit in the pocket of one's spouse. Lady Althea had simply bowed to the current fashion. But now her ladyship's reserve toward Lord Lynley was discussed at some length and exhaustively. Perhaps there was a reason for it. Perhaps behind the viscount's smiling facade, there lurked rejection of his wife because he had become aware of some transgression or other.

No one could actually link Lady Lynley's name to any one particular gentleman. She had taken such care to be discreet. But she was the daughter of a libertine. Kind reverted to kind. It was a pity, of course, but there it was.

The first weeks of May were the zenith of Althea's happiness, but the blush of the rose waned with the whispers. As the warmth of June approached, the days swiftly degenerated into her nadir.

Not all of Althea's friends and acquaintances turned against her. Indeed, the majority merely waited to see how matters would fall out and in the meantime behaved toward her with cool civility.

Althea swiftly found which individuals she could truly depend upon. One of those was Lady Greville, who was a staunch ally and who told Althea privately that she had inquired weeks ago of Mrs. Comstock the reason for that lady's pointed championship. "I was profoundly shocked, of course, when Margaret related to me the persecution that you had endured much of your life as a result of your unfortunate family connection. It is dastardly that your father's sins are visited upon your head, and him in the grave besides!"

Althea had expressed her gratitude to Lady Greville, most

sincerely. However, she could not but wonder, with a thread of cynicism, what would have been that lady's tack toward her if Mrs. Comstock had not foreseen this very situation and done what she could to counter it.

What complicated matters even further was that Althea had but lately come to realize that she had fallen in love with her husband. She had no inkling when it had happened, if it had come upon her suddenly and she had simply not recognized the emotion for what it was—for after all, when had she ever experienced true affection—or if it had grown slowly and surely and eventually overtaken her heart.

However it had happened, Althea was in love with her husband, and she was utterly wretched. She thought that she could have borne the slights and slurs that kept cropping up all about her better if only she had been able to bury her head upon Gareth's strong shoulder.

But she could not. When the whispers began, he was not in town. By the time that he had returned, all she could think of was that he would surely blame her for the taint of scandal that she had brought to his name.

But her fears were unjust, for when Lord Lynley learned precisely what was being said about his wife, it was a blinding rage toward the gossipmongers that first gripped him. He did not know how he extricated himself from the friends who had been concerned enough on his behalf to confide the rumors. Nor was he aware of returning home to catch Althea at dinner.

When he entered the dining room, Althea looked up in surprise, and what Gareth perceived as consternation. Her expression swiftly smoothed. "My lord! I did not expect you this evening."

He managed a civil smile and indicated the chair opposite her. "May I join you, my lady?"

"Of course." Althea signaled the footman to set another place. She cast a quick glance at her husband's somber expression. Lowering her voice against the servant's ears, she asked, "Gareth, what is it? Is there bad news from the frontier?"

"No, nothing of that sort. At least, not yet." Gareth passed a hand over his face. "I am merely more weary than usual." He looked over at his wife, his gaze suddenly keen. "What of you, Althea? How have you been keeping yourself? Since my return I have been at headquarters so much that I have not seen you more than a handful of times."

Althea hesitated. Her instincts urged her to confide in him. There was an expectancy in his eyes that encouraged openness. But she dared not take the leap. She could not bear it if his eyes should grow cold and his words form for the purpose of cutting her. She shrugged in a negligent manner. "It is all vastly entertaining, I suppose." Althea rattled off an amusing anecdote and from there relayed a few items of interest.

Gareth listened to his wife, a smile on his face. Inside, he was bitterly disappointed. Althea had not trusted him. He had hoped that if she felt herself to be in difficulty she would turn to him. She had appeared as though she had wanted to do so, but then she had pulled away again. Of course he could confront her with what he had been told, Gareth thought. But he would far rather have Althea come to him of her own volition. He felt that it was a test of the bond between them.

It had seemed to him, before he left for Ghent, that they had slowly been making progress in repairing the breach between them. Now he was not at all certain that was true. Perhaps this marriage of his was not worth the effort.

His fingers clenched on his thigh, out of sight beneath the table. It must be worth the effort, he thought grimly. He could not continue in the manner in which they had for the remainder of his life.

"Althea."

"Yes, Gareth?"

She looked at him with a wariness of gaze. Gareth could almost physically feel how she drew up her defenses. Feeling suddenly defeated, he sighed and shook his head. "It was naught; just a passing thought." He introduced a neutral topic.

Althea responded suitably, relieved that he had not brought up the rumors that were making the rounds in Brussels. Perhaps he had not heard what was being said. Even as she hoped that he never would, she knew it was a vain hope. The gossip was too pervasive, the society too insular, for Gareth to remain long in ignorance. But at least she had a reprieve in deciding how she would answer him whenever he did confront her.

She did wonder, however, about what Gareth had meant to say. For an instant there had been such an intent look in his eyes. She knew that whatever was on his mind this evening was not of small moment. He had denied that there was anything troubling the frontier and he had not once alluded to her troubles. She could not think of anything else that would put that grave expression on his face.

Suddenly, passionately, Althea wished that she was secure enough in her relationship with him that she could simply ask him. But there were barriers between them. Some had been set by her and some by Gareth. From an early age Althea had been adept at erecting barriers. She had never learned how to tear them down.

The distrust and fear that Gareth had aroused in her had been overpowering. She had reacted mindlessly, out of her own brutally scarred childhood. She could not say whether she had been right or wrong. In truth, it had come to matter very little to her. Time had blunted the ugly emotions.

What mattered was being able to convince Gareth that something had changed for her. She had learned that she did not want a marriage based solely upon mutual respect and a studied, casual, affection. She wanted full-blown, idiotic, romantic love. She wanted to share his burdens with him and know that he was equally interested in hers. Althea did not want to settle for anything less.

Yet how she was to bridge the chasm that yawned between her and Gareth continued to defeat her. More than once a declaration of her love was on the tip of her tongue, but Althea bit it back. She was so afraid Gareth might reject her. He might believe that she was saying these things only because she needed his support to protect her from the worst effects of the slanders.

Soon Althea knew that Gareth had heard the lies. There was a new tightness about his eyes, a certain sharpness when he glanced at her, that made it abundantly clear. He had withdrawn entirely from her, even excusing himself from escorting her on the mornings she rode. He treated her with distant courtesy, but rarely did he smile.

Althea greatly feared that Gareth suspected the gossip about her was true. She had never given any hint to him of the disquieting thought, nor of what a strain it placed on her sense of balance. Given how repugnant she found even the very notion, it was ludicrous to suppose that she could ever actually take a lover.

Standing alone, profoundly lonely, Althea kept her head proudly lifted. She had weathered this particular storm before, though never one of such intensity. Nor one for a greater prize. Gareth must come to believe in her, to trust her. Then perhaps she could go to him and open her heart. She recalled the force of his anger and wished that she could be confident of his compassion instead.

The group of those that Althea could truly call her friends seemed pitifully small. There was Lady Greville, the Salyers, the Creeveys, the Comstocks, a few British officers and their wives; the Duke of Brunswick was kind to her, as were the Duke and Duchess of Richmond. She was also recognized by Sir Charles Stuart, the British ambassador.

The Duke of Wellington was gracious enough to say an encouraging word to her. "My brother knew something of your father's reputation and once told me about the earl. You mustn't allow wagging tongues to defeat you, my lady."

"Thank you, your grace. I shall stand," said Althea quietly.

The duke had given his loud hoarse laugh. "That is the spirit!"

Several personages watching the short exchange between the Duke of Wallington and Lady Lynley were surprised by his grace's obvious enjoyment at whatever remark the viscountess had made. Lady Lynley's badly dipped credit rose a notch.

Among the Belgian coterie, the dePliers remained constant toward Althea throughout the ordeal. She was grateful for it, knowing that she could always count on an oasis of peace whenever she called at the dePlier home.

Gaston dePlier was not often in residence when Althea called. She deliberately limited her visits to times when she guessed that there would be others present as well, or when the tall handsome cavalry officer could reasonably be expected to be off with his fellow officers. The backbiting gossip was bad enough. It would be touched to fire in an instant if it was ever thought that she was keeping assignations with the baron.

Madame dePlier was an invalid, but the lady's sweetness of disposition made one forget her infirmity. Althea always came away from the widow's presence with a sense of well-being.

She gravitated more and more toward the dePliers, seeking the emotional support that she so badly needed and could not find anywhere else, not even with her husband.

Mademoiselle dePlier was two years younger than Althea, but in many ways she was the wiser. She rarely appeared to be ruled by her emotions or by what other people thought. She was unusually discerning. Fleurette dePlier had a unique strength of character. Early in their friendship, Althea had quickly recognized that quality and she had wondered at it. She, who was so battered by demons private and public, would very much have liked to possess even a tenth of the serenity that Fleurette dePlier brought to her days.

Althea was surprised one afternoon when Mademoiselle dePlier asked whether she would care to attend mass with her. She had known, of course, that the Walloons and the Flemish were devoutly Catholic. She had known, too, and accepted that the dePliers regularly attended services.

Indeed, most of the British in Brussels also customarily attended religious services. It was an accepted thing, especially in Brussels at that time. Those who were not sincerely worshipful in spirit nevertheless attended church along with the rest of their countrymen as an assurance to themselves and everyone else that their world was the same as it had always been. It was but another proof that there was nothing to fear from Napoleon Bonaparte.

Lord Lynley attended church services regularly whenever his duties permitted. More than once he had asked Althea to accompany him, but she had politely declined each time.

Unlike most of her contemporaries, who had been raised with the church as an integral part of their experience, Althea had never been comfortable with the principles of Christianity as she knew them. She was uncertain what she could expect of God and she certainly did not know what He expected of her. The experiences of her childhood had not encouraged her to trust in anyone or anything other than in herself.

In actuality, Althea had never given much thought to the matter. She knew that others regarded her as an anomaly because she did not attend church, but she disregarded that. She had always been different, in this as in everything else.

Certainly, society had thought it odd that Lady Lynley absented herself from formal worship, but not much had been actually said about it until the Earl and Countess of Hawthorne came to Brussels. Lady Hawthorne advanced the opinion, in the most complete confidence, that Lady Lynley's character was secretly so blackened that she could not bear to set foot inside of a church for fear of heavenly judgment. This delicious speculation went hand in hand with the gossip that was already circulating about Lady Lynley.

Mademoiselle dePlier's request took Althea completely by surprise. She had never expected to receive such an invitation. Her consternation must have registered upon her face because Mademoiselle dePlier smiled understandingly.

"You are English, of course, and Protestant, so do not feel obligated to go with me out of friendship or feel that you would insult me by refusing. I will understand," said Mademoiselle dePlier.

"I do not think that I have been in a church more than three times in my life," said Althea. "I do not know whether I am Protestant or not, Fleurette." She paused thoughtfully, wondering how a divine God categorized a person who did not attend His house of worship. "Perhaps I am nothing."

"Do not say such a thing! We are all something in the eyes of the good God. *Non,* Althea, you are important. Just as I am, or Gaston, or the Duke of Wellington," said Mademoiselle dePlier.

Althea laughed. "I do not think that anyone may be compared with the Duke of Wellington. He is a great man."

"Agreed; but he is still a man." Mademoiselle dePlier regarded her solemnly. "It has been a very lonely, hurtful time for you, my dear friend. I wish to show you something for your wounded spirit. Althea, will you come with me?"

Althea hesitated, but then she agreed. Despite Fleurette's assurances to the contrary, she did feel that she should humor her Belgian friend. Althea had discovered that she had few true friends and she was careful not to offend any one of them even by an inadvertent word. Thus, she found herself seated in a Catholic church, attending an afternoon mass.

She found the ritual strange and it was awkward to know when to kneel and when to rise. The priest spoke in Latin, a language with which she had only a passing acquaintance. She wondered what had possessed her to come. But as Althea glanced at Fleurette's face, she was startled by an expression of such radiance that it awed her.

As the younger woman lifted her glowing gaze to the crucified figure of Christ Jesus above the altar, Althea saw something that she actually envied. It was peace in all its serenity.

Afterward as the two women walked back to the dePlier home, Althea asked hesitantly, "What does it mean when you pray to the crucified figure of Christ?"

"It is not the wooden figure that I am praying to, Althea. That is but a symbol of our Christ. When I look upon it, I am not seeing it. Instead, I am looking beyond it to my resurrected Lord," said Mademoiselle dePlier.

"You always appear so . . . so serene. Is that the source?"

Althea felt intensely awkward. It was difficult to form her query. She almost felt that she was prying. It cost her, too, a measure of pride to acknowledge that she had seen something that she did not understand, but wanted.

She had no one and nothing to fall back on but herself. She wondered what it must be like to be able to rely on God, as did her Belgian friend. Althea realized in that moment the true and terrible depth of her aloneness.

"*Oui*, it is Jesus Christ. One day I hope that you will understand, my dear friend," said Mademoiselle dePlier. She turned her head and her dark eyes were somber. "Do you know what I pray most? I pray for a swift conclusion to the years of war. It is time for it to end."

Althea was struck by the genuine selflessness of her friend's concern and it gave her much food for thought.

A few days later Mademoiselle dePlier asked Althea to accompany her again, but Althea did not return to the church. She made some excuse and was relieved when Fleurette did not press her. But she did not forget what she had seen or what Mademoiselle dePlier had said. That, at least, remained with her whether she willed it or not.

That week when she looked around at whatever company she found herself in, she saw few gentlemen attired in dark evening clothes. They stood out like rare birds from among the sea of red and green and brown and blue uniforms. The world she had known was twisted into something unrecognizable and bizarre. Perhaps she, too, would pray for an end.

Chapter Twenty

The strain between Althea and Lord Lynley was palpable. The town house fairly vibrated with tension. The Belgian servants went about their business with hushed quiet. The majordomo and Lady Lynley's dresser exchanged sharp words on more than one occasion.

Althea had attempted to communicate something of her chaotic emotions to Gareth, but he had completely misunderstood what she had been trying to convey. She had closed her mouth then, regretting her rash impulse. Her abrupt silence, which Gareth had interpreted as condemning, had thoroughly angered him. He blasted her for her selfishness in coming to Brussels and finished by bitterly renouncing the day that he had wed her. It was too much to be borne. Althea had run from the room, blinded by tears, with her heart shattering into little pieces.

Since then, it had only been her pride that had sustained her.

Althea's one indulgence was still to visit the Place Royale to buy as many flowers as the carriage could hold, but the flowers seemed to stand in sad commentary of what had become the ruins of her life. One day in the drawing room, in a momentary frenzy of despair, Althea tore down a vase containing a large arrangement of lilies and roses, smashing the vase and spraying water and blooms everywhere.

The noise brought the servants running, the majordomo in the forefront. The servants crowded at the door and stared at their mistress, aghast. Althea had burst into tears. Pushing her way through the servants, she fled upstairs. John Applegate looked thoughtfully after her. When he heard the murmurings behind him, he turned on the Belgian servants and sharply rebuked them, sending them scurrying.

There were no longer companionable conversations between Lord and Lady Lynley. They avoided dining alone at home and rarely entertained at the town house, mutually preferring to be out among company.

Lord Lynley felt that his nerves would snap with very little more pressure. The outlook for war was very bad, and as aide-de-camp to the Duke of Brunswick he was in a position to know several things that were not public knowledge.

Despite the cold gap that existed between himself and his wife, he yet cared for her. He worried about what would happen when the attack came, as surely it must, and he had to leave Althea on her own in Brussels.

He spoke to Althea about returning to England.

Althea merely stared at him with her cool, unreadable gaze. She was magnificently gowned for the evening and she appeared as proud and untouchable as royalty. "I have no intention of leaving Brussels just now, Gareth. I am enjoying myself too much. What is there for me in England?" she said.

He drew his brows together, an indication of his shortened temper. "I am concerned, Althea. Things are moving more swiftly than you are aware. I would feel easier if you were safely away."

"Would you indeed! How chivalrous of you, my lord. But you have forgotten our bargain," said Althea.

He flushed. "You need not remind me of the devil's agreement between us, Althea! I wish to God I had never allowed myself to enter into it."

"As I recall you were rather adamant about it, and now, as a gentleman, you cannot go back on your word," said Althea. She brushed past him. She turned at the door, a half-smile playing upon her face. "I told you once that I am self-sufficient, Gareth. Pray believe me when I say that I shall take heed for my own safety. I do not wish you to occupy your thoughts on my behalf. You must attend to your duty. I shall do very well on my own, just as I have always done." With that, she had left the room.

Gareth smashed his fist down on the mantel, aware of how impotent he was in his marriage. His wife had completely spurned him, rejecting both his overtures of affection and his judgment. There was nothing that he could see to do that would change matters, short of physically removing Althea from Brussels. He did not want to do that, for he knew that she would never forgive him. But they were so estranged now that it might not matter in the end. His guts had become so twisted up inside him that he thought it would come as a relief to expend himself in battle.

For Lord Lynley, everything came to a head that same evening as he idly watched Althea while she talked animatedly with her friends. He was aware that his presence among her circle would not be welcome. Althea's expression had spoken eloquently and often enough of her distaste for his company.

Lord Lynley's eyes traveled over the individuals that paid his wife court. There were some new faces added tonight. Althea seemed to have weathered the worst of the gossip that had sprung up so unpleasantly and so inexplicably. Through it all, her composure had never broken, though at times he thought he detected a brittle quality to her laughter.

His wife started laughing at that moment and a strange hollow feeling edged with anger stirred within him. Althea never showed him a laughing countenance. She displayed cool civility toward him, always polite, always accommodating, always distant.

He had stopped going to her bedroom weeks before. It had grown to be too great a burden to make love to a wife who submitted solely because it was her duty. God, how he ached for her. If only she could come to care for him as he did for her, Gareth thought helplessly. But he had apparently destroyed any possibility of that in one careless night.

He must have been mad. Even the brandy should not have led him to do what he had done. Gareth had regretted it more than he had ever thought it possible, for from that night to the present Althea had maintained between them an impenetrable, invisible wall.

A fellow officer clapped Gareth's shoulder. "You do not dance, Lynley? Why, but listen to that music, man!"

Gareth smiled. "I shall take the floor in a moment. I am waiting for the musicians to play a favorite tune of mine."

The officer grinned. His eyes held a knowing expression. "A bit blue-deviled tonight, are you? You must not think so much, Lynley. It makes a man too sober. We shall have at the French soon enough, never fear!"

Gareth made an easy rejoinder and the officer went away, laughing. For a moment Gareth's eyes followed his friend. The officer confidently approached a young lady of his acquaintance and brought himself to her notice. Almost, Gareth envied the fellow. The officer had not a thought in his head except to enjoy himself as long as he could.

He suddenly noticed Lady Hawthorne sailing toward him. Inwardly he groaned, knowing himself to be fairly caught. He disliked Lady Hawthorne and avoided her whenever he was able. It was by far the wisest course. The woman had grown notorious for her biting tongue.

After greeting Lord Lynley cordially, Lady Hawthorne remained standing beside the viscount and inquired about the latest war rumors. "For I know that as aide-de-camp to Brunswick himself you must overhear a great deal, my lord," she said smilingly.

Gareth smiled slightly, shaking his head. "No, I am afraid not. I have never been one of his grace's confidantes, Lady Hawthorne."

The countess's smile grew a little frigid. Playfully she slapped at his arm with her fan. "Come, come, cousin! For I do think of you as my cousin, my lord, ever since you and Lady Lynley wed, you know. Surely you may drop your guard with me. I shall treat whatever you have to say with the utmost discretion, I assure you!"

"I am in no doubt of that, my lady," said Gareth, somewhat dryly. He was well aware that the woman was an inveterate gossip. There was probably not an individual in Brussels who had not found his or her name on the woman's malicious lips. "Unfortunately, it is just as I have said. I am not in his grace's confidence." The countess shot him a suspicious look, but his pleasant expression apparently convinced her that she had not heard that dry note after all.

"What a pity that you are not very well-trusted by your superior, Lord Lynley," she said with smiling spite.

Gareth inclined his head, not at all put out by her insult. It meant nothing to him. His ego was not so sensitive that such a clumsy attempt could move him. "As you say, Lady Hawthorne." Bored with her ladyship, his glance unconsciously strayed away.

Following his lordship's gaze, the Countess of Hawthorne allowed a grimace to cross her face. The sight of her beautiful cousin-in-law was not one that pleased her. She had assumed that by coming to Brussels she would naturally be feted by those of her own kind. As the Countess of Hawthorne, she had indeed generated interest, but she had never gained the popularity that she so craved. It had been a totally unwelcome revelation to discover that the accolades that she desired for herself were instead directed at Viscountess Lynley, who was certainly her inferior both socially and in breeding. It was galling, therefore, to find that Brussels society had not, in the end, agreed with her. Lady Lynley was still well received by anyone that truly mattered.

Fanning herself, Lady Hawthorne said, "Lady Lynley is extremely popular, my lord. For a short time, I quite thought that her star had fallen. But she is uncannily resilient in the face of censure. You must be very proud of her continued success."

Gareth turned his head to meet the woman's bright, considering gaze. He knew Lady Hawthorne's reputation well enough to reply warily. "Yes, of course. I have always believed that Lady Lynley is something quite out of the ordinary."

Lady Hawthorne laughed gently, as though he had uttered a witticism. "Indeed! She has quite taken Brussels by storm, one might say. Particularly the gentlemen. Several hearts have reputedly been cast at her feet, but she will have none of them—so it is said."

Gareth smiled, but the expression in his eyes had grown considerably colder. "I am not at all surprised, my lady. My confidence in my wife is deeply rooted. Lady Lynley is scrupulous to a fault. It is one of her most endearing qualities."

"Oh, quite! It is particularly admirable in one whose upbringing was so very shocking," said Lady Hawthorne. She shook her head, smiling ever so slightly. "How unfortunate for a certain Belgian gentleman whose attentions of late have been so very particular toward Lady Lynley. One feels most thoroughly for the brave cavalry officer. She has proven herself to be so very devoted to the gentleman's mother, too, I am told. It must be hard, indeed, for the gentleman to discover her in his mother's sitting room so very often."

Lady Hawthorne laughed, playfully slapping Lord Lynley's arm again with her fan. It was a stinging blow rather than the attention-getting tap of previously. "You must be careful, my lord. Lady Lynley is quite bewitching. I should think you would keep a more jealous eye upon her." Lady Hawthorne searched Lord Lynley's expression and she apparently saw something that pleased her. The countess fanned herself slowly and moved away, her restless eyes already searching for new prey.

Gareth scarcely noticed Lady Hawthorne's departure, so powerfully had her words operated upon him. It was true that Althea had appeared to bewitch every male that came within her scope.

Gareth had not before realized how potent her charms were or to what good effect that she used them. Now he gave it thought even as his eyes searched her out from the crowd. She had learned much since she had come out into society. Her poise and beauty had matured. Since the whispers had begun she had also wrapped herself about with an admirable air of dignity.

Lady Hawthorne had been referring to Baron Gaston dePlier, of course. Gareth's mouth tightened as his gaze fell on the tall, unmistakable figure who was even then bowing over Althea's hand. Damn dePlier's eyes! The Belgian's impudence was unconscionable.

Mindful of how Althea had recoiled from him, Gareth had thereafter treated her with tenderness and consideration. He had hoped to erase the ugliness of that one night. But it had not served. He had begun to believe that there was something lacking in himself.

Now he wondered whether there was not another reason for Althea's distance. She enjoyed the admiration of several gentlemen. Her reputation was unsullied, it was true; but perhaps even so she had taken a lover. Perhaps even at that moment she was making an assignation.

The insinuation so poisonously placed in his mind exploded into full-blown suspicion. It was like a body blow and he nearly doubled over with it. Gareth held himself stiffly, his breath sounding ragged in his own ears.

Althea's low laugh carried clearly across the short distance. He saw the sparkling glance that she bestowed upon Gaston dePlier. A bolt of unprecedented jealousy unexpectedly rocked his soul. She had never laughed like that for him or looked at him with that same softened, teasing expression.

Gareth found himself standing beside Althea with no recollection of how he had made his way through the throng that had separated them. With a smile, a word, he extricated his wife from her friends and escorted her onto the ballroom floor.

The selection proved to be a waltz. Gareth smiled, his eyes gleaming, as he took her hand and put his arm around her slender waist. He drew her closer than was seemly and he did not care. He led her expertly about the floor, spinning them ever closer together. On the sidelines, several personages began to take note of the Lynleys' shocking progress.

"You are making a spectacle of us, my lord," said Althea quietly as she caught yet another disapproving stare.

"Am I? I am glad to hear it. Perhaps some of your so very attentive admirers will realize that your hand is already claimed," said Gareth shortly.

She stared up at him, incredulous. "Why would you say such an odd thing? Do you suspect some gentleman of taking too great liberties with me? Really, that is just too ridiculous."

"Is it, my lady?" Gareth bit out savagely. "I believe that you must allow me to be the judge. It has come to my attention that you parade yourself with every man-milliner in town. I will not have it, my lady. You are mine, and you will remain so."

"I think you are mad," said Althea with conviction. She had been surprised when he had appeared to whisk her onto the floor, but a tiny flame of hope had sprung up at the interest he was showing in her. With his words that hope was snuffed.

The waltz ended. Gareth released her but he did not step back. "You are completely out there, my lady. I have never been more sane in my life. As of this moment, I am exercising my authority as your husband. We shall tell our hosts good night and take our leave."

"I do not wish to leave," said Althea, her own anger rousing in defense against his arrogance and insinuations. She started to turn from him, but he caught her wrist.

"Nevertheless, we shall do so," said Gareth.

"Why? Why should I go with you?" Althea demanded fiercely.

"Because it is my wish." Gareth smiled, not pleasantly. "Put a good face on it, sweetheart, for I assure you that I am quite capable of picking you up bodily and carrying you out the door."

Looking up into his implacable face, Althea had no doubt whatsoever that he would do just as he threatened if she did not comply. She fell back on her pride. Althea shrugged as though it had become a matter of immense indifference. She said brittlely, "Very well. I can scarcely refuse, can I?"

Without replying, Gareth drew her hand through his elbow and escorted her over to their hosts. Once the formalities were observed, it was but the work of moments to retrieve their wraps and step up into their carriage.

Chapter Twenty-one

There was not a syllable uttered during the drive through the streets to the town house. Althea stared out of the glass-paned window at the passing sights. She was still angry, but she was frightened, too. She had seen her husband only twice before in the grip of a compelling force. Tonight it was as though he was holding in an emotion so powerful that it threatened to explode.

There was nothing that she had said or done that could possibly warrant or justify such a reaction. Nevertheless, she knew that his fury was directed at her, and she shivered.

Lord Lynley politely handed his wife down from the carriage. She went up the front steps swiftly, passing into the house without him. He followed her, his lips tight. When he entered the house, he paused only a moment to give his coat and hat to the porter. Althea was already at the bottom of the stairs when he overtook her.

Gareth caught her elbow. She gasped, turning as if at bay. The wide fright in her eyes only infuriated him further. "My lady, I crave your company for a few moments. Pray join me in the drawing room," he grated.

Feeling the harsh hold on her arm, Althea had no choice but to cross the hall with him to the drawing room. He released her as they entered. Althea immediately moved to stand several feet away from him.

Her wariness was not lost on her husband. Caught up in his base suspicions, Lord Lynley interpreted her actions as indicating guilt. Gareth closed the door, his expression masklike.

When they were private from the ears of the servants, Althea asked, "Why have you done this, my lord? Why have you treated me so shabbily tonight?"

"I am exercising my rights as a husband."

The pupils of her eyes dilated. He knew instantly what she was thinking. It was like a knife twisting in his heart. He smiled rather grimly. "Pray do not misunderstand me, my lady. I have no intention of ravishing you. What I meant is that I have the right to expect my wife to behave circumspectly and correctly."

"When have I not?" asked Althea, amazed. "I have never given you cause for this jealous rage."

Gareth stiffened as though under a flail. His was a justifiable anger, not an unwarranted jealousy. He had had his own suspicions confirmed, though for the moment he chose to forget the source. "Your name is linked with Gaston dePlier. I do not care to be made a cuckold, madame. When my heir is born, I want there to be no question that he is mine!"

Without conscious volition, Althea moved. She slapped him. An angry imprint appeared upon his lean cheek. Bright color flew in her cheeks and her bosom rose and fell again, sharply. "How dare you!" she breathed.

Gareth threw back his head and laughed.

Althea's eyes blazed. She regained full use of her voice. "I am not to be so basely accused, my lord! I am not a common trollop. I shall not accept such insult! You are acting the fool, and so I tell you!"

"Then I have the fool's reward! Do you deny that you spend all of your time with all manner of various gentlemen fawning about you? God, it sickens me!"

"What else would you have me do, my lord? Hide myself away and pretend that I do not exist? What is it to you if I enjoy the companionship of other men?" Althea gave an angry little laugh. "It is quite apparent that you cannot stand to be around me. You have not shown me in more than two months by word or gesture that you desire my company."

Gareth took a step that brought him nearer to her. There was a glitter in his narrowed eyes. "Is that what this is all about, Althea? A bid for my attentions in your bed?"

"No!" She stepped back quickly. She could accept nothing from him that did not also bring with it his heart. Aware only of her own chaotic feelings, Althea did not realize with what wounding force her action would be misconstrued.

Gareth felt the rejection in all of its impact. His face froze. He clenched his fists. His voice was a bitter whiplash. "I did not realize that you found me so extremely repugnant, my lady. It is regrettable in view of that agreement we made before ever we wed."

Althea was white and trembling. "Yes! How I wish my part was done with. You have but the one use for me, have you not, Gareth? What a stupid, ignorant little fool I was. I thought that I knew you well enough. But I was wrong, so very wrong!"

She turned and fled to the door. Almost blinded by tears, she fumbled with the knob, but she got the door open at last and ran out.

Gareth stood quite still. He had not tried to stop her. He passed a hand over his eyes. It would have been pointless to do so, he thought wearily.

The painful scene replayed through his mind in excruciating detail. He stared into the middle distance, frowning darkly. Little by little the conviction grew on him that he had missed something important. There was a key somewhere in the words that Althea had flung with such bitterness at his head. Instinctively he knew it. But the meaning eluded his understanding.

In the first week of June, the Duke of Wellington took stock of the Allied armies that were under his command. It had been difficult to forge a cohesive force with so many nationals, but he had mixed the corps in thoroughly with the British troops and that seemed to stabilize the whole. Altogether, he had at his command a troop strength of 93,717.

On the twelfth of June, Napoleon Bonaparte was poised to cross the frontier into Belgium. The French army totaled 535,000.

Lord Lynley escorted his wife to Lady Conyngham's party on the evening of Wednesday, the fourteenth of June.

Daily, there had been rumors that the French had crossed the border into the Low Countries. The general anxiety of those in attendance was universally felt. When the Duke of Wellington arrived, he was asked if there was any truth in the rumor. He replied gravely that it was so. There was an immediate outbreak of consternated exclamations.

Althea gave as much heed to what the duke had to say as any other there, but she turned quickly to tell an amusing anecdote, which effectively lightened the sobered expressions of those around her.

Lord Lynley was not among those who chose to be amused by his wife. He had been playing cards. Upon hearing what the duke had said, he had thrown in his hand and wandered toward the windows. The windows had been thrown wide on that warm June night and he leaned against a column where the slight breeze could touch his face. He frowned out at the shadowed gardens.

An elderly dame, in passing, recognized him. She stopped and graciously inclined her grayed head. "Good evening, Lynley."

He roused himself to a courteous bow and smile. "Good evening, ma'am."

"The duke has confirmed that madman is now across the frontier. What think you, Lynley?" asked Lady Shotte, her shrewd eyes on his face.

"I suspect that it will not be long before the Allies see action at last," said Gareth gravely.

Lady Shotte cackled and nodded. "I thought that must be the reason why you were standing here lost in a brown study. The prospect of battle does that to some men. I have seen it before." Abruptly, she said, "Your wife was the previous Earl of Hawthorne's gel, was she not?"

Lord Lynley bowed again, immediately wary. He had learned recently that the rumors that had done so much damage to his wife's reputation had begun to circulate when the Earl and Countess of Hawthorne, his wife's cousins, had come to Brussels. He regretted having fallen for Lady Hawthorne's poisonous insinuations, for his resulting jealousy had all but ruined what had been left of his marriage. Since then, he had challenged every deprecating remark that was made within his hearing.

Lord Lynley's determination to put to rout the last of the spurious talk had been marked. The gentlemen, at least, had learned to say nothing that could be construed as disrespectful of Viscountess Lynley. The worst offender, one of those whom Althea had cut from her acquaintance weeks before, had found himself spitted on a sword. The duel over Lady Lynley's honor quickly became known and caused a scandal. Lord Lynley had been reprimanded by the Duke of Wellington himself, for his grace strongly disapproved of any disruptions among his officers. However, the message had been understood. Lord Lynley would not tolerate a word uttered by any man against his wife.

The ladies' set was immune to the code duello, however, and once in a while a catty remark still surfaced. Lord Lynley suspected that this was what he was faced with now. Unsmilingly, he said, "Yes."

The old woman shook her head. A profusion of diamonds flashed in her shriveled ears and at her scrawny neck. "Very bad blood there. The earl was a scandal, a libertine of the worst sort. My cousin was an intimate for a time. He was not a man easily shocked, but he swore that there was such stuff going on under the Hawthorne roof that it sometimes left him queasy. It would be wonderful, indeed, if that gel of yours was not fatally scarred by it all."

Gareth stared at the elderly woman, not at all certain that he wanted to hear more. But he felt himself compelled to ask. "What precisely do you mean, my lady?"

Lady Shotte shrugged thin shoulders. "She is a libertine's daughter. She was exposed to all manner of evil from her girlhood. It would be wonderful indeed if she had not lost her maidenhood early on. Aye, and continued on a progression like her father's."

"That was not the case," said Gareth stiffly. He was aghast at the old woman's blunt speech. He also very much disliked the position in which he found himself. It was one thing to challenge a man for a rash statement, but he could not very well take an elderly female to task in the same way. However, defending his wife's good name was an unpleasant necessity. "Lady Lynley was, and is, very much a lady."

The elderly dame cocked her head, her bright beady eyes considering him with worldly weariness. "That's the way, is it? Cold as ice between the sheets, I make no doubt."

Gareth flushed. "Madame!"

Lady Shotte did not heed his explosive protest. "The gel must be something indeed to have preserved herself whole.

Ah, but I was forgetting! My cousin mentioned that there had been a veritable battle-ax of a nanny. No doubt the dragon protected her charge fiercely. The door was always locked, I was told." She shrugged and yawned, fanning herself. "Just as well. It was whispered that some of those bounders had a fancy for Hawthorne's little girl. Hawthorne would have killed any one of them had she been touched. He was that sort. But who's to say he would have reached her in time, eh? No; it was the nanny and the locked door that saved her. That mother of hers was of no help, of course. A poor-spirited thing. The woman lived in fear of Hawthorne's displeasure. A black upbringing, my lord; very black."

Bored and done with her recollections, the elderly dame moved away. Gareth scarcely noticed. He turned his head to find his wife. Looking upon her graceful form, the perfection of her features, and catching the flash of her quick, beautiful smile, he could only wonder with a kind of numb shock what horrors were locked inside her head.

It was no wonder she had reacted the way that she had when he had gone to her with brandy fumes and anger clouding his judgment. Gareth had felt instant shame for what he had done, but now his entire being felt suffused with it.

His fists unconsciously clenched and unclenched. She had locked the door against him the following night. His fury had taken unequaled when he discovered it. But now he understood that it was not so much a rejection of him but rather of everything that must still have haunted her. God, how he had mismanaged his marriage.

With the clearness of hindsight, Gareth saw many things that he had misunderstood. He realized now the depth of her desperation when she had fled from her stepfather's unwelcome attentions. It must have seemed as though she was reliving a nightmare. But he had been there to rescue her, like a knight in splendid shining armor.

His armor had swiftly become tarnished, however. He had wed her and deserted her. When she followed him to Brussels, he had treated her very much like an unwelcome package. He had not listened to what she was saying. He had not tried to understand what she was feeling.

He had been so sure, so arrogantly certain, that he knew

what was best for them both, when in actuality it had been his own selfishness that he was serving. He had not wanted his wife in Brussels because he had not wanted the responsibility of caring for her. Of course there had been, and there was still, the horrible possibility that Brussels could be overrun by the enemy. In that much he had been right. However, he had shunned the prospect of protecting someone close to him as too daunting to even consider, and in that he had been wrong. Althea had a claim on his protection, not his father's.

He could not imagine what she had felt when she had been blackened with the brush of her deceased father's foul reputation. Again, he had failed her. She had stood alone, stoically enduring it all, without once attempting to defend herself. She had had to draw encouragement from friends, and it shamed him that he had shown himself so lacking.

Their last awful row blazed across his memory and he heard again Althea's bitter words. He had known there was something important hidden in them. Now he was stunned to realize what they had meant. Althea had indeed given herself into his keeping, more thoroughly than he had ever guessed.

Gareth closed his eyes for a moment. When he opened them again, he was looking at his wife. His wife. How hollow that title must have become to Althea.

He hoped that it was not too late.

Chapter Twenty-two

The following morning Althea went downstairs to breakfast not knowing what to expect. Through her dresser she had been informed that Lord Lynley awaited her pleasure in the breakfast room. Accordingly, she had attired herself in an almost severely plain pelisse. It was the most dignified dress she owned and she felt that she presented the appropriately somber appearance that such a summons warranted.

When she and Gareth had left Lady Conyngham's, he had been very quiet. Althea had grown used to his silences, but this one last night had had a different tenor to it.

Gareth had handed her out of the carriage and then had firmly drawn her hand inside his arm. She had cast a swift glance upwards at his face. In the lantern light his expression had appeared somber but not grim. He had not been angry or indifferent or mocking, as she had become accustomed to expect of him.

He had escorted her into the house and at the bottom of the stairs he had bid her a civil good night. Gareth had then turned away and walked away from her toward the library. She had stared after him, amazed; but catching the porter's curious eyes on her, she had quickly gone upstairs. Althea had almost expected Gareth to come to her bedroom later, but the connecting door had remained shut.

When Althea entered the breakfast room, she paused in the doorway. Gareth stood up at her appearance and bowed, indicating a chair. She saw that he was dressed in breeches and riding boots. Warily, Althea seated herself in the chair that he was holding. She glanced up at him as he went back around to his own place.

"I trust that you slept well, Althea," he said. He started to cut into his steak and kidneys.

"Exceedingly well, thank you," said Althea. She waved away the footman once he had poured tea for her. She was not hungry that morning. A certain tenseness had crept in upon her and disrupted her stomach.

"What are your plans for the day?" asked Gareth.

Althea narrowed her eyes, her thoughts busy. She could not decide what he was hoping to accomplish. He had not uttered one cutting remark. Nor had he adopted that air of indifference that he had so often employed when they were forced to be together. She decided that she must simply await events, so she outlined the calls that she planned to make and the invitations that she had accepted.

Gareth listened gravely, never once interrupting. When she had finished, he nodded and said, "I must go in to headquarters for an hour or two later this morning, but otherwise I will be free to escort you wherever you wish to go."

Althea was astonished and distrustful. What lurked behind this polite civility she utterly could not imagine or fathom. She couched her refusal in polite terms. "That will not be necessary, Gareth. I am certain that you have your own itinerary. I would not wish to disrupt your day."

"Not at all. I shall be only too happy to oblige you," said Gareth.

Althea said nothing more, but when he rose with her and followed her out of the breakfast room, it occurred to her that he meant to keep an eye on her for a reason. He did not trust her and believed that she had an assignation that day with some lover or other. She was humiliated and angered. She turned sharply around. "Gareth, really, there is no need to put yourself about for my sake. As you have no doubt realized, I have planned a very dull day."

He smiled at her. "I shall make an attempt to be an amusing companion. I have had the horses saddled for a ride this morning. I feel like a good gallop, do not you? I shall wait for you here while you change into your riding habit."

A flush mounted in her cheeks. Althea turned sharply around on her heel and swiftly went upstairs. She delayed as long as she could, but eventually she left the bedroom. It was either do that or remain in her rooms all day, for she had seen that obstinate look about Gareth's mouth. He meant to play her escort and that was precisely what he would do. There would be no persuading him otherwise.

Gareth was waiting precisely where she had left him. His expression was pleasant. "You are in looks this morning, Althea," he said quietly, looking down at her. The smart bonnet she wore framed her face and the color in her cheeks was vastly becoming. Her eyes flashed with sparkling annoyance, but she looked magnificent.

"Thank you, my lord," said Althea in a neutral voice. She tightened her fingers about her riding whip and turned away. She was aware of Gareth behind her as she went toward the front door.

The porter opened the door for them and ushered them out.

The carriage was waiting for them by the time they had changed their toilettes and they returned downstairs. Gareth opened the door and handed her up, then joined her inside. He latched the door and signaled the driver. Althea allowed Gareth to help her into the saddle and gathered her reins. She was determined to give him no satisfaction, and she preserved a stony silence as they rode to the Allée Verte. But she could not remain long in the sullens when she was horseback with a companion who entered so precisely into her own tastes. Before even the hour was up, Althea had thawed considerably and, after their return to the town house, even accepted Gareth's stated intention to accompany her on her morning calls with equanimity.

Althea was in Gareth's company very nearly the entire day. Not once did his courtesy waver. He was civil and set himself to the task of proving a good companion. He succeeded so well that Althea was betrayed into smiling up at him more than once. She even laughed at some witticism. By the end of that memorable day, Althea had come to the startling conclusion that Gareth was attempting to woo her.

Althea sat in front of her cheval glass while Darcy fixed her hair for the evening. She was preoccupied with her own thoughts and only absently replied to her dresser's comments.

The dresser cast a knowledgeable eye over her mistress's expression and smiled to herself. She had heard that his lordship had danced attendance on Lady Althea all the day. It was certainly past time that he should do so.

Althea was confused by Gareth's new way of dealing with her. She wanted to trust him, but she was unsure that she dared. She did not want to be hurt or betrayed again. Her heart had already taken such a beating at his hands. If she should respond to his present mode of behavior, what guarantee did she have that he would not turn his face against her yet again?

Althea went downstairs still torn by the decision that she felt was required of her. She could scarcely stand it any longer. She had to know why Gareth was acting as though he was courting her.

She went into the drawing room. Lord Lynley was waiting for her and at sight of her, he drew in an appreciative breath. She was attired in a sea-blue gown accented with knots of lace and ribbons. Her blonde hair had been drawn up to cascade in tiny tendrils about her face and nape. Sapphire studs adorned her ears and sapphires and diamonds graced her slender neck. He went forward to take her hand. Lifting it, he brushed a light salute across her gloved fingers. "You are beautiful," he said, his voice deepened.

Althea shivered. She did not want to feel vulnerable. She withdrew her hand from his. "My lord, you flatter me."

"I do not think so. If you knew what words I would like to say to you, it would make you blush," he said, a teasing smile lighting his face.

"Pray do not!" Althea said sharply. At the change in Gareth's face, as his expression altered to one of amazement, she drew in her breath. Clasping her hands together to stop their trembling, Althea said, "Gareth, you showed me a civility and courtesy today that I had not expected. I do not understand it."

"I realize that, Althea. I have been unkind toward you. Put bluntly, I have been the worst kind of monster. I should like to make it up to you," said Gareth slowly.

Althea stared at him. Her heart was tumbling in her chest. "But why? Why, Gareth?"

He shrugged. "Is it not enough that I desire to do so?"

Althea felt the thrust of sharp disappointment. Nothing had changed. He was acting purely out of his own self-interest. No doubt he had chosen this means to work his way back into her good graces and her bed, believing that he could persuade her to receive him warmly. She was almost sick with her conclusions.

Althea turned away so that he could not see her face. She had already accepted an invitation for that night or otherwise she would instantly have rushed directly upstairs for a hearty bout of tears. But it would be an insult to the duchess if she did not make her expected appearance.

Althea did not want to be with her husband. She did not want him to escort her to the Duchess of Richmond's ball and supper. Her voice was flat. "I would prefer to attend the duchess's ball on my own, my lord."

"What?" Gareth's brows snapped together. He did not understand what had gone wrong. He had been encouraged at the progress that he had made throughout the day. It had been difficult initially to maintain his patient wooing, but slowly he had had his reward. Althea's tension and obvious mistrust had gradually given way and she had become much more like the young woman that he remembered encountering at that inn.

Now her voice was cold; the tenseness in her slender back was eloquent of disfavor. Gareth stepped forward and took hold of her arm. He turned her around to face him. She raised her chin in that proud distant look that he had come to know so well. "Althea, whether you wish it or not, I shall escort you," he said quietly. "There will be no discussion of the matter. It is closed."

Althea's anger rose. How dared he lay down an ultimatum of that sort. He would not brusquely override her wishes. "I shall go, but alone!"

"You will go with me or not at all," said Gareth rashly.

"Then I shall stay at home," Althea snapped, her eyes flashing.

Gareth realized that their exchange was degenerating into a pointless battle. With difficulty, he caught hold of his fraying temper. "Pray do not be such a child. There is no one of consequence who will not attend. Do you wish to expose yourself again to ill-mannered gossip, this time for cutting the Duchess of Richmond?"

Althea stared up at him, hating that he had insulted her, hating more that he was right about the gossip. She had known that she could not offer such insult to the duchess. She relinquished the field to him. "Very well, my lord. I will allow you to escort me, but I do so under duress. I have no wish to be with you."

"As I am all too well aware," gritted Gareth.

The Duchess of Richmond's ball and supper was held on Thursday, the fifteenth of June.

Scarcely twenty-four hours earlier, Napoleon Bonaparte had crossed the frontier into the Low Countries. Since that intelligence became known, however, there had been no disturbing reports, and when the Duchess of Richmond had asked the Duke of Wellington for his advice, he had assured her that there was no reason to cancel her ball and supper.

So the duchess's plans for the entertainment of all of Brussels went forward. The Duchess of Richmond held the ball on the ground floor in a large room that had once served to house the former owner's coaches. One could no longer discern the ballroom's plebian beginnings. It was stunningly decorated and ablaze with candlelight.

The occasion was soon pronounced to be a crush and its success was assured. All the royalty of continental Europe graced it. Wave after wave of obeisances were made as the royals arrived. Eventually the formal entrances were at an end and the business at hand was attended to. Bright crisp uniforms contrasted pleasingly with pale gowns as flirtations were got up amid the music and dancing.

Lord and Lady Lynley arrived at the ball both determinedly presenting a smiling countenance to the world. After a few moments, when he became aware that it would be impossible to keep Althea at his side except by main force, Gareth let her hand slip from his arm. Within moments, Althea had deserted him to greet some of her friends. He watched her go, outwardly as pleasant-expressioned as ever, when what he wanted to do was to wring her lovely neck.

The Duchess of Richmond had brought in a special entertainment to surprise her guests. The regiment of Highlanders dancing to the wild skirl of the pipes, their bright tartans flying, were a spectacular success. The duchess's ingenuity was applauded by even the most jaded.

Althea made her way around the ballroom, amusing herself fairly well by conversing with her various friends. The Comstocks were still exclaiming in admiration of the Highlanders when she joined them.

After exchanging greetings with the elder Comstocks, Althea turned to their daughter. Eyes glinting with laughter, Althea inquired, "Surely you have not been so dazzled as to forget a certain Guardsman, Charity?"

Miss Comstock shook her head, her dimples appearing. "Indeed not! George outshines them all. Here he is now. I sent him for ices for Mama and me." She turned and tipped up her head, her eyes shining as she looked up into her betrothed's craggy face. Althea's heart was squeezed with envious pain at such obvious adoration. "George, here is Lady Lynley!"

The Guardsman, George Sanderson, bowed, slightly hampered by the ices in his big hands. His was a pleasant countenance and now he eased into a smile. "Your servant, Lady Lynley. May I get anything for you, my lady?"

"I thank you, but no. I have not done so much dancing as yet to make me warm," said Althea, laughing.

"That will soon be remedied, I suspect," said Mrs. Comstock with an impish smile.

"Pray spare my blushes, dear ma'am," said Althea, again laughing. After a few more words, she withdrew from the Comstocks' happy circle and passed on to other acquaintances.

Even as Althea talked and laughed, however, a familiar loneliness threatened to engulf her. Her friend Charity had found something very precious, which she herself had never been quite able to attain. Indeed, until coming to Brussels she had not known what love was. It was a pity that she had ever learned, for she had never been so miserable in her life.

Almost, she wished that she had never left Chard. If she had remained there, she would have retained that orderly outlook that she had once held on marriage. It would have been simpler and far less painful. She would never have come to love Gareth. If he had been killed in battle, she would have felt regret, of course, but little more. If he had returned to her after the war was done, as he had outlined, then they would probably have acquired an affection for one another.

But never would they have experienced the tempering threat of war together. There would always have been a part of Gareth, formed here in Brussels, that she would never have understood. She probably would not have had any great desire to do so, either. She would have been caught up in her amusements and perhaps even lavished her attentions upon a sturdy brace of children. Her husband would have remained what he had been in the beginning—the means to an end.

Appalled, Althea stood quite still. She had not realized how truly self-centered had been her decision. All of her life had been spent in surviving the circumstances in which she had found herself. She had never really thought about anyone else. She had never really given anything of herself to anyone.

Her friendships were strong, but there, too, she had used others to her benefit. The Comstocks had always stood in her mind as surrogate parents while Charity had been cast into the role of the sister that she had never had. She had used the Comstocks to buttress her own lack of family. The same was true of the dePliers and, to a much lesser extent, the Salyers.

Althea shook off her disquieting thoughts. It was not the time or the place for such blinding revelations. An officer of her acquaintance came forward and bowed to her. Althea smiled and graciously accepted his invitation to dance. Thereafter, she made certain that she was never without a partner and gave herself up to enjoyment of the moment.

Chapter Twenty-three

It was not quite ten o'clock when rumors that there had been a skirmish between the French and the Prussians began circulating around the ballroom.

Althea was standing with her friends the Salyers when they heard the rumor. Mr. Salyer echoed the general consensus when he voiced his opinion that it was but another false alarm. Mindful of his wife's pale countenance, he patted her shoulder reassuringly. "When the time comes you must be brave, my dear. Our boys will not want to see such distress upon their mother's face."

"Yes, yes, you are right. It would upset them dreadfully," said Mrs. Salyer. She turned to Althea with a wavering smile. "It is silly of me to be thrown into such sensibilities at every rumor, is it not?"

"I think, ma'am, that anyone with two fine sons in the army would be considered unnatural, indeed, if she did not express some concern," said Althea.

Mrs. Salyer squeezed her hand gratefully. "You are kind, Althea. Have I told you that May has now gotten up from her bed? The physician said that she could, but that she must rest as often as possible during the day since the baby *will* stretch his lungs at night!"

Althea laughed, shaking her head. "It is a wonder to me how one as soft-spoken as May came to have such a lusty child. Perhaps the baby inherited his lungs from his father."

Mr. Salyer had overheard and he expanded his chest in an exaggerated fashion. "The Salyers have always been a vocal lot," he said.

Upon the laughter that this sally provoked, Mrs. Salyer said, "Althea, you must come to dinner tomorrow evening. It will be a small party only, all of whom will be known to you. Pray say that you will, for I know that May will be delighted to see you."

"Then I shall," said Althea, pleased. "Pray let May know that I am looking forward to visiting with her. I hope that I may be granted the opportunity to take a quick peek at the newest young Salyer."

"Oh, there is not the least doubt in the world. We are all exceptionally proud of the boy," said Mr. Salyer.

They were joined by a young woman and her escort, one of the Duke of Wellington's aides. Althea and the Salyers greeted Miss Orde and her betrothed, Colonel Hamilton. After a few moments, Mrs. Salyer inquired after Miss Orde's mother, who was an invalid.

"She is not feeling as well as she should, ma'am, unfortunately. My stepfather stayed at home tonight to sit with her," said Miss Orde.

"Mr. Creevey is commendable in his devotion," said Mr. Salyer.

"Indeed, he is. I must call upon your mother soon," said Mrs. Salyer.

"What has Creevey heard, Hamilton?" asked Mr. Salyer.

Colonel Hamilton shook his head, smiling. "That you must ask him yourself, sir. I cannot keep abreast of the man, nor could anyone. Mr. Creevey has an extraordinary flair for knowing the news before anyone else."

"I should like to have heard his observations concerning this most recent rumor," said Althea.

"We shall all know soon enough, I'll wager," said an amused voice. "But right now I am more interested in going in to supper."

A general laugh was raised even as Althea turned to find Gareth at her shoulder. "Lynley! You startled me."

Lord Lynley exchanged compliments with the others and then offered his arm to his wife. There was a smiling determination in his eyes. "Pray do me the honor of going in with me, Althea."

Althea acquiesced gracefully. No one could have guessed her true feelings.

The Duke of Wellington was sitting after dinner with a

party of officers over the dessert and wine when an officer arrived with dispatches from Marshal von Blucher, the Prussian
commander.

The rumor that had circulated earlier was true. Blucher had
been attacked that day by the French. The duke was as calm as
ever. The troops were ordered to hold themselves in readiness
to march at a moment's notice, but no immediate movement
was expected.

There was now a feverish quality about the faces of everyone in the ballroom. The musicians played for all they were
worth, and not a single lady went without a partner. It was as
though every ounce of amusement had to be extracted from
each passing minute. Such an expectation was building in
every breast that it was felt that if it was not soon released
the very roof of the ballroom must be driven off.

A second officer arrived from Marshal von Blucher and the
dispatches were delivered to the Duke of Wellington in the
ballroom. At once animated conversations were abruptly suspended as everyone became aware of the delivery and turned
themselves about.

While the duke was reading the dispatches, he became so
completely absorbed in their contents that he forgot his surroundings.

All eyes were trained upon the duke. All conversation
hushed. The musicians had faltered to silence. It was as though
a collective breath was being held.

After the Duke of Wellington had finished, he remained for
some minutes in deep reflection. Upon forming his decision,
he gave clear and concise orders to one of his staff officers,
who instantly left the room. The duke then reverted to his
usual animated style.

Taking their cue from his grace, the musicians struck up
once again. The crowd was released from their immobility and
bright conversation and laughter once more filled the ballroom. If the flirtations seemed to have acquired a desperate
edge, if expressions had become rather fixed upon the faces of
those who were dancing, no one chose to point it out.

It drew past midnight. Except for the ongoing gaiety of the
Duchess of Richmond's ball, a heavy silence seemed to hover
over Brussels.

Suddenly, the drums beat the call to arms. The loud brassy call of trumpets was heard from every quarter of the city.

The attack had become serious. The enemy was in considerable force. Bonaparte had taken Charleroi and driven back the Prussians. The English troops were ordered to march immediately to support the Prussians.

In the duchess's ballroom, the ladies looked at the officers with a kind of glazed stare. Slowly, inevitably, reality broke upon company. Everywhere one looked there began to be tender leavetakings.

Miss Comstock took leave of her Guardsman with tears dimming her vivacious eyes. She turned and threw herself into her mother's arms, breaking down entirely.

"There, there, my dear," murmured Mrs. Comstock, a stricken look upon her face.

Mr. Comstock took the Guardsman by the hand and exchanged with the young man a crushing grip. "We will be praying for you, my boy," he said simply.

"Thank you, sir," said George Sanderson gravely. He touched his betrothed's shoulder gently, tenderly. Abruptly, then, he turned on his heel and strode away. He was quickly lost to sight in the crowd of others like himself who were leaving the ballroom.

Not all were so somber of countenance. Many of the younger officers were full of high spirits to be going to war at last. Some were as young as seventeen. It would be their first action. Visions of glorious contests and heroic deeds leaped from their heads and spun off their tongues in an excited babble.

One young officer pelted across the floor, too excited to heed his direction, and crashed into a Belgian cavalry officer. "A thousand pardons, sir!" he exclaimed, and hurried on.

Baron Gaston dePlier had ignored the impudent youngster, but not out of disdain. His expression was worried as he turned about, searching the milling crowd. When he saw Althea, his eyes lighted with relief. He went up to her quickly. "Lady Lynley! I must go at once. Fleurette is still here, without escort. I do not wish to send her home alone. She has gone to collect her wrap. Will you see her home safely?"

"Of course, Gaston," said Althea. "You know that you may rely on me."

The cavalry officer caught up her hand, pressing it in fervent thanks to his lips. Retaining her hand a moment, he looked down into her face and smiled. There was a rather odd expression in his ice-blue eyes. His thumb gently traced across her wedding band. "If you had not already been Lynley's, I would have tried to make you mine," he said. Before Althea could form a reply, he said good-bye and was gone.

Gareth had come up in time to see dePlier take hold of his wife's hand. He had hesitated, and then he overheard dePlier's quiet declaration. His face grew taut with full realization of his stupidity.

Althea turned slowly, an expression of distress on her face. When her gaze fell on her husband's stern visage, her eyes widened. Afraid that he might have misconstrued Gaston dePlier's leavetaking, she hurried to explain. "Baron dePlier has asked me to escort his sister home. He was Fleurette's escort this evening."

"Of course you must honor dePlier's request," said Gareth. It was with a welcome finality that he had discovered that his jealousy had been truly unbased. He wanted nothing more than to drag Althea into his arms, but instead he lifted her hand and held it in his. "I, too, must go. Althea, pray take care of yourself."

Althea stared up at him, the inclination of her heart in her eyes. "I shall, Gareth. Pray come back safely," she said. Such inadequate, calmly said words. She hated herself for them.

Gareth forced himself to be circumspect. A show of passion now would startle and frighten her. "Althea . . ."

He started to tell her that he loved her, but he changed it to a promise that he would return. "I promise you, too, Althea, that we shall start again," he ended quietly.

Althea nodded, not daring to trust her voice. Tears were suspended in her throat.

Gareth turned and left her.

She stood staring after him until he had disappeared into the crowd of all those who were still streaming from the ballroom. Then Althea went to find Mademoiselle dePlier. The ladies left together.

Althea's carriage had difficulty making its way through the streets. Wagons, carts, and horses crowded the thoroughfares. Jostling soldiers carrying their weapons and knapsacks made their way quickly toward the Place Royale. Families walked with the soldiers. Sometimes it was the soldier's own wife and children or parents, but often enough it was the Belgian family with whom the soldier had been quartered accompanying him.

After Althea had deposited Mademoiselle dePlier and politely declined the offer of refreshment, she ordered her driver to take her to the Place Royale. At the outside of the square she had the carriage stop so that she could watch.

The Place Royale gave the appearance of being something out of a madman's dream. Soldiers were assembling from all parts of the town, carrying their weaponry and knapsacks. Some were saying good-bye to their wives and children, others to their fathers and mothers. Some just sat down on the sharp pavement to wait for their comrades. Others curled up on packs of straw and went to sleep. The din was deafening. Bat horses and baggage wagons were being loaded. The artillery and commissioned trains were harnessed. Carts clattered in from the country loaded high with vegetables. Officers rode in from all directions. Many of the officers were still in ballroom dress, not having taken time to do more than retrieve their horses and swords. Everywhere was the high strident sound of bugles and the rumble of drums. Over it all, the flags flew.

The seeming confusion straightened out as the troops began forming up. At two a.m., the troops started to march down the Rue de Namur out of Brussels. Althea was not alone in her desire to witness what was happening. Hundreds of spectators stood all around the Place Royale to watch the troops leave. Column upon column, seemingly unending, passed out of the great square.

About four o'clock in the morning, the first rays of the dawn slanted across the still-moving columns and lighted the pale faces of those who were being left behind. For four more hours, the spectators continued to stand and watch, until the last of the Allied forces had finally gone.

Althea asked to be driven back to the town house. When she

went inside, she slowly climbed the stairs, clutching the banister at each step. The dresser was waiting for her in the bedroom. Waiting only until her ball gown had been removed, Althea dropped down onto her bed. She fell instantly into a deep, exhausted sleep.

Chapter Twenty-four

On Friday, the sixteenth of June, the Duke of Wellington and his staff rode out of the Porte Namur. A crowd watched them go by. The duke was in great spirits. He gave his braying horse laugh and remarked, "Blucher has most likely settled the business himself by this time, so I should perhaps be back to dinner."

Accompanying the duke was Sir Thomas Picton, that gruff old soldier, mounted on his charger with his reconnoitering glass slung across his shoulders. He, too, was in the highest spirits and gaily hailed his friends as he rode past.

When the duke's entourage had passed out of the city, the crowd slowly separated and dispersed.

It was shortly before eight o'clock in the morning. The streets, which had been filled with busy crowds, were empty and silent. The great Place Royale, which had been filled with armed men, was now deserted. The heavy baggage wagons remained under the guard of a few sentinels and were ranged in orderly fashion, ready to be moved whenever required.

Only the farmers who had brought in their carts of vegetables for market occupied the great square. But this market day was unlike any other in memory. There was no one to buy. The Flemish drivers slept in the tilted carts.

The populace of Brussels was without news the better part of the day. Some officers could still be seen riding out of town to join the army, but there were none returning. Though anxiety abounded, no one really expected that there would be any action that day. The army would likely see hours and miles of marching before the enemy could be engaged.

It was awful not to see the familiar uniforms in the streets, at the cafés, or in the drawing rooms. It was as though the earth had opened up and swallowed the entire Allied force, leaving Brussels deserted and vulnerable. Despite the heaviness of dread and tension in the atmosphere, most tried to pretend that this Friday was like any other.

Althea had wakened late, heavy-eyed and with a trace of headache. With an effort she shook off her malaise of spirits. At her dresser's insistence, she nibbled on breakfast while still lying in bed. Then she rose, dressed, and went downstairs.

Having recalled that the Flemish farmers had come in for market day despite the momentous events of the night, she sent a footman around to the Place Royale with orders to buy strawberries. She would take a basket of the fresh fruit with her when she called on the dePliers that afternoon. She knew that Madame dePlier would enjoy the strawberries. She would describe to madame and Fleurette what she had seen at the Place Royale and how bravely the troops had marched out of the city.

Thus, Althea put order into her day. She pretended that all was as it should be when inside her there was a waiting feeling of dread. She was not alone in her apprehension. Every personage left in Brussels was just as subject to it.

When Althea returned home from her visit with the dePliers, she recalled that she was to dine with the Salyers at their home in the Park. She took particular care over her toilet, choosing a new confection of pale green muslin set off by yellow ribbons tied at the bodice and cap sleeves. Her reticule and her slippers were also yellow.

She was being dressed when there sounded a furious round of dull repercussions. Darcy's hands stilled. Althea and the dresser both listened tensely. The booming repeated with crackling rapidity.

"Dear Almighty God," whispered Darcy. " 'Tis the cannon, my lady."

Althea was white. She went to the window and looked out. Without turning around, she asked, "What o'clock is it, Darcy?"

The dresser glanced swiftly at the clock on the mantel. "It is close to the half-hour, my lady."

Althea continued to stare out of the window. She saw several individuals hurrying down the street toward the ramparts.

Quite clearly she could hear the cannonading. "Have the carriage brought around, Darcy. I shall not wait until five o'clock. I want to drive to the ramparts."

"Yes, my lady." The dresser scrambled out of the bedroom, calling for a servant. When she returned, she found her mistress still standing at the window. There was a strange expression on her ladyship's face. "Shall I finish doing up your gown, my lady?"

"Yes, of course." Althea swept away from the window and returned to her dresser's capable hands. When she was ready, a shawl covering her shoulders and her net reticule dangling from her wrist, she suddenly grasped the dresser's arm. From the frame of her smart bonnet, her eyes entreated. "Will you go with me, Darcy?"

"Of course, my lady," said Darcy staunchly. She went to get her bonnet and shawl.

The women went downstairs and got into the carriage. The driver took them to the Park, where he stopped the carriage so that they could get out and walk.

Althea and her companion went up onto the ramparts. Several people had already preceded them. All were looking out over the ramparts in a listening attitude. For a long time Althea and her dresser stood among strangers, listening to the cannonading. As evening drew on, the sound was perfectly distinct and regular.

At last Althea turned away. "I have heard enough, Darcy. Let us go home," she said quietly.

"But what of your engagement this evening, my lady?"

Althea looked at her dresser blankly. Comprehension slowly entered her eyes. "I had forgotten. How very stupid of me. I must go around and apologize to Mrs. Salyer."

When she arrived at her friends' address, it was to discover that her tardiness had gone completely unnoticed. Other guests had simply not shown up at all so that it was a rather meager company that had actually gathered. All were known to Althea and she exchanged greetings. There were two couples older than she, the younger Miss Orde, who had come with the Comstock ladies, and Mrs. May Salyer. Althea was surprised and touched by the eloquent glance of relief with which she was greeted by the new mother, who whispered, "You are steady in your nerves, which is just what we need, dear Althea."

Althea's puzzlement was quickly enlightened within moments of her arrival.

"My dear Lady Althea, I am so glad that you have come. We shall serve dinner directly, of course," said Mrs. Salyer, looking vaguely around as though she was uncertain.

"It is of no moment, dear ma'am. Pray, have you heard any news?" asked Althea, drawing off her gloves.

Mrs. Salyer wrung her hands. "That is what I am waiting upon, my lady. Mr. Salyer and my youngest son, Edward, set out on horseback some time ago. I am in an agony of apprehension, as you may imagine."

Althea caught the eyes of the hovering butler. "Perhaps a little tea might refresh us all while we wait."

The butler nodded, as though he was glad for direction, and departed. Mrs. May Salyer lay back on the sofa cushions and smiled. She turned to direct a light observation to Miss Comstock and Miss Orde. Althea turned her efforts to drawing out the older members of the party.

An hour later Mr. Salyer and his son returned. Mrs. Salyer at once started up with a small cry, her hands reaching out toward them. Mr. Salyer caught his wife's hands, reassuring her that they were quite safe.

Mrs. Salyer indicated the small company, most of whom had already arrived before their host had set off. She then drew Althea forward. "And here is Lady Lynley, who has been good enough to help me amuse our guests."

Mr. Salyer greeted Althea cordially. "I am glad that you could come this evening. Have you dined as yet?"

"We were waiting dinner upon your return, sir," said Althea, smiling. She nodded to Edward Salyer. He was fifteen, too young to have enlisted, and she was glad of it. She had seen too many young men march out of Brussels that morning, she thought.

Mr. Salyer nodded. "Good. We will get out of our dirt at once. But first I must tell you that we have returned no wiser than we were when we left. There are a thousand different stories, all contradicting. Some say that Blucher has been completely beaten; others, that he has won a resounding victory."

"Some say that the French left thirty thousand dead on the field. We were also told that same number was advancing upon Brussels," volunteered Edward Salyer.

There were murmurings in the company, accompanied by somber expressions. Mrs. Salyer clutched at her heart. "Dear merciful God. Could it be true?"

Her son shook his head in disgust. "You may judge the truth for yourself, Mama. Your opinion or mine or any other expressed in this room is as likely to be as accurate as anything we have heard."

"We heard also that our brave British troops are in full retreat," said Mr. Salyer quietly.

At once a roar of outrage broke from several people. "That is a damnable lie!" exclaimed one gentleman angrily.

"I do not believe *that*, at least!" said Althea sharply.

Mr. Salyer barked a laugh. "Nor I, my lady. Our fellows will never turn tail. They have never been beaten and I'll warrant that they will not be this day, either!"

The company applauded their host's ringing declaration. He called for wine to toast the patriotic sentiment and the victory of the Allies was toasted by the entire company. On that brave note, Mr. Salyer excused himself and he and Edward went upstairs to change.

A quarter hour later, Althea sat down to dinner with her friends. It was a well-prepared meal. A barley soup was removed by herbed eel, *moules et frites*, and thick-backed hare in brown gravy, served with new peas, buttered cabbage, and several other vegetables.

Though the talk earlier had been brave, there was such an undercurrent of tension that everyone at the table seemed peculiarly occupied by their own thoughts. All evening, nervous or irritable glances were thrown at the windows as the heavy pound of the cannonading continued.

The food might as well have been so much ash in Althea's mouth, for she remembered nothing of what she had eaten when presently she took leave of the Salyers and returned home. Darcy had also eaten, in the servants' quarters, but she could not have said either what she had consumed.

When they reached the town house, the dresser asked if she

was wanted, but Althea shook her head. "I shall do very well on my own tonight, Darcy. Do you go on to bed," she said.

"Very well, my lady." The dresser glanced toward the window. The dull concussions of the cannonading still sounded without. "I doubt that I shall be able to close my eyes."

"Yes, I know."

The dresser withdrew and left her mistress alone.

Althea did not go up to bed. Instead, she went back downstairs, preferring to sit in the drawing room with her embroidery. There was no possibility of sleep with the distant noise of the battle dinning in her ears.

About ten o'clock the heavy cannonade became fainter. Althea raised her head, listening, her gaze riveted on the mantel clock. The minutes ticked slowly away. Soon after the hour, the noise died entirely away. Althea drew in a ragged breath. She felt weak with thankfulness that the dread noise had stopped at last.

Still she did not retire. She hoped that someone would come to give her some news. Who might do so, she did not know. But surely one of her acquaintances would remember her and send someone if there was news of any kind.

The silence after the cannonading was oppressive. Her taunted nerves were such that she could scarcely bear to sit still any longer. After tangling her threads for the umpteenth time, Althea threw aside her embroidery hoop. For want of something better to do, she grasped the fire iron and stirred up the logs until flames and sparks leaped.

There was a banging upon the front door. Althea startled nearly out of her skin, dropping the fire iron with a clatter. Her glance flew to the mantel clock. It was close on eleven o'clock. She went quickly to the entrance of the drawing room.

The majordomo was coming up the hall from the back of the house. He had a pistol in his hand and he handled it quite capably.

Althea's gaze dropped to the pistol for a second, then her eyes rose to meet his cold gaze.

"Pray go back inside, my lady," said John Applegate quietly.

Without a word, Althea retreated into the drawing room and closed the door.

When he was certain that her ladyship was out of sight, John Applegate gestured to the waiting porter to unbar the front door.

The porter did so and warily cracked open the door. When he saw who stood on the step, he threw wide the door, exclaiming in gladness.

"Get out of the way, man!" snarled the majordomo. The pistol was up and poised in his fist.

The tall figure on the step gave a laugh. "I hope that you do not mean to shoot me, John. It would annoy me, when I have dodged French bullets all the bloody long day."

The majordomo bit back an exclamation and lowered the pistol. "My lord!" He stepped forward quickly, ordering the porter. "You! Go see to his lordship's horse! My lord, are you well?"

Lord Lynley stepped into the house. He was battered and bloody, but his eyes were alert. "I am well, John, never fear. Where is Lady Lynley?"

"In the drawing room, my lord," said John Applegate. He could see no wounds and with relief concluded that it was not his lordship's blood that had stained the torn uniform.

Lord Lynley strode swiftly down the hall. He turned suddenly. "John, let me know when it is midnight. I must return then."

"Very good, my lord." The majordomo hurried away, his thoughts already busy upon what he could do for his lordship.

Chapter Twenty-five

Lord Lynley thrust open the door. He stood quite still, his eyes devouring the sight of his wife.

Althea had started up when she saw him. Her face was perfectly pale. "I am glad you are come," she managed to say.

"The Duke of Brunswick and young Lord Hay are dead. I escorted their bodies into Brussels," said Gareth in abrupt explanation.

"Oh, dear God," breathed Althea, her hand rising to her throat. The carnage that had raged that day was brought home to her with those familiar names. She looked upon his uniform with horror. "Gareth, you are hurt!"

"No; it is not my blood. I am unscathed, thank God," he said. He shut the door behind him. "I must return to headquarters at midnight."

Althea's eyes flew to the mantel clock. She was dismayed. "So little time."

"Yes," he agreed.

Silence, taut and terrible, filled the space between them. Much had happened in the last two days. War had befallen them. Their world had been turned upside down. Those things that had separated them and that had seemed to be such unscalable walls now just faded away. They stood, shorn of pride, staring into one another's eyes.

They both knew that this might be the very last time that they ever saw one another. The knowledge shadowed Gareth's eyes. Althea knew that her own reflected the same uncertainty.

"Gareth . . ." she said on a whisper. Unbidden, her hand reached out toward him.

He took a quick step and snatched her hand to his lips. His

fingers crushed the bones in her hand, but she did not care. "God, Althea!" he exclaimed hoarsely.

Of a sudden, not knowing how she had gotten there, Althea was in his arms. His arms were iron bands that bruised her ribs. Their lips met hungrily, fervently, greedily. Althea felt his hands rough on her body, pulling her into intimacy against him. She reached up to pull him closer, her fingers entwining into his hair, and her mouth opened under the demanding assault of his.

Gareth lifted her into his arms and took a few unsteady steps. They tumbled down onto the settee.

There was no finesse, no pretty lovemaking. They came together frantically, desperately. The consummation was explosive.

Afterward, there was only the mingled harshness of their shortened breathing and the inexorable tick of the mantel clock.

Gareth's body pressed her into the settee. Althea's arms clasped him tightly against her breast. He shifted, his weight lifting. But he did not rise. Instead, he tucked her comfortably against his side, her head resting upon his shoulder. "I never thought to love a woman so thoroughly," he said hoarsely.

Althea smoothed the soiled fabric of his uniform coat. "I am glad that it was I." She raised her head so that she could look into his eyes. "I am glad, Gareth," she repeated emphatically.

With one hand he brought her face close and kissed her slowly, lingeringly. Then against her forehead, he murmured, "I must go soon."

"Yes."

They listened to the steady, unending tick of the clock that marked the all-too-fleeting minutes.

"Althea, if I am killed . . ."

Hastily she put her fingers over his lips, stilling the words. "I shall return for a time to Chard, Gareth. Until I am certain. But do not ask more of me now. It does not bear thinking of."

He sat up, raising her with him. "We shall not speak of it, then. But you must listen to me in this. If the battle turns against us, the city will be overrun. No, you *must* listen! If the need arises, John is sworn to see you to safety. There are funds in the strongbox inside my wardrobe. You are to take them and make your way to Antwerp. There you will be able to buy passage for yourself, for Darcy, and for John."

"John will see me to the coast. But he will almost certainly return for you," said Althea, quite certain of the henchman's loyalty to his master.

Gareth shook his head impatiently, as though he could not quite grasp the significance of what she had said or simply because it was at that point irrelevant. "You must promisee me to do as I ask, Althea. I will be easier in my mind for it."

"You have my word." Althea laid her hand gently alongside his roughened jaw. It struck her as incongruous that Gareth, always so immaculate, was unshaven. "You must take your razor," she said unthinkingly.

Gareth laughed, his whole countenance lighting up all at once. He caught up both her hands in his and turned them so that he could kiss her palms.

There was an urgent knock at the door. They looked at one another, appalled.

Gareth leaped up from the settee, calling out, "One moment." He quickly rearranged his clothing.

Althea stood and straightened her gown, unsuccessfully smoothing the skirt which was wrinkled beyond repair. She sat down again. Hoping that she looked half-decent, she looked up to meet her husband's amused gaze. He now stood posed against the mantel, looking for all the world bored with the world. She started to chuckle. "We are a degenerate pair," she whispered.

He grinned and called out, "Enter!"

The door opened and John Applegate entered. He cast a swift glance from his master to his mistress. If he guessed what had so recently transpired, he kept such conjectures out of his expression. He focused firmly on Lord Lynley. "My lord, there is a messenger without. Your presence is urgently required."

"This is it, then." Gareth stepped away from the mantel. Althea rose and went into his arms. His kiss was strong and reassuring. Then he gently, reluctantly, set her aside. He smiled into her eyes and strode out of the room.

The majordomo followed him. "My lord, I have rather

hastily put together a basket of food and two bottles of wine. I am sorry there was not time to do more."

"Bless you, man," said Lord Lynley simply and gratefully, accepting the basket. He reached out with his other hand and grasped the majordomo's shoulder in a tight grip. "You gave me your word, John. Remember that."

"Aye, my lord. I will see her ladyship to safety if need be, never fear," said John Applegate.

Lord Lynley nodded. He turned on his heel and swept out of the house to where the porter was guarding his horse. He swung into the saddle, spoke briefly to the waiting messenger, and then put spurs to his mount.

After Gareth's departure, Althea went up to bed. She was anxious still, but she was peculiarly happy as well. She knew now that Gareth loved her.

She found that Darcy had not gone to bed, but instead had simply lain down in her dress on top of her mattress.

"Oh, Darcy! You should have tried to rest," said Althea.

"Never you mind about me, my lady. It is you who ought to take more care," said the dresser tartly.

Althea gave a tremulous laugh. "We shall each nag at the other, then. I shall rest if you promise to do the same."

" 'Tis impossible, but all the same you have my word," said Darcy, sighing.

Darcy had just undressed her mistress when suddenly they heard the rapid rolling of heavy carriages in long succession. Doors banged open. Loud cries and frightened exclamations rose outside in the street.

Althea threw on a wrapper and hurried to throw open the window. Darcy was right at her elbow. The noise came from the direction of the Place Royale. Faster and faster, louder and louder. They listened for some minutes in silence, their faces tense, their hearts racing.

There was a knock on the bedroom door. Althea turned sharply. "Enter!"

The door was opened by John Applegate. "Begging your pardon, my lady. I have been to the Place Royale. I thought you might wish to know what is happening. The artillery is leaving the town."

"What are they saying?" Althea waved one hand toward the window. "I cannot make it all out."

"A panic has broken out, my lady. Some are saying that a large body of French have been seen advancing through the woods to take Brussels and that they are only a half an hour away. The Belgians are shouting that the English are in full retreat," said the majordomo.

"Dear God Almighty," murmured Darcy.

John Applegate shook his head. "It cannot be true, for I saw with my own eyes that the artillery is advancing. Do you understand, my lady? *The artillery is going up to the field.* It is *not* retreating out of Brussels."

"Thank you, John. You have greatly relieved our minds. We shall be able to sleep now," said Althea.

The majordomo grinned at her for the first time. His cold eyes had even warmed a trifle. "That's the ticket, my lady. We'll not be leaving Brussels just yet."

"No, John, we will not," said Althea, her own smile tremulous.

A look of perfect, unexpected understanding passed between her and the majordomo. He backed out and softly closed the door.

"Will you really be able to sleep, my lady?" asked the dresser.

"I think that we must, Darcy. For there may be few opportunities for rest later," said Althea composedly.

The dresser regarded with sheer amazement the cool strength in her mistress's expression. "Yes, my lady," she falteringly agreed.

The dresser returned to her room and Althea lay down on her bed. Althea did not go to sleep for some time. Later, she was even unsure that she had done so at all. But she was fitfully dozing when she was jerked upright by loud hammering on the front door below. Incoherent shouting accompanied the frightening noise. There was the clatter of hoofbeats and the rumbling of carts in the streets.

The dresser hurried into the bedroom. She had thrown a shawl over her shoulders. Her dress was badly wrinkled because she had not put it off. Dark circles underlay her eyes. "My lady! You must get up and dress at once!"

Althea did as she was bid. She shot a fleeting glance at the mantel clock. It was 5:30 a.m. "What is happening, Darcy?"

The dresser's fingers were trembling as she did up the last of the buttons on Althea's dress. "The French are said to be entering the city!"

Althea swept around, casting a shawl about her shoulders. "Where is John Applegate?"

"I-I do not know," said Darcy.

Althea ran out of the bedroom and out onto the landing. She grasped the banister until her knuckles whitened. Her eyes fell on a footman standing below in the entry hall. "You! Where is John Applegate?" She started quickly down the stairs.

The footman shrugged, turning out his hands helplessly. "He is not here, my lady. There was pounding on the door. He ran outside and he has not returned."

Althea stood quite still in the entry hall, thinking furiously. The dresser came up beside her.

"My lady, what are we to do?" asked Darcy, clutching the ends of her shawl tightly.

"Do? We will wait for John Applegate to return," said Althea. At the dresser's half-formed protest, she snapped. "I said that we will wait for John's return! While we do so, we will prepare to leave this house. We will need food, wine, blankets, bait for the horses. See to it, man. Darcy, pack nothing that is frivolous. There will not be room for much baggage."

Their expressions relieved that they had been given something to do, the footman and the dresser hurried off. Althea went in search of the housekeeper. She would need to see about closing the house should they be forced to flee, and the housekeeper had charge of the keys.

After much searching, Althea found the housekeeper hiding in the linen closet. The woman's apron was thrown over her head and she was moaning as she rocked back and forth. At Althea's touch, the woman screeched and began screaming for mercy.

Servants came running from all directions. None of Althea's pleas or her attempts to soothe the housekeeper did the least good. The woman's hysteria was uncontrollable. Althea saw the white-eyed glances that were beginning to be tossed among the other servants. Fear was taking hold.

Althea narrowed her eyes. She could not have unreasoning panic set in. Sharply, she slapped the housekeeper. The mewling screams stopped on the instant. She gestured to the two shocked housemaids. "You! Take her to her room. Her nerves are overwrought. She must rest."

The maids did as they were bid, looking askance at Althea as they edged past her. They took hold of the softly crying housekeeper by the arms and, murmuring encouragements, they led her away.

The chef bowed deeply in respect to the mistress of the house. Then he turned and shooed the kitchen staff back to their interrupted duties.

The footman that had been entrusted with Althea's instructions had returned. "My lady, the horses have been put to the carriage and those things which you ordered have been placed inside. Do you wish to leave now?"

"Have you seen John Applegate?" Althea demanded.

The footman shook his head.

"I will stay. Summon the household, please," said Althea.

When all of the servants, with the exception of the housekeeper, had come together in the entry hall, Althea stepped up onto the bottom step so that she could be seen and turned to face them.

"We have heard dire reports this morning. I have ordered a carriage made ready in the event that these reports are true," she said.

Murmurings rose from the servants. Althea raised her voice. "I am staying in this house. But if there are any among you who wish to leave, you may do so. I know that most of you have family for whom you are apprehensive. They will be fearing for you, as well. It is best that you are together if, indeed, we must all flee Brussels."

The servants glanced at one another. None seemed anxious to speak up. The chef snorted suddenly. He stepped forward. "I stay," he stated flatly, his head held proudly. The new footman, his nephew, threw back his shoulders and also stepped forward.

Althea's eyes glittered with tears as one by one most of the servants stepped up to add their number to those who had chosen to remain. "Thank you. Thank you all," she whispered.

It was then that the front door was thrust open and John Applegate stood on the threshold. He regarded the stupefied expressions of the faces that had turned toward him with a glare. "What is this door doing unbarred, pray?" he barked.

The porter started forward with abject apologies. The majordomo slammed shut the door and roundly cuffed the servant. The porter accepted this rough treatment stoically and set about barring the door.

"John! What have you found out?" demanded Althea, stepping down from the stair.

The majordomo shook his head, disgust showing in every line of his face. "It was but a panicked troop of foreign cavalry, my lady, galloping through La Montagne de la Cour at full speed and yelling at the top of their lungs that they were pursued by Boney himself. The whole town took fright, of course!"

"But what of the wagons we heard?" asked Althea.

"The fear set off those with the carts and the baggage wagons in the Place Royale. The square is deserted now." John Applegate pretended not to notice that the servants were still hovering about with their ears open, but he raised his voice slightly. "As for the French being in town, it is no such thing!"

Expressions all around relaxed and the servants slowly left the entry hall, discussing the newest false alarm.

"I am glad. I had some things put into the carriage and the horses readied. I suppose that I was a bit beforehand," said Althea.

The majordomo regarded her unsmilingly. "Not at all, my lady. It was an excellent decision. I will go out to the stables and see that the horses are put away, but I think that we will leave the carriage just as it is."

Althea looked at him for a moment. "Then you are saying that we may have to flee at a moment's notice."

"No, I am not saying that, my lady. But it is always best to be prepared," said John Applegate.

Chapter Twenty-six

The majordomo bowed and left for the stables. Althea had turned to go back upstairs to help Darcy with the packing when there sounded a knock at the front door. The porter glanced toward her questioningly. Althea nodded. The man opened the door and Mademoiselle dePlier entered.

"Fleurette! Pray come in," said Althea, going forward at once with her hands outstretched.

Mademoiselle dePlier met her in the middle of the entry hall. She reached up on her tiptoes to kiss Althea on the cheek. "My dear friend. I have come to ask a favor of you, Althea."

"Why, you may have anything you wish. Come into the drawing room. I will send for tea to warm you, for I know it is still cool this morning," Althea said, leading her visitor into the drawing room. Althea remained at the door long enough to ask the footman to relay her request for hot tea before she joined her friend. "Pray be seated, Fleurette. You know that you do not need to stand on ceremony with me."

Mademoiselle dePlier sat down and drew off her gloves. She reached into her reticule while she spoke. "I have brought you something to read, Althea. It will explain much. But first I must tell you that the wounded started arriving in the city last night."

With a startled look, Althea took the sheet that Mademoiselle dePlier had taken from her reticule. Althea saw that it was a proclamation published by the mayor of Brussels, Baron Vanderlinden d'Hooghvoorst. She perused it quickly and looked up. "A hospital established! And they are asking for mattresses or palliasses. Is it already so bad?"

"I have been there this morning. It is worse. You see that the major makes an appeal for all sorts of linens and blankets and lint. It is all to be deposited with the parish priests. I am acting for my parish. I am asking everyone I know to send with me what they can," said Mademoiselle dePlier.

"Of course I shall help! I was just going upstairs. You must come with me and take whatever you need from the linens and blankets," said Althea, rising to her feet. "We shall go up at once."

Arm in arm the ladies left the drawing room. Althea requested that the remaining footman follow them as they went up the stairs. Althea threw wide the door to the linen closet and invited her friend to take whatever she wished. The footman was soon loaded down and Mademoiselle dePlier instructed him to deposit the sheets, blankets, and bolsters inside the carriage that she had left waiting for her in the street.

Darcy came up just as the ladies were turning to go back downstairs. "Begging your pardon, my lady, but I was wondering what to do with those things that we shan't be able to carry away with us."

"Simply leave them where they are, Darcy."

"But if the house is looted, my lady—"

"It will not matter as long as we are well away before it happens," said Althea with a quick smile.

Mademoiselle dePlier frowned a little, but she said nothing until she and Althea had returned to the drawing room. A pot of hot tea had been brought in and the ladies poured for themselves. Mademoiselle dePlier tasted the tea, appreciating the bitter warmth because it had been in truth a chilly morning. Then she set down the cup. "Althea, I could not but overhear. Are you preparing to leave Brussels?"

"I am preparing to do so, yes. Whether I actually set out remains to be seen," said Althea. She leaned forward to place her hand on her friend's knee. "I would never do so without first saying good-bye to you and your mother."

Mademoiselle dePlier nodded, smiling fleetingly. *"Oui,* I know. I will tell you why I am curious. Many English fled yesterday to Antwerp."

"Well, I am staying until I have heard which way the battle has gone," said Althea.

"Some of those wounded who have come in this morning are French prisoners," said Mademoiselle dePlier.

Althea stared at her, attempting to grasp the implications. "Then . . . Oh, Fleurette, does it mean we have won?"

Mademoiselle dePlier shook her head. "I do not believe so. Not yet, for the wounded talked of the battle being renewed this morning. We must continue to pray, Althea."

"Yes, of course," said Althea, wondering if her prayers would do any good. She had never given much thought to God. Would He have given any thought to her? Yet at such a time as this perhaps every prayer, no matter by whom it was said, was needed.

Mademoiselle dePlier pulled on her gloves. "I must go now. I have many doors to knock on this morning, but I wished to call first on you." She rose to her feet and, as Althea also stood up, Mademoiselle dePlier embraced her. There was a smile in her dark brown eyes. "You must come to us if you need anything, Althea. I think of you as my sister, you see."

Althea felt tears start to her eyes. "I promise you that I shall." She saw Mademoiselle dePlier out. When she turned away from the front door, which the porter closed and carefully barred, Althea glanced thoughtfully around the well-appointed entry hall. It seemed terribly stupid to simply sit about waiting when she could be doing something useful like her young friend.

The majordomo was returning from the back of the house. On impulse Althea called to him. "John, may I have a word with you?"

John Applegate followed her into the drawing room. Althea closed the door and turned toward him. "John, I wish to be doing something."

He frowned at her as though uncomprehending. "What do you mean, my lady?"

Althea gestured impatiently. "There must be something that I can do to help. Surely you heard or saw something while you were out? I do not want to spend the day hiding in the house waiting for the news."

The majordomo frowned, pulling down the corners of his mouth. "It would not be wise for you to go out, my lady."

"Nevertheless, I believe that I shall. I mean to call upon the Comstocks," said Althea, opening the door.

"My lady, you should know that I have put a guard on the

stable. Horses are as precious as gold in this city, and as rare. If you drive to the Comstock house, I must insist that an armed servant accompany you to guard the team from thieves," said John Applegate.

"But Mademoiselle dePlier did not seem overly concerned," said Althea, slightly alarmed on her friend's behalf.

The majordomo smiled almost sourly. "You did not look out to see the burly man on the box nor the horse pistol in his hand, my lady."

Althea shook her head. "It is scarcely believable."

"Just so, my lady."

Althea went upstairs to put on her pelisse and bonnet. Her dresser was unexpectedly outspoken about Althea's intentions.

"You have no business cavorting about the streets, my lady," said Darcy, visibly upset. She smoothed a wrinkle out of the skirt of the pelisse.

"I am not going to cavort, Darcy. I am merely going to call upon the Comstocks. You need not accompany me if you are so nervous. I shall understand, I assure you," said Althea, tying the ribbons of her bonnet under her chin.

"Aye, and wouldn't I be the proper maid if I sent you off alone," said Darcy bitterly, bowing to the inevitable. She flounced off to get her bonnet and a wrap.

Althea laughed, making certain first that her dresser was not within hearing. Her spirits were lightened and not even the sight of one of her stalwart footmen with a pistol thrust into his belt and sitting up beside her driver had the power to dim them.

Althea was sobered, however, before ever her carriage reached its destination. Mademoiselle dePlier had told her that the wounded had started to come in during the night, but she had neglected to say that they were on every hand.

Wagons filled with broken and bloodied men rolled past. The streets were filled with pitiful, even horrifying sights. The dead bodies of those that had simply dropped lay on the sidewalks and in the road. Here and there, weeping families had gathered about their loved one who was lost to them, and Althea suddenly recalled how Gareth had described just such scenes to her. How long ago that seemed now and how naive she had been.

The wounded that were still on their feet shuffled forward, their clothes bloodstained and ragged, their faces white and exhausted. Althea saw residents come out of their houses and stop the men, to lead or carry them indoors. "Darcy, I had no notion," said Althea, breathing deeply. The sight of so much blood and suffering made her stomach rebel.

The dresser did not reply and Althea turned toward her. Darcy had put a handkerchief over her mouth and tears streamed down her face. Althea took hold of her dresser's hand and they sat that way, mistress and maid, their hands clasped, for the remainder of the drive.

At the Comstocks', Althea was warmly welcomed. She was dismayed and surprised to learn that Mrs. Comstock and Charity were not at home, but Mr. Comstock assured her that they must return before many more minutes had passed. She was borne off to the drawing room by her host while Darcy went her way to the servants' hall.

Mr. Comstock was full of news. "George Sanderson came in last night on errands for the general and was able to visit with us briefly. He told us of the battle. The British were attacked by overwhelming odds and under every possible geographical disadvantage, but our troops completely repulsed the enemy and remained masters of the field! What do you think of that, my lady?"

"It is wonderful, indeed," said Althea, but in her mind's eye she was once more seeing the wounded that she had passed on the way in. "I was told, however, that another bitter battle will be fought today."

Mr. Comstock nodded. "George said that the duke expected the attack to be renewed this morning. But our forces are now collected and they are joined by both the artillery and the cavalry, so that this engagement will be more decisive still."

"You said joined by the cavalry? Were they not engaged yesterday?" asked Althea sharply.

Mr. Comstock looked grave. "Most of them were not, having gone up at the close of the action. The British infantry bore the brunt of the enemy's cavalry as well as their infantry the whole day."

"Dear God," breathed Althea, horrified.

"It was a nasty business, of course. But our fellows managed," said Mr. Comstock.

At that moment the drawing room door opened and the ladies of the house entered. Miss Comstock rushed to greet their visitor. "Althea! I recognized your carriage downstairs and came directly in. Oh, you will not believe me when I tell you what we have been doing this morning. She will not, will she, Mama?"

"No, indeed! We have been at the church scraping lint and making cherry water to be used for those poor unfortunate young men. Mr. Comstock, we must go back almost immediately. We have only come home for a moment so that we might tell you. There is such a need for bandages and other things that there is no keeping up with it," said Mrs. Comstock.

"Of course you must go back," said Mr. Comstock gravely. "Pray do not forget that we have two wounded upstairs. They will be wanting tea and soup presently."

"You must have the maids see to it," said Mrs. Comstock. "Those boys are the fortunate ones, having only the slightest of injuries. I have seen such sights this day that I shall never forget. I held a young man's head in my lap as he died. I was never more affected than when he thanked me for the little bit of cherry water which I gave him."

"Perhaps Charity should not be allowed to accompany you," said Mr. Comstock, frowning.

"Oh no, Papa! You cannot forbid me, pray! What if one of them is George and there is no one to give him water or to care for his wounds? Papa, I cannot stay here thinking of that," said Miss Comstock.

"Charity, have you been tending the wounded?" Althea asked, shocked.

Her friend looked at her, surprised at the question. "Of course. At least, we had started to do so when we decided to come home and let Papa know that he need not worry about us. There are a great number of ladies who are doing the same."

"I shall go with you, Charity. I have wanted something useful to do and this will suit admirably," said Althea. "Only let me inform Darcy and I shall be ready."

The dresser was horrified by her mistress's intent. "What would his lordship say if he knew, my lady?"

Althea laughed, shaking her head. "He would not be the least surprised, Darcy. He knows that I must have my head."

Althea sent her dresser home in the carriage with a message to John Applegate, informing the majordomo of her whereabouts. The Comstocks would see that she returned safely home.

Althea had been shocked and subdued by the sights that she had already seen. But when she accompanied the Comstocks to the Place Royale, which had been made over into a huge bivouac for the wounded, she was stunned. The wounded lay any which way on pallets or piles of straw, if they were fortunate, and on the rough paving stones if they were not. Shattered limbs and gaping wounds abounded upon all sides. A low collective moan filled the air as the wounded called for water or mumbled in pain.

Mrs. Comstock had had the forethought to bring a huge turret of thin soup. She proceeded to dispense the lukewarm liquid, cup by careful cup, to the parched and helpless soldiers.

Althea and Miss Comstock moved through the raggedly defined rows, cleaning and bandaging those injuries that they could, trying to make more comfortable the sufferers. Other ladies also worked among the wounded, indefatigably and as swift as they could.

As many wounded as possible were gotten inside. Every house in the city opened its doors. But still the wounded were carried in from the battlefield. The dead were mixed with the living. There was a sea of faces and Althea had stopped looking at any one of them as a separate entity.

However, as her gaze chanced to fall on one young soldier who had died, she looked back quickly. Her brain fumbled. Numbly she realized that she was looking at Harry Salyer, who had just days before become the father of the newest Salyer.

Althea sank down to the pavement and cried then. She cried for them all. She cried because somewhere in that horrible place, or perhaps somewhere else, Gareth could also be dead.

That afternoon the sky had turned black. Suddenly a violent thunderstorm cracked and crashed overhead. Cries of warning rose on all sides that the wounded must be moved. Before much could be done, however, it was too late. The skies opened and torrents of rain sluiced down. The wounded that lay out in the open square and those who tried to tend them were instantly drenched. There was nothing that could be done to shelter the poor soldiers and they lay stoically enduring.

Althea was dragged to her feet by her arm. Her straw bonnet was a sodden shambles. She turned up her face, the misery plain in her expression, and met John Applegate's unreadable eyes.

"It is time to go home, my lady," said the majordomo.

Althea nodded. She was too weary to protest. But she gestured down at poor dead Harry Salyer. "Bring him, please, John. It is the Salyer's son. We must take him home to his family."

The majordomo glanced down. His face wooden, he bent and lifted the body. Without a word, he turned and walked away with Harry Salyer cradled in his arms, leaving his mistress to come as best she could.

Althea lifted her soaked skirt and docilely followed John Applegate through the rain and the wounded to the waiting carriage.

At the town house, Althea went directly upstairs. She was shaking with cold and her teeth were chattering. Darcy stripped the wet things from her mistress and bundled her directly into bed after running a hot warming pan between the sheets.

"And you are to stay there, my lady!" she ordered sharply.

Althea gave a thin laugh and turned over and went to sleep.

Chapter Twenty-seven

It rained all night. When Althea awakened, she learned from Darcy that John Applegate had asked to see her as soon as possible. Fearing the worst, Althea rose immediately and dressed. She passed swiftly downstairs to the drawing room, where the majordomo awaited her.

He bowed. "My lady, there have been many reports while you slept. Terror and confusion are rife in the streets." He briefly studied her face. He was satisfied with what he saw. Her ladyship was not one to get all in a flutter. "It has become known that the Duke of Wellington fell back on the town of Waterloo yesterday afternoon. The Belgians are convinced that the duke's retreat means that the Allies have been put to flight and they expect at any time that the army will run into the city hotly pursued by the French."

Althea grasped the back of the chair. Her face was pale. "What are you trying to convey to me, John? Have we lost, then?"

The majordomo's visage was grim, even a little savage. "No, it does not mean that. However, it is time for a decision. Great numbers set off for Antwerp last night, those who were without horses determined to walk the thirty miles. Others took to the boats in the canal. We still have horses, safely under guard. Shall I have them hitched to the carriage, my lady?"

Silence, but for the ticking of the mantel clock.

"It was your promise to see me safely to the coast if the situation warranted," said Althea finally. She was looking closely at the majordomo's face for a clue to his thoughts.

"Yes, my lady."

"I do not think that you wish to leave," said Althea slowly.

By a slight widening of his eyes, she knew that she was right. She straightened. "Very well, John. We shall stay."

John Applegate permitted himself a smile. "Thank you, my lady. I will be leaving shortly, but I have left instructions with the footman. I am unhappy to inform you, my lady, that three of our staff have deserted us."

Althea brushed aside the reference to the diminished household. "Where are you going, John?" She did not need to be told. It was in his eyes. "You are going to look for his lordship. I am going with you."

"My lady, you cannot!" exclaimed the majordomo. "It is not safe, especially not for a female."

"I ride better than many men. You will give me a pistol. I shall go up to change into my habit," said Althea, moving toward the drawing room door. She turned back, her eyes very bright and hard, to say, "And if you leave without me, I am perfectly capable of setting out on my own."

She was followed out of the room by a bitten-off curse.

When Althea returned downstairs and went out to the stable, John Applegate was waiting, already astride a horse. He held the reins to Althea's saddled mare. From the instant he caught sight of her, he began arguing the inadvisability of her going. Althea mounted and gathered the reins. "Give over, do, John. You shan't change my mind."

The majordomo muttered something, but fell into reluctant silence. Althea and the majordomo left the stable and rode down the street. Before they had gone more than a few blocks, a man rushed down the steps of a town house and seized the bridle of Althea's horse. The horse snorted, jibing in agitation.

"Let go this instant!" Althea exclaimed sharply, attempting to free her horse.

The man paid no attention. He reached up to catch hold of her habit and started to pull her down off the back of the horse. Althea slashed her assailant across the face with her whip and he cringed, but he did not let go.

John Applegate turned his horse to come around in front. He smashed a pistol butt down upon the man's head. The man's eyes rolled up in his head and he crumpled to the ground. The majordomo shook his head. "A desperate thief, indeed. He'll waken with a bit of the headache. Come, my lady. We must be off."

Shaken more than she wished to admit, Althea gathered her reins and put spur to her mount. She rode close to John Applegate as they left the city behind them.

Althea had never seen such a mass of confusion as that which greeted her eyes when she saw the road that led to Waterloo. It was practically impassable. Woods bounded the road on both sides. Baggage wagons and carts had been overturned or driven up the embankments into the trees. Horses were still tangled in their traces. Wounded and dead were everywhere. Officers, infantrymen, and civilians were all trying to pass in one direction or the other. The enormity of their task burst upon her. "John, what are we to do?" she asked faintly.

"We go on, my lady," said the majordomo.

They had just put their horses into motion, when a hoarse voice hailed them. "Lady Althea! For pity's sake, stop!"

Althea looked around, startled. At first she did not recognize the smoke-blackened and bloodied figure that came limping up to her, leading by the reins a lamed horse. Then her eyes widened. "Gaston! You are alive!"

The Belgian laughed, his white teeth flashing. He sketched a weaving bow. "As you see, my lady. And not only myself." He pulled on the reins, turning the horse. An inert officer was bent over the saddle, his wrists tied around the horse's neck. A filthy bandage wrapped his head.

Althea stared, her breath suspended. She was freed from her frozen amazement by the majordomo's hoarse cry. "Gareth! It is Lynley, John!"

The majordomo had thrown himself off his horse. He touched the viscount's shoulder gently, but Lord Lynley merely uttered a low groan. "He is wounded, my lady."

"We must get him home." Althea reached down to take the reins of the lamed horse from Gaston dePlier. He smiled up at her, somewhat wanly. Althea easily read his expression. She said softly, "You dear fool, Gaston. I shall not leave you behind." Straightening, she said, "John, help Baron dePlier up to ride with you."

The majordomo had remounted and now he held down a hand. Gaston dePlier grasped it and swung up behind the majordomo. The Belgian sighed with profound weariness. The majordomo said roughly, to cover his very real concern, "Don't you let go, sir. I would have to leave you otherwise."

"Do not be concerned for me, my friend," said Gaston dePlier. "I may sleep, but I will not fall."

The small cavalcade returned slowly to Brussels. Althea kept glancing back to satisfy herself that Gareth was still in the saddle. She had no inkling how badly he was hurt, but he was alive and she was taking him home. That was all that mattered.

They reached the town house without incident. Gaston dePlier practically toppled off the horse. He sagged against the rough wall of the stable for several moments as though he had not the strength to stand. Exhaustion carved deep lines in his face.

John Applegate cast the Belgian a glance. He was cutting the rope that had kept Lord Lynley on the lamed horse. "Let me but get his lordship upstairs, sir, and I will be back to help you."

"Nonsense. I will do well enough on my own. Just take care of Lynley. He has been through more than I," said Gaston dePlier. He had forced himself upright and now pushed himself away from the stable wall.

"Go right in, Gaston. Tell whomever you see that you are to be given food and a bed," said Althea. She had braced herself to help catch Lord Lynley's weight as John eased the unconscious man out of the saddle.

Gaston dePlier did not reply, but simply did as he was bid.

John took his lordship's full weight. "I've got him, my lady. Let's get him upstairs to his bed."

The advent of the master of the house was greeted with a general outcry of concern. Althea spurned all urgings to relinquish the burden of Lord Lynley's weight to another. "John Applegate and I have him firm. Darcy, the bed!" Darcy ran ahead to fling down the covers of his lordship's bed and prepare water and clean cloths for cleaning the wounds.

It was difficult to work his lordship's dead weight out of his torn and bloodied clothing and boots. Althea feared that the inevitable mauling would give pain to Gareth, but the necessity of the operation was undeniable.

In a very short time, Lord Lynley was between the sheets of

his own bed. He had not regained consciousness, though his eyelids had fluttered momentarily and he had groaned something.

Althea and the majordomo soon discovered that besides the injury to his head, Lord Lynley had sustained a grave wound to the hip. They bathed the gaping wound and bound it as best they could. Without a word, Darcy took away the bowl of bloodied water and cloths. The maid's departure went unnoticed by Althea and the majordomo.

"We'll need a doctor to him, my lady. I suspect there's a bit of shrapnel still in that, and as ugly and swollen as it is, I wouldn't want to try digging it out myself," said John Applegate.

"No, indeed," agreed Althea, shuddering. She looked down at her husband's feverish face and brushed back a lock of his tumbled hair. "Will you go find one, John?" At her touch, Gareth moved his head fretfully and muttered something unintelligible.

"You do not need to ask, my lady. I will turn out every building in this city," said the majordomo fiercely, and left the bedroom.

Althea poured more water and wrung a cloth in its coolness. She bathed Gareth's heated, filthy face. It seemed to ease him a little, for he sighed and lay quieter.

Althea pulled a chair over close to the bed. She sat down and clasped Gareth's hand between her own. His skin felt hot and dry, and she wondered anxiously whether his fever would mount.

Her fears were realized. As Gareth's fever rose, he began to thrash around on the bed, muttering and calling out disjointed words. Althea did her best to quiet him by bathing his face often, but the grip of the fever and his nightmarish memories of the battle would not be contained. Once, he started up on his elbow to stare through her, horror writ in his unseeing eyes. Althea tried to ease him back down. Gareth gave a hoarse cry and flailed out, the back of his wrist striking hard against her cheek. Tears started to her eyes, but Althea did not abandon the unequal struggle. "Darcy!"

The maid ran in and exclaimed at the sight of her mistress fighting to keep the wounded man in his bed. It was only with the combined efforts of the two women that Lord Lynley was forced back down onto his heated pillows. The struggle appeared to have exhausted him and he lay quiescent, his breathing harsh and shallow. A white line etched his mouth.

"We cannot be having this, my lady," panted Darcy, pushing back a loose strand of hair. "He'll tear open the wound and start it to bleeding again."

"I know." Althea raised frightened eyes to the maid's grim face. "It's the fever, Darcy. What are we to do? John Applegate went out for a physician more than an hour since, and he has not yet returned."

"Drat the man." Darcy compressed her lips, thinking. "Let me go downstairs to look over the household apothecaries, my lady. Perhaps there will be a packet of fever powder."

"Yes, do that," agreed Althea, relieved that there was something constructive to be tried. "I shall stay here."

"I will send up someone to help you, my lady, if his lordship should become restless again," said Darcy, exiting at once.

Not too many minutes later a servantman entered the bedroom and took up his post at the door. Althea glanced around and vaguely recognized him as one of the kitchen help. She offered a wan, preoccupied smile.

Within a short time Darcy returned, triumphantly bearing the hoped-for packet. Lord Lynley was made to swallow the powder, not without difficulty, but enough to satisfy Darcy that he had gotten a decent dose. "That should do the trick," said the maid with relief. "You should go rest, my lady. Jacques and I will watch his lordship."

Althea shook her head. "No, Darcy. There are others to attend. I will stay. I want to be here when John Applegate returns or-or his lordship wakens." She tried to smile. "I shall manage, never fear."

"Very good, my lady." Darcy left the bedroom, bearing the servantman off with her. She glanced back just before closing the door.

Lady Althea was once more sitting in the chair beside the bed, Lord Lynley's hand clasped between her own.

There she remained until a few hours later when John Applegate returned with the doctor.

At the doctor's request, Althea left so that she would not

hinder the man in doing his job by fainting or some such thing. Althea waited an anxious half hour before she was joined by the doctor in the drawing room. She jumped up at once. "How is he, sir?"

The doctor's face was drawn with fatigue. He had not seen food or bed for two days; therefore he spoke impatiently. "His lordship is a fortunate man. I was able to extract all the shrapnel. Barring gangrene, the wound should heal very nicely. As for his head, I suspect that he'll be concussed for several days. Your man is sitting with Lord Lynley now." The doctor's sharp eyes studied Althea's strained face. "My suggestion is rest for all, my lady. I bid you good day."

Althea went up to Gareth's room. She went in quietly. Waving back the majordomo when he would have risen to his feet, she said softly, "Send Darcy in to me if he begins to waken, John. I am going to lie down for an hour."

"I shall do so, my lady."

Althea left and entered her own bedroom. She lay down on her bed, intending only to doze. Instead, she was quickly fast asleep.

She was roused some time later when Darcy shook her shoulder. "My lady, his lordship is asking for you."

Althea bolted up from the bed and ran to Gareth's room. She stopped just inside the door, suddenly afraid. Suppose that he had forgotten what he had said to her. Suppose it had just been the passion of the moment.

But then he turned his head and smiled at her. There was exhaustion in his haggard face, and pain. But his eyes were tender. "Althea." He lifted his hand scant inches above the blankets.

She went to him then and fell to her knees beside him, clutching his hand to her face. "Thank God you came back," she said in a choked voice.

"I promised you, did I not?"

"My dearest love."

"What did you say, Althea?" There was wonderment in his voice. "I never thought to hear those words from you."

She looked at him, a smile trembling upon her lips. His fingers softly traced her jaw. "It is true. Oh Gareth, pray forgive me. I have been such a wretched wife to you! When I thought you might die—"

He pressed his fingers against her lips. "Quiet, my life. It is I who must crave forgiveness. I who treated you so monstrously! I did not understand, then." His eyes were very clear. "I asked Darcy several pointed questions before the Richmond ball. About Sir Bottlesby and a recurring nightmare of yours. Althea, was that dream true?"

Color had risen in her face. She did not drop her gaze as she might once have done to hide from him. The time for disguise was past. "When I was a child my father saved me from rape. He savagely beat the man who had attempted it. I-I have never quite forgotten the incident."

Gareth searched for her hand, encompassing her fingers warmly. "You will have no cause for ugly dreams any longer, Althea. I swear it. We will have a good, loving life together."

Althea laughed, a bit hoarsely for the emotion choking her. She dashed her free hand across her cheek to catch an escaping teardrop. "Shall we live at Chard, then, Gareth?"

He shook his head. The shadow of a grin lit his somber expression. "With my parents? I thank you, no! I have a London town house. Shall you dislike that, Althea?"

She shook her head quickly, wanting to tell him that it did not matter where she lived, as long as he was with her. But all she could manage past the constriction in her throat was "It sounds lovely, Gareth. Truly it does."

Outside the window there was heard a great commotion. Church bells began ringing madly and the roar of many voices rose. Both Althea and Gareth turned startled faces toward the glass panes.

Suddenly Gareth raised his head sharply from the pillow. "What are they saying?" He turned his head toward her, a blaze of sheer joy in his eyes. Tears suddenly streamed down his face. "Althea! Do you hear it? Do you hear it?"

She laughed at him, her own tears cascading. Her very soul rose in spontaneous thanksgiving. Repeating the gathering tumult outside, she chanted, "Boney's beat! Boney's beat!"

He reached out for her and she fell into his arms, still laughing.

The malignant clouds of war had finally cleared and the sun had broken out to shine the way into a new beginning.